Silver Lining

Silver Lining

Wanda B. Campbell

www.urbanchristianonline.net

Urban Books, LLC
97 N18th Street
Wyandanch, NY 11798

ISBN 13: 978-1-60162-668-4
ISBN 10: 1-60162-668-1

First Mass Market Printing August 2014
First Trade Paperback Printing August 2011
Printed in the United States of America

10 9 8 7 6 5 4 3 2 1

Distributed by Kensington Corp.
Submit Wholesale Orders to:
Kensington Publishing Corp.
C/O Penguin Group (USA) Inc.
Attention: Order Processing
405 Murray Hill Parkway
East Rutherford, NJ 07073-2316
Phone: 1-800-526-0275
Fax: 1-800-227-9604

Silver Lining

Wanda B. Campbell

For those who have failed,
but had the courage to get back up again,
this work of ministry is for you.

*O LORD my God, I cried out, and you
healed me. O LORD, you brought my
soul up from the grave; you have kept
me alive, that I should not go down to
the pit.*

Psalms 30:2–3 NKJV

Acknowledgments

I'm amazed at releasing my fourth novel in as many years. This journey has truly been awesome!

As always, I give all honor and glory to my **Heavenly Father**. Thank you for trusting me with this great ministry. Thank you for every mountain I had to climb. It was in the clefts and crevices that I really learned to love you and myself.

Craig, much love for loving me with your best.

My children, **Chantel, Jonathan**, and **Craig Jr.**: It has always been my prayer that you follow your dreams and strive to fulfill the purpose God has for your life.

Recently, I had the honor of becoming a grandmother. **Little Dinari** is my heart, and, yes, I've spoiled him rotten.

To **Readers** and **Book Clubs** everywhere: Thank you for your continued support. Thousands of books are placed in the marketplace every year. I appreciate the investment of your time and money to support me.

Prologue

Shivers that chilled to the bone caused Marlissa to reach for covers that weren't there. Like the two previous attempts to cover herself, she came up empty. Frustrated, she tucked her bare arms inside her shirt and shook vigorously, hoping the friction against the musty carpet and her jeans would ignite some heat. Her frivolous effort resulted in a sore shoulder to go along with her already stiff back. Sleeping on the floor in a cheap motel definitely held its disadvantages. Yet, it beat a park bench or homeless encampment.

She moaned and turned her chilled body in the opposite direction to block out undisputed evidence that she'd lived to see another day in what she considered hell on earth. This had to be hell. Mentally, she'd died and gone to hell. She was just waiting for the physical manifestation. Desperately, she prayed that the demons assigned to transport her into the deepest, uttermost part of

Hades would hurry. Just how long could a person survive on a diet of Hennessy, vodka, and Cisco, anyway? Hopefully, by evening the devil would be in desperate need of her company, since she didn't have a dollar to her name and didn't trust her luck at securing another bodily fluid–stained carpet to lay her head upon.

She grunted, thinking of her beloved husband resting comfortably in his king-sized bed on a pillow top mattress. Like bile, envy collected in her stomach and traveled up her esophagus. With force, she swallowed the melon-sized lump in her throat. It wasn't Kevin's fault that she preferred alcohol over him. She'd made her bed and now she'd lie in it, but next time she'd make sure she had an actual bed to lie in.

She peered at the snoring mass beside her and wondered how anyone could sleep so soundly on this filth. Obviously, her drunken comrade had more experience with this lifestyle than she did. The wrinkles and red hue of his skin were indications that he enjoyed the depressing effects alcohol offered just as much as she did, if not more. She wanted to wake him and thank him for the shelter, but first she had to remember his name.

Chapter 1

Marlissa stared intensely at her reflection. The woman looking back at her certainly was not the same hurting, reckless woman who tried to self-destruct almost two years ago with her friends: Hennessy, vodka, and Cisco. Physically, she was the same, except now the red eyes and ashen skin were gone and her hair was longer and thicker. She was also twenty-five pounds heavier now that she was eating her dinner instead of drinking it. Her clothing size had jumped from size eight to size ten. Marlissa didn't mind because with the added weight, her five foot eight frame didn't resemble that of an anorexic anymore.

Emotionally, anxiety and grandiosity, along with isolation, started their retreat the night she walked down that long aisle to the altar at Restoration Ministries. With only inches separating her and the minister, Marlissa dropped to her knees and surrendered her life to the Lord. At the time, Marlissa could not say she really believed in God, or was even sober for that matter, but the words spoken by the preacher sparked hope in the core of her wounded being. Real hope; that was something she had not felt in years.

As a child, Marlissa's grandmother sent her to church on a regular basis. During Sunday School, Marlissa had listened intently to what she called the greatest fairy tales she had ever heard. On Christmas and Easter, although Marlissa recited her preprinted speech with style, she could not feel or relate to the words on the index card. Marlissa viewed Jesus as a Prince Charming or superhero who would one day come and clean the world of all the bad people. He would take away the rain and the thunder. The world would be covered with green grass and people and animals would live in the fields together. Jesus was the person to call on in trouble. But on her day of trouble, He didn't come for her. Marlissa never called Him again until that night she and Leon staggered into church, sloppy drunk.

That was a year ago. Now Marlissa had two new friends: Jesus and Leon Scott. Ironically, she had met Leon at a club during one of her drinking binges. Both being alcoholics, the two understood each other and instantly bonded. Needing a place to live other than on the streets of Oakland, the two became roommates. Together, they accepted the Lord and stopped drinking. Every day was an uphill battle, but each worked hard, and encouraged the other to lean on the Lord, stay sober, and work on mending the fences each had mowed down with a semi truck. Their first order of business was to restore the hearts and relationships their addiction allowed them to break.

"Are you sure you don't need me to come with you?" Leon asked from the doorway of her bedroom, interrupting her thoughts.

Marlissa's eyes traveled from her mirrored image to the legal-sized envelope on her nightstand. In slow, deliberate motion, she shook her head from side to side before answering. "Thanks, big bro, but I have to do this by myself."

Marlissa sometimes called Leon "big bro" because his last name was the same as her maiden name. At thirty-four, Leon was three years older and treated her the way a brother would treat a younger sister, always trying to tell her what to do. Marlissa molded with ease to the role of a nagging sister. Being an only child, Marlissa had always wanted an older brother, someone to look out for her. She did not have a big brother to run home to back then, but, no matter what happened today, Leon's shoulder would be waiting for her.

"Are you sure?" Leon offered again.

Her eyes moved back to her reflection. "I've made my bed and now I have to lie in it. Alone, I might add."

"Don't remind me," Leon responded. He was more familiar with an empty bed than he'd like to have been. His alcohol addiction had cost him his wife of five years and two small children. "Do you know what you're going to say?"

Marlissa turned to face him and hunched her shoulders. "Other than I am sorry, what do you say to the man you promised to love until death, then twisted his heart until it crumbled?"

It was Leon's turn to shrug. "Maybe he'll give you another chance?"

Marlissa turned and began searching her jewelry box for her dangling beaded earrings. "I doubt if that happens. What I really want to do is clear the air. You know, take responsibility for my actions and hope he doesn't hate me forever."

"He's a Christian, remember. He can't hate you."

"He is saved, but even saved people have their limit. And trust me; I pushed him past his breaking point." Marlissa glanced at the envelope again and her eyes watered. "I messed up. I really blew it."

Leon quickly entered her room and held her, and, for the third time in as many days, allowed her to cry on his shoulder. "We both have, but God is able to restore. Isn't that what Pastor Drake teaches every Sunday at Restoration Ministries?"

Marlissa sniffled. "Yes." She then listened as Leon prayed for her pending divorce proceedings and for his reunification with his wife. She couldn't help but laugh when he made her recite Pastor Drake's motto: "If God can't fix it, it can't be fixed."

Chapter 2

"Do you think she'll show?" Kevin asked his lawyer, trying to hide his anxiety of coming face-to-face with his estranged wife. Marlissa was already five minutes late, but that wasn't unusual for her. Kevin had vivid memories of waiting into the wee hours of the morning for her to come home. Or for the police to call and say they found her passed out on the highway somewhere.

"I doubt it. Neither she nor an attorney responded to the petition. My guess is she probably didn't read it." Tyson Stokes pursed his lips. "Then again, I could be wrong. Now that you're divorcing her, she might sober up long enough to try to take you for every dime."

Kevin could not believe that, but, then again, he could not believe he had allowed himself to fall in love with and subsequently marry an alcoholic. Kevin thought he was much smarter than that. In hindsight, he saw every warning sign, every flashing red light. He heard every siren, including his mother, Pastor Rosalie Jennings, preaching.

"That woman is not saved, she's pretending," is what his mother constantly barked. "She's hiding something." Kevin made a habit of discarding anything his mother had to say about the women he liked. No one was ever good enough for her only son. During many lonely nights he reconsidered his practice of tuning out his mother's voice.

Kevin checked his watch for the umpteenth time. "Ten more minutes and I'm out of here. I have a full schedule this afternoon."

Riding the elevator to the sixteenth floor en route to Lightfoot & Stokes, attorneys at law, Marlissa reflected on the day she first laid eyes on Dr. Kevin Jennings.

She was rushing through the grocery store entrance as he was leaving, and she banged her leg on his cart.

"Ouch!" she screamed.

"I'm sorry, miss. Are you all right?" The deep voice was enough to make Marlissa temporarily lose focus on the pain. The face and body that accompanied the voice were more than

enough incentive for her to put homeboy Cisco on hold, for a while anyway. He was six foot three, she estimated, dark chocolate, with the most developed upper body she had ever seen. It was as if every muscle in his arms and chest had been chiseled by a master designer, then slowly developed. His clean-shaven face housed soft, yet the sincerest, brown eyes she had seen. They instantly drew her into his essence.

"I'm fine. I just banged my leg a little," she finally answered.

"Can I take a look? I'm a doctor," he asked. "I just want to make sure the injury is superficial."

Marlissa did not like the idea of a strange man touching her, but for reasons she could not explain, she did not want to leave this stranger's presence, not this soon. When she did not respond, he extended his hand to her.

"Hello, I'm Kevin Jennings. And you are?"

"I'm Marlissa Scott," she answered after bringing her mind into focus. She then gave him a light, impersonal handshake.

"Now that we've been officially introduced, follow me to my car and I'll take a look at your leg."

Marlissa wasn't following this strange man anywhere, no matter how fine he was. "Why can't you check me right here?" she asked, leaning against his cart.

"*My prosthesis won't allow me to kneel.*" Kevin pointed to his lower right leg. "*If you sit down, I'll be able to examine you better.*"

Suddenly, Marlissa wasn't smitten anymore. "*Hold on, I thought you said you are a doctor. How can you be a doctor and be a cripple? That's a lame pick-up line and I am not impressed!*" Marlissa went on a rampage, shaking her head and waving her finger in his face. "*You all up in here talking about follow you outside so you can look at my leg. Humph, for all I know you could be a rapist or something!*"

"*Hold on!*" Kevin raised his voice above hers. "*I am not a rapist and I'm not trying to pick you up. I'm a doctor, an ophthalmologic surgeon to be exact. I'm impaired, not crippled. I operate with my hands, not my leg.*" Kevin stepped back behind his cart. "*I was just trying to help, but for all I care, you can go and sit five hours in the emergency room.*" Kevin shook his head and walked away, grumbling, "*Crazy woman.*"

For a reason Marlissa couldn't explain, she didn't want him to think she was really a basket case. "*Hold on,*" she called after him. When he didn't stop, she tried to run to catch him, but couldn't ignore the pain shooting through her leg.

"*Ouch!*" Her agony was enough to get his attention. Against his better judgment, Kevin stopped and waited for her.

"I'm sorry, I didn't mean to offend you. I mean, you never know who to trust these days." Marlissa hoped her smile would soften his stance.

For the first time Kevin took a good look at the crazy woman who had just called him a rapist. Touched in the head or not, she was an attractive woman; tall and leggy and the color of coffee with two servings of cream. The bob haircut outlined high cheekbones and a set of full lips. Her elongated nose revealed her African American and Indian ancestry.

"Maybe you should just go to the emergency room," he suggested, but not nearly as firmly as before.

"No, I want you to examine me. It'll save me a lot of time."

"I'm parked over there." He pointed to a silver SUV.

They walked to his vehicle in silence. Marlissa watched his every step. Aside from a slight limp, Kevin walked normally and with ease.

"Sit here," Kevin said after opening his trunk.

Without protest, Marlissa sat down on the base of the vehicle and lifted her pant leg. As Kevin gently examined her, she tried to make conversation.

"What happened to your leg?"

"Car accident when I was a sophomore in high school, severed my right leg below the knee," Kevin answered without taking his eyes away from her leg. "Does this hurt?" he asked, extending her leg.

"No."

"Point and flex your foot."

She obeyed. "How long have you had an artificial leg?"

"I've worn a prosthesis since I was sixteen." He released her leg.

"You've adapted well. If you hadn't told me, I wouldn't have known."

"Nothing's broken, but you do have a slight bruise. Ice it tonight and you'll be fine." Kevin stood upright, signaling that it was time for her to leave. Marlissa sensed his defensiveness and made the first move.

"Kevin, excuse me, Dr. Jennings, thank you for helping me. I really didn't mean to upset you back there."

Kevin shrugged. "These days it's understand-able, but it still doesn't feel good to be called a rapist."

"It's not exactly a compliment to be consid-ered certifiably crazy either."

They let down their defenses and shared a laugh. When they said good-bye twenty min-utes later, they'd exchanged numbers and made plans to meet for dinner the following evening.

That was almost four years ago. After a year of dating, they were married in a lavish ceremony at his mother's church. Marlissa had wanted a small, private wedding, considering she didn't have much family. She'd never had the honor of meeting the man who'd participated in her conception, and her mother had died during childbirth. Her grandmother had suffered a stroke and died, suddenly, the day after Marlissa turned twenty-one. The only family members Marlissa knew of were a couple of aunts and distant cousins. However, Pastor Jennings had insisted on a grand affair. In Marlissa's opinion, Rosalie Jennings cared more about making her church friends jealous than she did about her son's happiness. Their wedding had more to do with her than Kevin and Marlissa. Pastor Jennings chose the colors, the flowers, and the bridesmaids and their dresses. She even selected the favors.

The elevator's wooden doors parted, bringing Marlissa back to the present. Walking down the hall to suite 1621, she forced the tears back. In a few minutes, she would see the man she'd vowed to spend the rest of her life with. The man who was supposed to be the father of her future children. The man she had intended to forsake all others for. The only man she had ever loved and still loved.

Kevin stood and walked over to the window after reading the conference room clock for the third time. In a way, he was relieved his estranged wife had not shown. When he last saw her, eighteen months ago, she looked and smelled like death to him. As deeply as she had cut him, Kevin couldn't stand to see her destroy herself, so he stopped looking for her. From the sixteenth-floor window, his eyes traveled down to the streets of downtown Oakland, wondering if Marlissa was sprawled out in an alley somewhere. Kevin knew she was still alive; at least, she had been a month ago when Tyson handed her the divorce petition at her current job site.

"Mr. Stokes, Marlissa Jennings is here."

Kevin's breath caught upon hearing the receptionist's voice over the intercom. No sooner had he exhaled and turned to face the door than his wife stood no more than five feet away from him.

"Sorry I'm late. Parking downtown is horrendous," Marlissa offered, mainly to soften the daggers Kevin's eyes threw directly and instantly at her. It was then that she saw how deeply his anger for her was embedded. The softness she once found in his eyes was gone. Aside from that, Kevin looked wonderful. From the beginning, Marlissa had labeled him the "finest man ever created."

Being the no-nonsense business man he was, Tyson Stokes cut to the chase. "Mrs. Jennings, will your lawyer be joining us soon?"

"I don't have a lawyer."

"Mrs. Jennings, the letter I gave you advised you to obtain representation."

"Mr. Stokes, I don't know a lot about divorce proceedings, but from what I do know, if the divorce is not contested, the process is less complicated," Marlissa offered.

"That's correct, but you still need representation to protect your interest in the marital estate," Tyson explained.

Marlissa nervously wrung her hands. "Mr. Stokes, I don't have any interest in the marital estate."

That statement took both Kevin and Tyson by surprise. With the two of them gaping at her like she was an alien, Marlissa took control of the situation before she lost her courage. "Tyson, Kevin, can we sit down? There's something I need to say." Without waiting for them to take their seats, Marlissa pulled out her chair and sat down. Once Kevin was settled, she took a deep breath and began.

"Kevin." When he didn't respond, Marlissa wanted to leave, but her heart wouldn't allow her. If she was ever going to move on with her life, she had to close this door, despite how painful and heavy it was.

"Kevin," she continued, "when I married you I was a wounded little girl in a woman's body. I didn't love myself. I didn't even like myself. For that reason alone I shouldn't have married you. I didn't know how to love you."

Kevin shifted in his seat but still didn't speak.

"About a year ago, I found the Lord. Actually, He found me. Since that night, I've learned a lot about myself. I've stopped drowning my pain with alcohol and I am learning to face my issues head-on. That's why I'm here. I need your forgiveness."

"Mrs. Jennings, my client is dissolving this marriage," Tyson interrupted.

"I understand, but please let me finish." Marlissa directed her attention back to Kevin. "Kevin, I am so sorry for the many ways I hurt you. I'm sorry for the lies and the broken trust. I am sorry for rejecting the love you freely offered me. You were a good and patient husband, and I'm sorry I couldn't love you the way you deserve to be loved. I am sorry I couldn't let you inside." Marlissa placed her hand over her chest and felt the erratic beat of her heart. "Kevin, can you please forgive me?"

Kevin looked away without answering.

"Mr. Stokes," she pressed on through Kevin's silence. She had to finish before she fell apart. "I understand California is a community property state. However, I don't want anything, not even alimony. If you draw up the necessary document, I'll sign it before I leave."

Tyson was always prepared. "Give me a few minutes and I'll have a notary here." Marlissa nodded her consent and Tyson left the conference room. Kevin walked back to the window. Marlissa did not miss the message his body language sent. Her husband did not want to have anything to do with her; he couldn't even sit at the same table with her. After a few cold moments, Marlissa conceded total defeat.

"Kevin, I pray that one day you'll forgive me. More than anything, I want you to find someone who will love you the way you deserve to be loved."

Kevin continued looking out the window.

When Tyson returned along with the notary, Marlissa signed the documents in complete silence. The second after the notary sealed the document, Marlissa pushed away from the table.

"Good-bye, Kevin." Marlissa remained composed long enough to get past the receptionist, but the long walk to the elevator was too much.

She needed a private place to release her pain. In the solace of the bathroom stall, Marlissa cried until there weren't any tears left.

Chapter 3

"Son, you're doing the right thing. It's time for you to move on with your life."

A month ago, Kevin could not have agreed with his mother more. But that was before he had seen Marlissa. The woman who walked into the conference room dressed in the black business suit was not the drunk who nearly had made him lose his mind and robbed him of his self-esteem in the process. Marlissa didn't even look the same. Her hair was longer and she'd gained a few pounds. The alterations enhanced her natural beauty to the point that Kevin thought she looked more beautiful now than she did on their wedding day. Marlissa sounded different, too. It wasn't her voice that had changed; it was the words she used and the gentleness in which she spoke.

During the year they had lived together, Marlissa was never as considerate or sincere as she had been in that conference room. She was always combative and defensive toward him, especially when it came down to lovemaking.

Kevin had known she wasn't experienced, but neither was he. His relationship with Marlissa was the first in which he'd let his protective shield down long enough to fall in love. Most women were either infatuated with him because he was a doctor or because they felt sorry for him. But not Marlissa. Not one time did she bombard him with questions about his bank account or assets. In fact, she did not accept any gifts from him until Kevin presented her with a new Lexus as a wedding present. As for feeling sorry for him, Marlissa didn't lower her expectations of him because of his impairment, nor did she sugarcoat her words. Back then Kevin appreciated her realness. Later, he would resent her, and the venom from her mouth would almost destroy him.

"Mom, you're probably right, but I shouldn't be discussing this with you, you've never liked Marlissa."

Pastor Jennings chose her words carefully. "Baby, it's not that I don't like your wife. I just think there's someone else better suited for you."

Kevin maneuvered from his mother's office chair. "You mean someone you've chosen for me, someone like Reyna?"

Reyna Mills had grown up in Pastor Jennings's church and under her teachings. Reyna's mother and Rosalie were old friends, with over thirty years of history. Pastor Jennings was present at Reyna's birth, performed her baptism, and, if she had her way, Pastor Jennings would have the honor of officiating Reyna and Kevin's wedding ceremony. At thirty-three, Reyna was only a year younger than Kevin and an almost exact replica of his mother. Reyna dressed like Pastor Jennings, even talked like her. That alone was the reason Kevin could not take Reyna's attraction to him seriously.

"This is not about what I want for you," Pastor Jennings defended. "But if you had listened to me, you wouldn't be in this predicament."

"Mother, you can save the 'I told you so' speech."

Pastor Jennings walked around her desk and interlocked her arm in her son's. "Baby, I won't say I told you so, but I will say this: you are too young to be miserable. Your life with Marlissa was never good. The two of you are unequally yoked. You made the mistake of marrying her, but you don't have to spend the rest of your life with someone who cares more for a bottle than she does for you." Pastor Jennings paused to let her words settle. "Marlissa has moved on, shouldn't you?"

Kevin smiled at his mother then kissed her on the cheek. "I have to go. I'll see you at Bible Study tomorrow night."

Pastor Jennings admired Kevin's graduation picture from medical school long after he'd left. She was so proud of Kevin. Following his accident, Kevin had refused to sulk and feel sorry for himself. Already a B student, Kevin quickly adjusted to using the prosthesis, and studied so rigidly he graduated high school a year early, went straight to college, and then to medical school without taking a break.

In the beginning, Pastor Jennings had hoped Kevin would work alongside her in the ministry, but Kevin didn't have the desire. Her disappointment was appeased when Kevin was offered a position as an ophthalmologist, specializing in corneal repair and corrective eye surgery at the top medical center in the Bay Area. At age thirty-four, Kevin was the youngest local eye surgeon, but also the most sought after.

Pastor Jennings replaced the picture then lifted the phone receiver. She needed to make sure she and Reyna were in accord.

"How do I look?"

"The same," Marlissa responded without looking up from her book. Leon had asked that same question five minutes ago and ten minutes before that. He was both nervous and excited about his wife, Starla, coming over for a visit.

"You could at least act like you care," Leon retorted, and stomped into the living room.

"I do care," Marlissa replied moments later from behind the Formica bar countertop. "That's why I picked these up for you." She held out a floral bouquet. "I knew you wouldn't think of it."

Leon was smiling again. "Thanks, brat, appreciate it." He took the flowers and placed them on the kitchen table.

"I'm glad things are working out. Keep this up and you'll be back at home before Thanksgiving."

"I wouldn't say all that just yet. Starla's coming to check out my living environment to determine if she'll let the boys visit me," Leon replied.

Marlissa quickly walked into the living room, directed her attention to the couch, and proceeded to rearrange the couch pillows so she wouldn't face Leon when she made her next statement. "Bro, I'm a little jealous, because even if you and Starla don't reconcile, you'll still have your kids to love. I don't have anyone."

Leon placed a hand on her shoulder. "Marlissa, you've helped me out of my deepest hole, and for that, you'll always have me." Marlissa offered her friend a slight smile. "Of course, I'm not the great Dr. Kevin Jennings, more like Melvin the milkman, but I'll always be your friend."

"Promise to bake some cookies to go along with that milk, *Melvin*?" Marlissa mused just as the doorbell sounded.

Leon gasped. "She's early."

"Get the door. I'll be out of here before she sits down." Marlissa rushed into her bedroom for her jacket and purse.

Before opening the door, Leon sprayed rain-forest air freshener and said a quick prayer. "God, please let this be a new beginning for us."

Leon held the door and gazed at the stranger glaring back at him. It only took a moment for Leon to recall why the man looked familiar. "Hello, I'm Leon. I've heard a lot about you," Leon greeted the visitor, and extended his hand.

"Kevin?" Marlissa called from behind Leon before Kevin could return the salutation. "What are you doing here?"

Kevin glanced over Leon's shoulder at Marlissa. "I didn't know you had company. I should have called first. Sorry to have interrupted." He started to retreat, but Leon's words stopped him.

"Hold on, man, I'm not company, I live here."

Kevin looked from Leon to Marlissa for an explanation. "Kevin, Leon is my friend and roommate. I'm pleasantly surprised to see you, but this really is a bad time. I was just leaving so Leon can spend time with his wife."

"That would be me," a female voice said from behind Kevin. None of them had heard the elevator open.

"Starla, come in." Leon smiled nervously.

Kevin, looking confused, stepped aside to let Starla enter the apartment.

Knowing how important and valuable Leon's time with his wife was to him, Marlissa moved expeditiously. "Starla, it's nice to finally put a face to a voice. From Leon's bragging and our brief phone conversations, I feel as if I know you already. I'm so sorry for intruding on your time with Leon. Kevin and I are leaving." She then started for the door and gestured for Kevin to follow, which he did.

"Do you have your cell phone?" Leon called after her. That was a part of their accountability pact. Whenever they left the house, they had to be accessible by phone, just in case they needed support or prayer or found themselves in a compromising position.

"Yeah, talk to you later," Marlissa answered.

"Nice meeting you, Marlissa," Starla added before closing the door.

Once Marlissa was alone in the hallway with Kevin, she began to fidget. She was still in shock by his sudden appearance. She wanted to know why he was there, but was afraid to ask for fear he would disappear.

"I didn't know you were living with a man," he stated, almost accusingly.

"It's not what you think. Leon is in love with his wife and is trying to do everything possible to win her back." Kevin remained silent. "I was going to catch a movie, but if you want we can go somewhere and talk." Marlissa assumed he would decline, but he didn't.

"Sure, but it won't take long to say what I have to say."

Marlissa ignored his defensive posture and started for the elevator. "There's a Starbucks around the corner," she said, at the same time pushing the down button. "We can walk."

Marlissa had never been claustrophobic, but tonight she was. It was the way Kevin's cold, lifeless eyes examined her, like she was a lab experiment gone bad or a two-headed freak. Love and adoration had vacated the premises a long time ago; now disgust and contempt took up residence. Marlissa, desperate for a distraction, searched her purse for a mint.

"You look healthy." Kevin's voice sounded just as she popped the peppermint into her mouth.

"Thank you." She wanted to say more, but for the moment couldn't articulate her thoughts. She decided to wait until she had the comfort of a tall chai tea in her hand.

The short walk to Starbucks was revealing for Marlissa. She had made the stroll down Piedmont Avenue on countless occasions, but on this mid-spring evening she actually noticed the stores and window displays. Like most Bay Area upscale neighborhoods, Piedmont Avenue was always crowded. Noted for its quaint boutique-style stores and neighborly restaurants, the mile-long strip bustled with activity from the crack of dawn well into the wee hours of the morning.

Marlissa gasped and stopped in front of a craft store. When Kevin finally noticed she'd stopped walking, he was three doors down. Marlissa was still admiring the African American angel molded figurine in the store window when he retraced his steps. Marlissa was so engrossed in the twelve-inch heavenly being, she nearly jumped at the sound of Kevin's voice.

"Do you still collect figurines?"

"I would love to have this beauty, but I can't afford to these days. Eventually, I'll start back." Marlissa reluctantly backed away from the window and continued down the busy sidewalk.

Marlissa walked the remaining distance in silence, while giving Kevin's torso a thorough visual inspection. Just as her eyes began to journey downward, he stopped abruptly, causing Marlissa to bump into him. "Sorry," she offered, as she steadied her balance without any assistance from Kevin. He did, however, hold the door to Starbucks open, and allowed her to enter.

He walked in behind her and didn't say one word during the ten minute wait in line. His lips remained sealed while Marlissa paid for her drink. When the barista greeted him, Kevin rewarded the pretty young woman with a warm smile and small talk about the weather. Disheartened, Marlissa added Splenda to her beverage, and then went to find a table.

Seated at a corner table facing the street, Marlissa prayed inwardly for Kevin. The frame seated inches from her was just the casing of the man she had fallen in love with. He was still gorgeous, but Kevin's softness was gone. She waited for him to take a sip of his black coffee. This was another indication of how much he had changed. Kevin had always taken his coffee with two creams. He liked his coffee the same way he liked his woman: two creams and lots of sugar. Marlissa had the cream part covered, and although they hadn't had premarital sex, she'd supplied him with lots of sugar.

"Kevin," she began. "You said you had something to say to me?"

Kevin leaned back and stretched his leg. "Yes. How have you been?"

"Wonderful. I don't know if you can understand this, but I have never been so content with myself before."

"You look great. Have you really given up the bottle?" His tone was soft, but far from gentle.

Marlissa set her cup down. "Yes, I have, and I'm saved for real this time."

Kevin's face twisted as if he was reflecting on the few times she'd accompanied him to church. She didn't participate in the service at all, and at home she let him do all the praying.

"How did that happen?"

Marlissa didn't miss the sarcasm in his voice, but that was expected considering their history. "I have Leon to thank for that."

"Leon?" Kevin frowned. "How does he fit into all of this?"

Marlissa took another sip of tea before recalling the events that changed her life. "You know the saying, 'God works in mysterious ways'?" Kevin nodded. "That's the only way I can explain what happened. I met Leon in Jack London

Square at The Zone about three months after I left you. We spent the evening flirting back and forth. We were good and drunk by the time we headed to the hotel room he rented."

Kevin braced himself for what was coming next by taking a big gulp of coffee. Marlissa chuckled. "We were so drunk, we fell asleep on the floor in the doorway. The next morning after we sobered up, got a good look at each other, and learned we shared the same last name, we realized sleeping with each other was something neither of us really wanted to do. Turns out, we have a lot in common. From that day on we've been friends. We became each other's keeper. Actually, he's more like the big brother I never had. He made sure I didn't get into too much trouble and I did likewise for him."

"I still don't understand how a drunk, like yourself, led you to salvation."

Marlissa didn't dodge the dart he'd thrown, nor did she fire back. "One night, we were both drunk and broke. I followed Leon to the church his mother attends so he could con her out of some money. We made up this story about me being homeless with two kids and needing money for a hotel room. Actually, that was true, minus the two kids, of course. I was going to use the money for alcohol."

Kevin pursed his lips, but didn't comment.

"We sat in the back of the church, sloppy drunk. So drunk that I didn't know I was in a church. Watching all those people yell and dance around the room, I thought I was at a new club. Leon was probably too wasted to remember that Friday was Revival Night at Restoration Ministries." Marlissa smirked. "Anyway, as I sat there, I was drawn into the preacher's words. He was speaking about the love of God. It wasn't that I hadn't heard those same words before, but for the first time I felt as though God was talking directly to me. Before I knew it, I was on my knees at the altar, crying and begging the Lord to love me." After wiping the happy tears that slid down her cheek, she added, "It wasn't until the saints finished praying over me did I notice Leon at the other end of the altar, begging for forgiveness. We joined church that night and haven't had a drink since. That was a year ago."

"And you haven't had a drink since?" Kevin repeated.

"No," Marlissa answered, shaking her head from side to side. "God really delivered me that night. Now, I'd be lying if I said I haven't wanted a drink. Once I went as far as to purchase liquor, but I couldn't drink it. I poured a good bottle of Hennessy down the sink. I read the Bible often, pray a lot, and have people praying for me. It's not easy, but I'm working hard to maintain my deliverance."

Kevin swallowed hard. "Although I'm happy you've found your peace, I can't celebrate with you. I always thought that if I loved you enough, I'd be the one to lead you to the Lord. Not some drunk."

Marlissa pressed forward. "Brother Atkins hired me as a secretary at his insurance office, but the salary isn't enough to cover the rent and food. In the beginning, Leon's job at the gas station didn't cover his rent either, and the occupancy regulations at his mother's senior facility prevented him from moving in with her, so we became roommates." Marlissa took a long overdue sip of tea. "Now that he's working on renewing his contractor's license, he'll be starting his business up again and hopefully reuniting with Starla and his two children soon. That's why I'm working two jobs, trying to save enough money to afford a nice one bedroom after he moves out."

"Tyson didn't tell me you have two jobs," Kevin interjected.

"I work retail four nights a week at Macy's Bayfair."

Kevin smirked and looked out onto the street. As his wife, Marlissa hadn't needed to work, but she forfeited that luxury the day she left him.

"Enough about me, how are you doing, Kevin? You look great." Marlissa didn't want the spotlight any more. Although proud of her progress, it was still hard reliving the past.

Kevin shot her a look she interpreted as, "How do you think I'm doing?"

"I'm busy as usual, still performing surgery three days a week. I also have clinic Monday, Wednesday, and Friday afternoons."

Marlissa glanced at his hands and longed to feel the gentleness of his touch. "How's Pastor Jennings?"

Kevin nearly frowned. "Mother is Mother. She still has members, so she's happy."

"Are you happy?" It just slipped out.

Kevin sat up straight. "I'm working on it. That's what I wanted to talk to you about." He paused. "Thank you for not contesting the divorce. This thing doesn't need to get any uglier than it already is."

"Kevin, I meant everything I said. I am sorry."

He didn't acknowledge her apology then and wasn't going to now. "I'm happy you've turned your life around," he said, suddenly standing. "This is a nice neighborhood. You should be safe walking back home. See you around." Then, just as unexpectedly as he appeared, Kevin was gone.

Chapter 4

Father, I thank you so much for giving me this opportunity for redemption.

Leon repeated the simple prayer constantly in his head, grateful that God would give him the chance to repair the home he had destroyed. After five years of marriage and receiving the gift of two precious children, Leon had allowed the pain and guilt of his younger brother's murder to swallow and then drown him in the pit of despair. Leon remembered the day like it was yesterday.

On the morning of Thursday, July 15, 2004, Leon didn't think his world could get any better than it was. He had finally acquired an ample staff of reliable and qualified workers, which was good because he had more than enough work for his construction business. Star Construction, named after his wife, Starla, was the most sought-after name in the flooring industry from Oakland to Fremont for both residential as well as commercial. Starla had given birth to their second son six months prior and Leon was in the process of finding land to one day build Starla a brand new house on. The three-bedroom home they owned was nice, but Leon felt Starla deserved something better. "You're my star, the light that lights my path," is what he constantly told her. It didn't matter the quantity or quality of compliments Leon received for his workmanship from his customers; coming home to Starla and his babies was the highlight of his day. As fulfilling as his natural life was, his spiritual life lacked just as much.

Leon had grown up in the church, his late father being a deacon and his mother an evangelist. Leon and his three siblings had Jesus preached to them for breakfast, lunch, dinner, and snacks in between. That was the problem. As a child Leon heard so much preaching he heard it in his sleep. In his teenage years, he tried to fake being saved around his family and imitate a thug at school, but neither act was convincing. Leon just gave up and did what he wanted to do.

Although he no longer attended church, Leon continued to pray from time to time and sent his tithes to Restoration Ministries on a regular basis through his mother. Believing that children *needed a strong religious foundation, Leon sent Starla and the children to the neighborhood church. Starla's receiving salvation still wasn't incentive enough for him to attend.*

"I went to church three nights a week, five if you count choir rehearsal and miracle healing service, plus twice on Sunday. I've had enough church to take me to heaven twice," was Leon's response whenever Starla or his mother would invite him to service. Eventually, Starla and his mother stopped talking and started praying for him.

That particular afternoon, Leon's brother, David, came by his jobsite asking for money. David, five years younger, was a heroin addict living on the streets of Oakland. David didn't own a car or cell phone, but he always knew how to find Leon. Normally, Leon would give him money, mainly to keep him from stealing it from their mother. But on that day, Leon had had enough of David. Three days prior, David had found him way out in Union City and nagged Leon out of $100; now he was back for more.

"Man, I told you the other day, I'm not giving you anymore money," Leon yelled at his brother. "I have a family to support."

"Y . . . You look like you're doing all right to me," David stuttered, looking around and scratching himself at the same time. "W . . . What about me? I . . . I ain't family no mo'?"

"Baby bro, I'm not hearing that today. Go somewhere else with that nonsense."

"Lee-man, you know if you don't give it to me, I'm gon' steal it from somebody."

Leon shook his head at his brother. He knew David was telling the truth, but he still didn't give into his manipulation. "Bro, do what you have to do, because I'm not giving you a dime."

The two brothers stood there, arguing back and forth for several minutes, before Leon walked away. David wouldn't give up; he tackled Leon from behind and tried to take his wallet. Leon reminded David that he was still his big brother by beating David until he begged him to stop. Then Leon did the brotherly thing and helped him to his feet, and told him to take his foolishness someplace else. This time David did what he was told and left.

That was the last time Leon saw David alive. Three hours later, sitting at his kitchen table, he received a call from his mother informing him that David had been shot to death by the gas station attendant he had attempted to rob.

From that moment on, Leon blamed himself for his brother's death, for not giving David the money he'd begged him for. Everyone tried to convince him that David made the wrong choice to hold up a gas station and threaten to kill the attendant with a plastic gun. And that, long before that, David, a magna cum laude college graduate, had choosen to give his life away to heroin. Leon didn't receive any of that. He couldn't when he was constantly tormented with nightmares of David telling him it was his fault. Trying to escape the voices, Leon made the choice to drown his sorrows with alcohol.

On the spiral journey downward, Leon had lost everything: his business, his house, and his family. The one silver lining behind the dark clouds that ruled his life for three years was that, in the end, he accepted Jesus Christ as his personal savior. Today, Leon didn't mind going to church so much. He even went to church at home by watching as many religious programs as possible.

Today was a new day and a new genesis for him. After her visit three nights ago, Starla agreed to allow him an unsupervised afternoon with the boys. She still wasn't ready to make any decisions about dissolving or restoring their marriage, but Starla consented to a date once in a while. Leon eagerly received every token Starla offered. The one thing he was certain of, aside from the love of God, was the love in Starla's heart for him. If the love had dissipated, Starla would have divorced him when he left her and the boys, bottle in hand, causing her to lose their home and move in temporarily with her mother. But she didn't; she cried and yelled, even hit him, but not once did Starla stop referring to him as her husband. She may have added the adjectives low-down, trifling, or stupid first, but always ended with the noun husband. Starla's wounds ran deep, but so did her love.

Leon opened the refrigerator. "Thanks, brat," he whispered. Marlissa had packed a picnic basket for him and the boys to take to the zoo before she'd left for work. Leon grabbed the basket and headed out the door.

"Are you sure that's a good idea?"

Starla switched the phone to her right ear and pondered Lewis's question. Lewis Mason was a deacon at her church who'd befriended her and the boys.

"Leon is doing better," Starla answered. "Besides, he has a right to see his children."

Stiff silence filled the line until Lewis cleared his throat. "Montel hasn't seen his father in over two years and Jaylen doesn't know him at all. The boys were only three and one when Leon left. They don't know him; it's like you're sending them off with a stranger."

Starla sighed. "For that reason alone, Leon needs to spend time with the boys. They need to know their father."

Lewis played the trump card. "Did you pray about this?"

"Of course I did. I even went to his apartment and checked it out."

"Did you also check out his girlfriend?" A slight chuckle escaped. "What's she like?"

"Her name is Marlissa, and she's not his girlfriend," Starla reminded him. "I also met her husband. They're actually a cute couple. I've been praying for things to work out for them."

"Are you still praying for your marriage to work out?"

Starla knew that Lewis had intended to be sarcastic, but she didn't care. "Lewis, I'm praying for the Lord's will to be done."

"Amen," Lewis whispered, then added, "I have to stop at the station I'm considering buying. I'll call you later and see how the boys are doing."

After hanging up, Starla restyled her braids and refreshed her lip gloss. Inside her bedroom, she dabbed on her favorite scented oil and found

the perfect mules to match her capri pants.
Normally, the ensemble was idiotic for this
time of year, but due to the unusually dry late
February weather, it worked. Before answering
the doorbell, Starla unbuttoned the top button
on her denim shirt. After all, it was her stupid,
but saved, husband at the door.

Chapter 5

"Mom," Kevin called after placing his jacket on the ottoman. Normally, he'd have hung his jacket in the closet, but tonight the visit with his mother would be brief, just long enough to grab his favorite dessert.

"I'm in the kitchen," she called back.

Kevin walked through the sunken living room, past the formal dining room, and into the kitchen.

"Baby, I didn't know you were coming by this evening," Pastor Jennings said, looking up from her organizer.

Kevin looked upward after kissing his mother's cheek. "Lord, please hold the lightening until I leave." Pastor Jennings slapped her son on the arm. "Prophetess Evangelist Preacher Teacher Pastor Jennings, you knew I'd be over here once you texted me the words 'banana pudding.'"

Pastor Jennings smiled, but from the doorway Kevin heard his mother's laugh coming from another source. *Not today*, he thought before greeting Reyna.

"Reyna, how are you this evening?" Kevin smiled, and his mother's clone nearly tripped over her own feet.

"I'm fine," Reyna said once she regained her composure. "How about you, Dr. Jennings?"

"Reyna, you've known me forever. You can call me Kevin."

"No, I can't." Reyna slowly shook her head from side to side. "Dr. Jennings, a man of your caliber and accomplishments deserves the highest level of respect. You deserve the best."

This act was getting old, quickly. "Reyna, I'm no greater than my name. If you can't address me by my name then don't speak to me at all." Kevin didn't miss the silent eye language exchanged between his mother and Reyna.

"If that's what you want, Kevin." Reyna had gotten the message, and so had his mother, or so he thought.

"Son, have a seat next to me. I have some dates to go over with you."

Kevin sat down next to his mother, and Reyna exited the kitchen, only to return seconds later with a large bowl of banana pudding.

"Thank you, Reyna, but I could have served myself," Kevin said just before depositing an ample spoonful into his mouth.

"It's my pleasure to serve you." Reyna lowered her eyelashes before adding, "With all the stress you're under, you deserve it."

Kevin paused before enjoying another helping. Pastor Jennings stated that she suddenly needed something from her bedroom, and left.

"My job is not that stressful. I love what I'm doing," Kevin explained.

Reyna clarified her statement. "Honey, I'm sorry. I didn't use my words clearly. I was speaking of your divorce."

Kevin wished she'd saved the clarification. "I'm not surprised my mother told you, but it's not final yet."

"It will be." Reyna gently touched his leg. "Kevin, you have nothing to be ashamed of. You gave Marlissa the best you had to offer. It's not your fault she was too drunk to appreciate how extraordinary you are."

If there were a degree for manipulation, Reyna would have a double PhD. With master skill, Reyna pulled the scab back from his deepest wound and used it to her benefit. What shredded Kevin's self-esteem most was knowing that he did, in fact, give Marlissa the best he had to offer, and that she'd rejected his best constantly. Kevin set the bowl down on the table, his favorite dessert suddenly tasting bitter.

"Would you like me to package this to go?" Reyna asked when Kevin stood.

"No, I've had enough. I'm going home."

Reyna stood next to him and took his hand. "Kevin, I know this is hard for you. If you ever need to talk, I'm just a phone call away."

"I wouldn't expect anything less." He was certain she'd mistaken his smirk for a grin.

Later, a strenuous workout in his home gym left Kevin exhausted. Maybe now he would be able to fall asleep. Reyna's contaminated words broke the levee that held the painful memories at bay. He didn't doubt that Reyna's intention was to draw him closer to her, but what she'd succeeded in doing was saturating his mind with thoughts of Marlissa and their intimate times together.

After removing his prosthesis, he turned the water as hot as he could stand and hopped into the oversized stall. Letting the hot pellets massage his skin, Kevin thought back to the day he and Marlissa first saw the house he now lived in alone.

She'd fallen in love with the house, and thought the large shower was perfect for his large frame and shower chair. He liked the shower too, but for a different reason. He anticipated the memories and melodies they would make together inside the shower. Those fantasies quickly faded on their wedding night. They were both virgins, and Kevin expected it would take a while for them to figure things out, but nothing could have prepared him for what happened.

Kevin was so nervous; he sat on the bed praying while Marlissa undressed in the bathroom of the bridal suite at the plush Ritz-Carlton in San Francisco. This was more than his first sexual experience; it was also the first time he would openly expose his disfigurement.

Whereas his professional accomplishments had earned him multiple accolades from professors and colleagues, they had done nothing for his insecurity of having a missing partial limb.

Kevin considered himself attractive and so did most women. With his developed upper torso he hooked his share of bait, but once he revealed that the slight limp in his step wasn't due to his "coolness," things would change. His apprehension of being physically able to satisfy a woman carried more weight in his decision to remain sexually pure than the idea of fornication. He came close to testing the waters a few times in college, but just when he trusted someone enough to reveal his frailty, his ability was called into question and Kevin retreated.

With Marlissa it was different. She never probed him about his abilities in that area, because she didn't have any intentions of sleeping with him. Marlissa told him so on their first date and her actions proved it. It would be a month before he was allowed to hold her hand and an additional month before he had the pleasure of her soft lips. Kevin guessed that she enjoyed their first kiss, because, afterward, she kissed him all the time. Much to his delight, she also hugged or held on to him every chance she got. The final test of Marlissa's genuineness came one evening while they watched *A Walk to Remember* at his apartment.

Kevin went into his bedroom, changed into a pair of shorts, and returned without his prosthesis. Marlissa didn't gawk, gape, or stare at him with his crutch. She simply made room for him on the couch, then cuddled against him like she'd always done. During the final movie scene, Kevin shed silent tears that had nothing to do with the images on the television screen.

Their honeymoon night at the Ritz was supposed to be the night he had dreamed about, but ended up being the beginning of a horror film, with Kevin playing the leading role.

The venue was perfect, with soft music and pillar candles. He'd heard her mention that she liked chocolate-dipped strawberries, so he ordered some to accompany the non-alcoholic champagne. Marlissa loved tulips, so, instead of rose petals, Kevin sprinkled tulip petals over the king-sized sleigh bed.

From the moment Kevin held her, he felt the tenseness in Marlissa's body. He took his time using his skillful, surgical hands to familiarize himself with the curvature of her body. His carefulness relaxed her, but the reprieve was short-lived. The second he removed the white silk from her skin, Marlissa started shaking. Kevin assumed she was self-conscious of her body, and thought that if he revealed his full, deformed frame, it would relieve her anxiety. He couldn't have been more wrong. Marlissa turned into someone he didn't know.

"Stop!" she screamed, jumping off the bed and grabbing the cover.

Kevin stood balancing on his one leg, and with his long and strong arms tried to bring her to him, but she wouldn't allow it. Marlissa screamed and punched and pushed until Kevin fell back onto the bed. "Get away from me!"

In a haze, he watched her run into the bathroom, and then minutes later storm out of the suite. He didn't see her again until the following morning when the manager brought her back, drunk.

At first, Kevin thought it was an isolated incident, but soon he learned that was not the case. The hangover had barely worn off when Marlissa started on new bottles of Cisco and vodka. For a week, Kevin tried talking to her, but all she would say was that she wasn't ready to be with him intimately.

In the weeks that followed, Marlissa softened enough to where she felt comfortable enough to touch and kiss him again. Kevin patiently took every bone she threw his way. Then it happened. Kevin came home one evening and Marlissa was ready. Kevin's bubble deflated somewhat when he smelled alcohol on her breath, but he continued, guessing that after the first time Marlissa would settle down.

She appeared to have enjoyed their first experience, but told him that it wasn't something she wanted to do often. She was content with kissing and cuddling. If his pride wasn't wounded and his heart not broken, he would have recognized that there was a deeper problem. What he perceived was that his body was so disgusting to his wife she had to be drunk in order to have sex with him.

Kevin soon recognized that Marlissa's drinking increased more and more. The harder he prayed for her, it seemed, the more she drank. Eight months into the marriage, Marlissa stopped attending church with him and became combative when he questioned her, accusing him of only wanting her for sex, although he'd stopped approaching her. He moved out of their bedroom to prove her wrong. Eventually, Marlissa started spending more time away from home than she did at home. Shortly after their one-year anniversary, she left for good. Now she was back and he was more confused than ever.

Kevin lathered his sponge for the third time. Thinking about Marlissa's rejection always made him feel extra dirty. Some days Kevin felt like he'd gotten what he deserved. When he proposed to Marlissa, he knew she wasn't saved and was only going to church to appease him. But he was in love, and, outside of accepting salvation, Marlissa was everything he wanted. Kevin believed that if he lived a sanctified life before her, Marlissa would eventually accept Christ as Lord of her life. Kevin's parents were married for thirty years and enjoyed, for the most part, a decent marriage. However, his father didn't receive salvation until the year before his death, thanks to his mother placing the ministry before her marriage. Kevin shook his head. Marlissa would probably make it to heaven, but without him.

Kevin rinsed and turned off the shower. He dried himself, and then reached for his crutch and wondered if he would ever trust another woman with his heart. Since he didn't trust his own judgment anymore, he seriously considered taking his mother's advice and giving Reyna a chance. Reyna was available and cared for him, almost to the point of obsession. With Reyna, he wouldn't have to worry about loyalty. All that made sense when he filed for divorce, but once he saw Marlissa, Kevin realized that, despite his hurt and anger and, now, bitterness, he still loved Marlissa and always would.

Chapter 6

Marlissa kept busy by cleaning and reorganizing the Estée Lauder fragrance counter. Tuesday nights were always slow at Macy's. She used to fill the downtime with frequent trips to the adjacent shoe department. That stopped once she realized her little paycheck couldn't handle one hundred–dollar shoes and transportation every week. How Marlissa longed for the days when she didn't have to worry about money. Being married to Dr. Kevin Jennings had certainly had its benefits. She'd have even settled for the days before Kevin when she worked as a human resources manager for a pharmaceutical company. "I've made my bed and I'll lie in it. This bed is hard and lumpy, but, Lord, I thank you for the few pillows," Marlissa mumbled as she locked the display case.

"Hello, Marlissa."

She spun around to find Kevin looking handsome, but stern. For some reason his sudden appearance didn't surprise her. Maybe because she was still in shock from his unexpected visit to Restoration Ministries on Sunday. He sat in the back and remained for the benediction, but didn't speak to her. If Leon hadn't tapped her shoulder to alert her to his presence, Marlissa wouldn't have known Kevin was there. Here he was again.

"Hey, Kevin," she answered, trying to redirect her thoughts. At that moment she wanted to feel around her those muscles bulging through his shirt.

"Is this a bad time?"

"What's on your mind?"

Kevin seemed to fumble for words. "I was on my way home when I thought I would pick up a couple of ties. I visited your church on Sunday. Nice service."

Marlissa smiled slightly. Kevin wanted to see her. "I'm glad you enjoyed the service. Would you like me to help you pick out some ties?" she offered.

Kevin looked confused. "Ties?"

"You said that's what you came for."

Kevin casually shrugged and replied, "Sure."

Marlissa asked her coworker at the Clinique counter to cover for her, and led Kevin to the men's department. Her suspicions regarding

Kevin's motives were confirmed the minute they stepped into the department. Kevin wasn't interested in anything Marlissa or the sales associate showed him. To save face, Kevin did purchase a pair of white dress shirts. A doctor could never have too many of those.

Back at her counter, they made small talk about church until Marlissa checked her wristwatch. "We close in ten minutes. I'd better start counting my drawer so I don't miss the BART train."

Kevin frowned. "Don't you have a car?"

"No, but I have BART and bus."

"It's not safe to ride the BART and bus alone at night." He sounded concerned, but she didn't put much stock in it. That was just Kevin being his normal considerate self.

Marlissa smiled. "I'm not alone, I also have Mace." They both chuckled. "Plus those big wings."

Confusion was etched on Kevin's face. "Please tell me that's not some sort of drink."

"Of course not! You know them angels that camp all around us." She was still smiling, but he wasn't. "What's wrong?" she asked.

"It's strange hearing you reference scripture. It's nice, but strange," he finally answered.

"I also dance in the Spirit, but you saw that on Sunday."

The store manager's overhead announcement of the store closing broke the awkward silence that followed.

"I don't want to hold you up," Kevin said, and picked up his shopping bag. "Thanks for your help. I'll see you later." Then he was gone.

Marlissa briefly watched him walk away. *Lord, I need another pillow,* she thought.

Twenty minutes later, Marlissa punched out and started the sprint to the BART station. Halfway across the parking lot, a white Jeep Cherokee with the window rolled down pulled alongside her. Marlissa tightened her grip on the Mace in her pocket.

"Get in."

She didn't recognize the vehicle, but she'd have known that voice anywhere. She leaned into the window. "Kevin, I thought you were gone."

He shrugged. "Decided to wait."

"Thanks," she said after climbing in and fastening her seat belt. "I appreciate it, but you didn't have to."

"I know." His terse response was Marlissa's cue to be seen and not heard. She concentrated on the jazz and easy listening station coming through the satellite radio. The late, great Luther Vandross was singing about dancing with his father.

"Do you take BART every night or does Leon pick you up sometimes?" Kevin's question disrupted her imagined picture of Luther's dance.

"Leon works most nights and he doesn't have a car either."

A long moment passed before Kevin inquired, "Do you have any other male acquaintances who can help you out?" He looked straight ahead, although his jaw flexed.

Marlissa knew exactly what he was asking her, so she chose her answer carefully. She sensed the answer was important to him. "Kevin, I haven't been with a man in any form since the last time you and I were together." She wondered if Kevin meant to exhale as loudly as he had.

Luther finished his dance with his father on the entrance ramp to Interstate 580. A soft ballad followed, featuring Chanté Moore and Kenny Lattimore performing a remake of The Commodores' "Still." They listened in silence as if pondering the words. Marlissa thought the song was both sad and beautiful: sad because of the pain the lovers inflicted on each other; beautiful because in the end love remained. Chanté was passionately telling Kenny that she still loved him when Marlissa dared to gaze at Kevin. He was already looking at her, but instead of holding eye contact, Kevin suddenly looked away and refocused his eyes on the road. Neither said anything until Kevin pulled in front of her building.

"Thanks for the ride." She reached for the latch while trying to hide the tears that trickled down her cheeks. Why couldn't she and Kevin be like Kenny and Chanté? Why couldn't they love again? Before she stepped inside the lobby, Marlissa turned to wave good-bye, but Kevin was already gone.

"Hurry up, brat, it's time to go to church." Leon banged on Marlissa's door on his way to service.

"I'm coming, just let me grab my stuff," Marlissa yelled back.

By the time Marlissa made her "CP Time" entrance, Leon was already at church and yelling his agreement with the preacher's topic. This was their routine: Marlissa and Leon went to church every Wednesday and Friday morning at seven o'clock on the local gospel network right in their living room. The services were so uplifting, many times Marlissa would have to throw her towel at the screen and yell, "You better say that!" or dance in the Spirit. Today it was Leon's turn.

"Come on now!" he roared as the bishop said something about instead of judging your brother, you should pray for him. "We need to raise that man an offering," Leon joked on his way into the kitchen for his morning bowl of cereal, once service was over.

"The bishop's offering will have to wait, I need to get to work." Marlissa fished a glass from the dishwasher and placed it on the counter. "Speaking of work, guess who gave me a ride home from work last night?"

"Your husband," Leon answered, and handed her the cranberry juice.

"You mean soon-to-be ex-husband. How did you know?" Marlissa seemed surprised that he knew.

"Because I am a male and I know how males operate. He's checking you out."

Marlissa waited until Leon swallowed before asking, "What do you mean?"

"He's doing the same thing to you that Starla's doing to me. Kevin is trying to see if your change is legit. That's why he keeps showing up when you least expect it; he's trying to see if it's real."

Marlissa shook her head. "He's already made up his mind to divorce me. Why would he care?"

Leon lifted his bowl and slurped the remaining milk before answering. "He doesn't want a divorce; he loves you. I saw it Sunday at church. He watched you more than he watched Pastor Drake. Trust me, he wants a divorce about as much as Starla does."

"Then why won't he say something?"

Leon placed his arm on her shoulder and sighed. "The same reason Starla won't let me move back home yet. You hurt him and he doesn't know if he can trust you again."

Marlissa let the words digest. Was it possible that Kevin still cared for her? Last night the hardness in his eyes appeared to have softened a little, and that would explain why he'd made up an excuse to stop by Macy's, which was totally out of the way. But the fact remained that the divorce proceedings were moving forward and he still hadn't acknowledged her apology.

"At least you and Starla are making progress," Marlissa stated.

"She's allowing me to see the boys as often as I want now without supervision." Leon smiled.

Marlissa twisted her lips. "That explains the hickey on your neck and the lipstick stain on your jacket," Marlissa teased. "Your boys must really enjoy being with you."

Leon laughed when he looked down at his jacket. He hadn't noticed the outline of Starla's lips until Marlissa mentioned it. He hesitated momentarily then cleaned his jacket.

"I'm really happy for you," Marlissa called after him before he walked out the door.

"Me too."

Three hours later Marlissa looked up from the monitor at the insurance office to find Tyson Stokes standing on the other side of the customer counter in what was no doubt an $800 suit. Tyson's pale complexion and stout physique gave him a strong resemblance to Fred Hammond. The only things Tyson lacked as a man were a sense of humor and the ability to relax.

"Hello, Mrs. Jennings," Tyson greeted her.

"Tyson, do you always have to be so formal? You can address me as Marlissa. You were the best man at our wedding, for goodness' sake." Tyson Stokes was more than Kevin's attorney; he was also his best friend.

"Marlissa, this is not a social call, it's business." Tyson exposed the legal-sized envelope from inside his jacket, and immediately Marlissa felt the muscles in her chest tighten. She glanced around the empty office and prayed it would remain that way until she finished the breakdown she was sure to have after Tyson handed her the divorce papers.

"Of course it's business. You're always the bearer of bad news."

"Don't look a gift horse in its mouth." Tyson smirked then got right to business. "My client has altered the divorce settlement."

Marlissa wanted clarification on what that meant, but Tyson pushed forward before she could voice it.

"Dr. Jennings is giving you possession of the Lexus he purchased for you as a wedding present." Marlissa's jaw fell open as Tyson placed the envelope on her desk. "Here are the keys, title, and proof of insurance. The car is parked outside." Marlissa gaped from Tyson to the envelope and back again. "He'll carry the insurance until you are financially able to afford the premium."

Tyson stopped talking long enough for her to respond. "Why did he do that?"

"Honestly, Marlissa, I don't know. This is totally against my advice, but, then again, Kevin has been doing a lot of things lately that don't make sense to me."

Curiosity got the best of her. "Things like what?"

Tyson smiled for once, and Marlissa knew a snide remark was coming. "Marlissa, if you want to know the answer to that question, do what you should have done a year ago: talk to your husband while he's still your husband."

Marlissa retreated in her chair, resting her chin against her hand. "I want to talk to him, but he puts up an iron wall guarded by two pit bulls when it comes to me."

"I don't know who is worse, you or him." Tyson shook his head. Marlissa knew the friend was now speaking and not the lawyer. "Look closer, Marlissa. It could be that those pit bulls are nothing but baby Chihuahuas."

She thought about Tyson's words long after he'd left. Could Leon be accurate in his assessment of Kevin's feelings toward her? In the wedding vows he'd written and recited to her, he'd vowed to always love her. The mere fact that he provided her with a vehicle one day after finding out that she didn't have one showed that Kevin still cared for her. *But how much?* Marlissa wondered.

Tyson knew Kevin better than anyone, and for him to suggest that Kevin still harbored feelings for her carried a lot of merit. One thing was for sure: Marlissa would have to be assertive and aggressive if she wanted to succeed in getting Kevin to open up to her again. She would have to make the first move.

***

"God, please don't let me make a fool of my-self. Father, please help me find the right words to say," Marlissa prayed, walking down the sterile halls of Sutter Hospital where Kevin's reputation in eye surgery was worshipped. His patients loved him and refused to see anyone but him. Some waited up to three months just for an appointment. She stopped and admired Kevin's photo hanging on the wall of the specialty clinic. The image staring back at her was everything she'd ever wanted in a man. His smile was wel-coming and his eyes gentle. *Gentle,* she thought. Kevin had always been gentle with her body the few times she'd allowed him to make love to her, but she'd never shared that with him. Marlissa tightly clutched the pastry box containing the banana cream pie from Kevin's favorite bakery, and prayed he would accept her small token of thanks.

After a light knock on Kevin's office door, she heard him invite her in. All hope and optimism vanished when Marlissa stepped inside and found Kevin having lunch with Reyna.

"I . . . I'm sorry. I didn't know you had com-pany. I . . . I'll catch you later." Marlissa set the box down on his desk and turned to make a quick exit.

"Marlissa, don't leave," Reyna called from behind. Marlissa stopped, pasted a smile on her face, then turned around. "How have you been?" Reyna asked, now standing next to Kevin, whose eyes were glued on Marlissa.

"I'm fine, Reyna. How about yourself?" Marlissa was determined to act like a lady—a saved lady.

"We're wonderful," Reyna replied as she placed a hand on Kevin's shoulder. "We're just finishing up lunch. There are plenty of leftovers. Would you like some?"

Marlissa could have sworn she saw a smirk on Reyna's face. "No, thank you." Marlissa smiled. "You're the expert on handling leftovers." Before Reyna could continue the catfight, Marlissa made eye contact with her husband. "Kevin, I'm sorry for interrupting your lunch date. Maybe—"

Kevin cut her off. "It's not a date. Reyna brings me lunch from time to time, that's all."

Marlissa glanced over to see Reyna glaring at Kevin.

"I assume you saw Tyson today?" Kevin asked.

"Yes, that's why I'm here. I wanted to thank you."

Kevin checked his watch. "My first afternoon patient should be ready; maybe another time?"

"Sure," Marlissa said, and then retreated toward the door.

"You've picked up some weight." Reyna had to throw one more dagger. "Does that mean you're attending AA regularly?"

Marlissa left before she reached across the desk and slapped both Reyna and Kevin. Until the judgment was signed, Kevin was still her husband, and she didn't like seeing him with his girlfriend. Marlissa was so angry at herself for thinking that she could have another chance with Kevin, she kicked the wall while waiting for the elevator. By the time she made it to her car, Marlissa was in tears. Trying to collect herself enough to drive, she phoned Leon and explained to him that Kevin was seeing Reyna.

"Calm down. It's not over yet." Leon sounded unusually calm to her.

"I know, but it feels like it." Marlissa pouted. "I know it's a long shot for me, but I never imagined he would ever be serious about Reyna Mills!"

"Brat, give it some time—"

"Hold on, I have another call." Marlissa placed Leon on hold and answered the incoming call.

"Marlissa, are you free for dinner on Thursday or Saturday? We can talk then." It was Kevin.

Marlissa was too stunned to say much or to ask how he had gotten her number, and she was too mesmerized by his deep, suave phone voice to care. "I'm off Saturday evening."

"I'll meet you at Mexicali Rose at six o'clock."

"Fine."

Marlissa was about to press the end call button when Kevin added, "Thanks for the pie. It's delicious."

"You're welcome." Marlissa was so happy, she forgot Leon was on the other line. She placed her phone back on the clip without telling him good-bye. "I've got a car and a date with my husband," she sang all the way back to the insurance company.

Chapter 7

"This is ridiculous, wearing a turtleneck two weeks before spring," Starla scolded herself, trying to hide the evidence of Leon's last visit with the boys.

She knew it was risky to have him linger around after the boys were in bed, but things were going so well. The boys quickly adjusted to Leon's presence, and Montel's behavior in school had improved drastically. Truth be told, Starla enjoyed having Leon around; he made her life feel normal again. His visits reminded her of the security and stability she experienced in their earlier years; and the attention—Leon was never short on affection when it came to her. That's why today she had on a turtleneck to hide her neck from Lewis.

Lewis wouldn't understand why she would let the man who'd abandoned her and their two children touch her again. Lewis wasn't the recipient of Leon's skills, so he wouldn't understand.

Leon, an average-looking man, always handled her like he was created just to please her, which was why she nearly made love to him on the couch last night. "Thank God for common sense," she whispered. In Starla's opinion, making love to Leon would have been a major mistake. She did love him, and he was her husband, but she wasn't ready to completely reconnect with him. She'd lost too much when he left. More than a home and financial security, Starla had lost her trust and faith in Leon.

When they married, they'd vowed to always be there for each other; to never put anyone or anything before the other. She'd held up her end of the bargain, but when David died, Leon pushed her away, forbidding her from being there for him. What hurt the most was that Leon threw their relationship away for a bottle, something that caused him more harm than good. He chose the comfort of a cold bottle over her warm body, which shredded her self-esteem.

Did she still love him? Yes, and she always would, but traveling down that road again wasn't a chance she was willing to take. What would happen the next time tragedy struck? The uncertainty was too great to overlook when there was a more stable alternative.

Starla had long ago recognized Lewis's interest in the boys as his way of getting closer to her. She didn't discourage or encourage his advances; more like ignored them. When Leon wasn't around that was easy to do. She didn't have to think about her feelings or make any decisions about her marriage. She was simply the abandoned woman with two kids. But between Leon's desire for reunification and Lewis's interest in her mounting, Starla was forced to deal with her feelings.

Was she attracted to Lewis? No, but Lewis, being ten years her senior, could offer her the stability and security she longed for. Lewis, a successful businessman, presented himself as conservative and saved. He never drank and wasn't prone to risky behavior. Lewis was also noble, never forcing his feelings on her. Instead, he gave her the time and space she needed to sort through her emotions. "I'll join you in prayer," was what he told her when she shared Leon's request for reconciliation. The boys adapted to him easily, too, although now they mentioned their father more than they did Lewis. The funny thing was that the boys never mentioned Lewis to Leon. It was like they were holding on to Lewis just in case their father disappeared again.

"Mommy, Deacon Lewis is at the door," Montel called from the living room.

"I'll be right out." Starla pulled her braids back into a ponytail and wondered if it was a good idea to allow Lewis to take her and the boys to the preseason baseball game. She was sure to burn up in that turtleneck. "Forget it," she grumbled, and changed into her Oakland A's T-shirt. "So what if Lewis sees my neck? I don't have to give him an explanation about what goes on between me and *my* husband."

Starla greeted Lewis with a big smile minutes later. If Lewis saw the red spots against her caramel skin, he didn't act like it. As usual, Lewis greeted the boys first, then Starla.

"Are you ready?" He smiled at her.

"Lead the way." *That went well,* she thought, until Lewis buckled the seat belt in his Escalade.

"I see the visits with the ex are going well," he said casually.

Starla faked interest in a passing billboard. "The boys are enjoying him."

"It appears that you are too." Lewis half smiled. "You must have received an answer to your prayers."

"Not yet." Starla smiled back.

"I'll turn up the heat then," Lewis said light-heartedly, but Starla knew her behavior infuriated him when his brakes screeched midway through an intersection.

***

Leon took a break from studying. Renewing his contractor's license was harder than he'd expected. A lot had changed in three years, but Leon believed that God would give him the grace to obtain his license, and the finances to restart Star Construction. He prayed every day for God to help him retain the knowledge he needed for the state exam, but finances were another story.

Outside of tithes, rent, and basic living expenses, every dime he made from his two jobs at two different gas stations went to Starla and the boys. With his personal bankruptcy, it was going to take a miracle to secure a business loan. But miracles were something God specialized in. He didn't have money, but he had a whole lot of faith. He walked over and fell onto the couch; his mind instantly went to his last visit with his family.

Things were progressing well. The boys felt comfortable enough to call him "Dad" instead of "Leon." Starla was softening too, but, then, he'd known that given enough time and the right touch she would.

"Have you seen my keys?"

Leon sat up and smirked at Marlissa. Just like his blood sister, Debra, Marlissa had mastered intruding on his quiet time by demanding his attention.

When he didn't verbally respond, Marlissa slapped his shoulder. "Come on, Leon, I don't want to be late."

Leon smirked again. "Woman, if you didn't want to be late, you wouldn't have gone for a hair, manicure, and pedicure appointment on a Saturday afternoon. It's not like the brotha's going to see your feet anyway," he said, referencing the brown mules she'd slipped her feet into.

Marlissa raised an eyebrow. "You never know. Besides, I feel better when my feet are pretty."

"Brat, relax. Dr. Jennings expects you to be late. He's married to you, remember?"

"That's why this date is so important, I have to show him that I've changed."

Leon looked down at his wristwatch. "You won't show him tonight. It's five–fifty-five and Mexicali Rose is ten minutes away."

Marlissa yelled out in frustration, "Where are my keys?" Leon laughed uncontrollably, and that infuriated Marlissa more. "What's so funny?"

He stood and marched her to the bathroom mirror. "Oh," she moaned. Her keys were hanging around her neck.

Kevin took a sip of Coke, leaned back in his corner booth seat, and absorbed his surroundings. Being a lover of authentic Mexican food, his favorite spot had always been Mexicali Rose. Located on the edge of Oakland's Jack London Square, Mexicali Rose was a popular hangout spot for both the weekday after-work crowd and weekend partygoers. He and Marlissa, who also loved Mexican food, had spent many evenings trapped in the very booth Kevin now sat in, emerging once in a while to share a slow dance on the crowded dance floor.

Kevin checked his watch; it was six-ten. Marlissa wasn't late yet. Marlissa had a self-made fifteen-minute grace period. He was confident she would show by her response to finding Reyna in his office. Kevin hadn't missed the commingled expression of hurt and anger, he just hadn't addressed it. He hadn't planned it that way, but it was way past time for Marlissa to get a taste of what she'd been dishing out. What Kevin didn't like was Reyna implying that they were a couple.

"Hey, handsome, mind if I join you?"

Kevin hadn't seen Marlissa approach the table, and was glad he hadn't, for fear he might have choked on his drink at the sight of her. She was beautiful, dressed simply in jeans and a V-neck pullover sweater. She'd worn similar outfits on most of their visits there, but now her jeans looked a whole lot better. She also used to greet him in the same manner.

As a courtesy, Kevin stood and waited for her to be seated. "I took the liberty of ordering for us."

"You knew I'd be late." Marlissa smiled.

"Some things never change."

"Chihuahuas, not pit bulls," she mumbled.

"Excuse me?"

She cleared her throat. "With the help of God, people do change."

Unprepared for her response, Kevin said nothing, opting to take a swig of Coke.

The waitress placed a glass of iced tea in front of Marlissa, and Marlissa smiled at Kevin. "You still know what I like."

"As I said, some things never change."

"Kevin, I wish you'd soften, because I'm not leaving until we've made peace."

He ignored her declaration.

"This place hasn't changed much." She looked around, trying to make small talk. "Do you still come here often?"

Kevin looked at her like she'd said something wrong before answering. "Marlissa, I haven't been here since the last time you and I were here. Too many memories."

Before she could respond, the waitress set a small plate in front of them, then a mountain of Carne asada and *pollo* nachos. The steak half was for Kevin; the chicken for Marlissa.

Kevin bowed his head and said grace, but Marlissa studied him. Kevin remembered everything. "Maybe all is not lost," she whispered once Kevin concluded the prayer.

As if time hadn't passed, the two dug in like old times: Marlissa, careful not to touch the guacamole, and Kevin the beans.

"Thank you for the car. I really wasn't expecting that after everything that's happened," Marlissa said.

Kevin finally held eye contact with her for longer than a second. "Marlissa, I don't hate you and I don't wish you any harm. The reason I gave you the car is because you needed one, and, remember, that was my present to you for becoming my . . . well, you know."

"But can you give me your forgiveness?" Marlissa blurted. He didn't answer, so she pressed on. "Kevin, I am so sorry, but I can't change what happened. I need you to forgive me. Please, it's important for me to have your forgiveness."

Kevin dropped a chip back onto the plate and leaned back against the booth. "Marlissa, I'm trying to forgive you," he answered honestly. "I have to if I'm going to have a future."

"Does your future include Reyna?" Marlissa asked directly.

Kevin shifted in his chair. He didn't know the answer to that question. Marlissa took his silence for his answer.

"How long have you been dating?"

"We're not," he finally answered.

"It didn't look like that the other day."

Kevin smiled; Marlissa was jealous. "Green doesn't suit you."

"And Reyna doesn't suit you. Now open up." It was their tradition to share their half with the other.

Kevin gazed at her, but it wasn't a cold stare. "Come on," she prodded.

Kevin opened his mouth and she gently fed him the loaded chip, but not without smearing his mouth with sour cream. In the old days she would have kissed the sour cream away. Tonight she used a napkin. As her fingertips dabbed the corners of his mouth, Kevin held her gaze.

"Your turn," he said. His anxiousness surprised him.

"Sorry, gorgeous, but if I get any bigger—"

He cut her off. "Marlissa, you're beautiful. I . . . I mean you wear your size and hair well."

"Thanks," she said, then calmly took his hand in hers. "Kevin, can we please call a truce and try to be friends? I know you're moving on with your life and I'm trying to move on with mine, but I need your friendship."

Kevin swallowed hard, trying to suppress the lump that threatened to choke him. Why did she have to sound so sincere, and why on earth did she have to be so beautiful? Why was he even there with her in the first place? Kevin didn't trust himself to speak, so he just nodded his consent.

They sat there for a long time talking about church. It wasn't until Kevin used his left hand to take a swig of Coke that Marlissa realized she was still holding his right hand. He didn't say anything and neither did Marlissa. Kevin was sharing with her the details of his nomination for Physician of the Year at Sutter Hospital for his work in repairing retinal and corneal defects, when the music changed from the festive beat to a slow, mellow tune. It was one of their favorites; one that always made him think of her.

"Dance with me," Marlissa insisted. Kevin was taken aback by her request. "Please, I won't bite."

He wanted to tell her no, but they'd made a truce and Kevin was a man of his word. Besides, they'd danced to the tune countless times before.

At first it was awkward trying to slow dance and, at the same time, keep a safe distance from each other. Marlissa knew Kevin well. He wanted to be closer to her; he just didn't know how to tell her. Marlissa decided to open the door for him.

As Melba Moore and Freddie Jackson crooned the words to "A Little Bit More," Marlissa leaned into him and laced her fingers around his neck, then rested her head against his chest. The two instantly fell into sync, and, for a while, nothing else mattered.

"I want to hold you in my arms forever," the duo bellowed, and Kevin reacted by pressing her even closer. Kevin wanted to restrain himself, but couldn't. He didn't mean to squeeze her so tightly, but it had been a long time and she felt so good. He certainly didn't mean to moan, but for some reason his body seemed to be controlled by what was in his heart and not his brain. Kevin wanted to kick himself for surrendering to her so easily.

It was evident that neither wanted to let go when the song ended. They stood there, holding each other. Finally, Marlissa raised her head, only to find him staring intensely down at her. He didn't say anything, but the rapid flexing of his jaw muscles spoke volumes. He wanted the same thing she needed.

"Kevin, I don't want a divorce. I love you," she whispered, then raised her mouth to his. At first he was hesitant, like he was trying to digest her words, but she persisted and he joined her lips on a sweet but passionate ride. When she finally released him, he was panting for breath. Without saying a word, Marlissa took him by the hand and led him off the dance floor.

"Reyna who?" she mumbled victoriously, heading back to the table.

"I think we should be going." Kevin pulled out enough bills to cover the check and a nice tip.

Marlissa nodded her agreement. She'd put the ball in Kevin's court and he needed to be alone to chart his next move.

Kevin walked quietly with Marlissa to her car and waited for her to unlock the door.

"Thanks for dinner and the dance," she said once she'd fastened the seat belt. Kevin looked perplexed, like he wanted to say something. "Kevin, what's on your mind?"

He exhaled deeply. "Marlissa, I heard what you said in there, but I don't understand. You've been saved and sober for a year, why didn't you come back? If I hadn't filed for divorce, I wouldn't have known if you were dead or alive."

Marlissa reached for his hand, but this time he placed his hand inside his pocket. "Kevin, I was coming back at the beginning of the year, but your mother asked me not to."

"Marlissa, what are you talking about?" Now Kevin was really confused.

"Our office handles the insurance for her church. Pastor Jennings came in there one day in December. She was just as surprised to see me as I was to see her. I told her about my recovery and that I was attending church. When I asked her about you, she asked me not to contact you. Said you had moved on with your life and I would only be a distraction." Kevin shook his head. "I honored her wish because I knew how deeply I'd hurt you, and because I didn't want to hinder your progress. A short time later, Tyson informed me you were filing for divorce."

Kevin closed his eyes in an attempt to hide his anger, but was unsuccessful. He hit the hood of the car then stomped away.

Once inside his SUV, Kevin punched in Tyson's number. He answered on the third ring. Kevin didn't bother with a greeting.

"How did you find Marlissa?" Kevin barked.

"Can a brotha get a hello?" Tyson retorted.

"Not until you answer my question. How did you find Marlissa?"

"I was speaking with Pastor Jennings after church one Sunday, when Reyna interrupted to say she'd seen someone who looked like Marlissa at the insurance company. I sent my guy to check it out and there she was. Why?"

"When was that?"

"Sometime before Christmas. What's up?"

"Never mind," Kevin said before ending the call.

Chapter 8

"Be not deceived, God is not mocked, whatso-ever a man sows that shall he also reap." Pastor Jennings paused to wipe beads of sweat from her forehead with the hand towel inscribed with the word "Pastor" in white letters. "Truth is, we reap what we sow. Lemon trees don't spring up from apple seeds."

"I know that's right, Pastor," someone yelled.

"We live this life thinking that we can do what-ever we want and however we want to do it. Saints, God is a just and fair God. He won't let you reap where you haven't sown. If you've sown good, He'll send you a good harvest. But if you've sown deceit and discord among your brothers and sisters, God will still love you, but He'll stand back and watch you reap a harvest of *payback*." Pastor Jennings moved her head from side to side, then walked the length of the platform. She always did that when she felt the Spirit real strong, like the

Lord had just dropped a divine revelation in her spirit. "And another thing the Lord told me to tell you all: stop being nosey!" she hollered.

"Say that in the mic, Pastor!" one of the deacons yelled with his hands raised.

"Stay out of everyone else's business and let the Lord teach you how to manage what's going on in your own life. Stop trying to make people into what *you* want them to be, and learn how to do what God has called *you* to do." Pastor Jennings was feeling real good now. She waved her hands frantically, then started dancing.

"Incredible." Kevin smirked from his front-row seat. Not only was his mother having conniptions, so was Reyna. If he hadn't grown up in the church, the "do as I say and not as I do" attitude would have shocked him. But Kevin had seen it all growing up in the home of Pastor Rosalie Jennings.

Pastor Jennings was skilled at preaching words that she herself could not live. Kevin believed that was part of the reason it took so long for his father to receive salvation. At church, Pastor Jennings was patient and kind, portraying the love of Jesus. Once she entered the doors of her home, she transformed into a bossy control freak. Everything had to be her way, and if someone wanted to stay in her good graces, they made sure they did everything according to her wishes.

For most of his life Kevin had done just that. Then he married Marlissa. Up until then, Pastor Jennings was the only woman in Kevin's life he cared about pleasing. Naturally, he downplayed her possessiveness as motherly love, but last night's revelation was sobering. His mother didn't have any intentions of allowing Kevin to navigate his own path.

When Pastor Jennings finished greeting her congregants, Kevin was waiting in her office for her and her sidekick.

Pastor Jennings greeted her son as usual, with a smile and a big hug. "Hey, baby. The presence of the Lord was surely in this place today." She didn't notice that Kevin didn't return her embrace.

"Mother, where's Reyna?"

"Right here," Reyna answered. Like a genie, Reyna appeared next to Kevin.

A wide, satisfied grin creased Pastor Jennings's face. "I hear y'all have been spending time together."

Ignoring her zeal, Kevin stepped away from them both and walked over to the other side of the room.

"Reyna," he began. "Before last week, when was the last time you saw Marlissa?" He didn't allow Reyna time to answer. He turned to his mother. "Mother, when was the last time you saw Marlissa?"

Kevin folded his arms and watched the two women. He'd have bet his annual salary that they tried to transmit telepathic answers to one another.

"I hadn't seen Marlissa since the last time she came to church," Reyna answered honestly.

Kevin tilted his head. "Really? Then why did you tell Tyson to look for her at the insurance office?"

Reyna lowered her head, suddenly finding her shoes interesting. Pastor Jennings spoke in an unknown tongue.

Kevin pressed past the dramatics. "Mother, I'll repeat the question. When was the last time you saw Marlissa?"

"Well, I . . . I can't remember the exact date," Pastor Jennings struggled.

Kevin took a step forward. "Pastor Jennings, let me help you out, so you can practice what you've just finished preaching. You saw Marlissa in December at the insurance office, then had Reyna feed the information to Tyson."

"I . . . I, well—"

"Save it, Mother!"

Rosalie gasped at Kevin's forceful tone.

"I'm a grown man. I don't need you or Reyna manipulating my relationship with Marlissa. You had no right keeping her whereabouts away from me"

"Baby, I—"

"Mother, that's the problem. I'm not a baby. I can make my own decisions."

"No, you can't!" Pastor Jennings screamed. "That's how you ended up married to a drunk in the first place!"

Seeing Pastor Jennings rattled was enough to make Reyna retreat quietly into a corner.

For the first time Kevin verbally questioned his mother's integrity. "Mother, tell me what's worse, a drunken wife or a manipulating preacher. Sin is sin. Your manipulation is just as bad as Marlissa's drinking. At least she admits her sins. You hide behind a collar and a robe."

Reyna gasped as Pastor Jennings raised her right hand to strike Kevin's face. He knew it was coming, but he didn't dodge the blow. Once the sting wore off his face, Kevin slowly backed toward the door.

Pastor Jennings glared at him, trembling. "How can you . . . How can you stand here . . . After all I've done for you . . . How can you disrespect me?"

"Mother, I told the truth, now deal with it. I love you, but that doesn't change the fact that you're wrong." Kevin then faced Reyna. "You should listen to what my mother said today. Stop trying to fit into her mold, and be the person God created you to be."

Just before Kevin closed the door, Pastor Jennings yelled, "Are you trying to tell me that you still want that drunken heathen?"

"I'm asking you to let me live my life." The words spoken in simplicity went right over Pastor Jennings's head. She stood glued in place with a confused expression.

Sunday evenings were the highlight of Marlissa's busy workweek. With working a regular nine-to-five and part time four nights out of the week, Sunday evenings were the only time she had to regroup and prepare for the week ahead. While Leon worked the swing shift, she enjoyed the solace and tranquility that only an aromatherapy bubble bath by candlelight could provide. Bubble bath and candles from the Dollar Store were the only luxury items she could afford. During these extended periods of self-indulgence, Marlissa immersed herself in her journal, chronicling the previous week's events and accomplishments. She recorded every triumph and every failure and her emotions at the time. She noted her response to adverse situations and evaluated how to better handle them the next time around. Marlissa ended each entry with a closing prayer, and thanked God for being sober and in her right mind. Tonight she also added a thank you for the progress she'd made with Kevin the night before.

Watching Kevin storm away with that cute limp, Marlissa second-guessed her decision to come on so aggressively, but then she remembered the firmness by which he'd held her. Kevin needed the connection just as much as she did. "He's right, some things never change." Marlissa sighed and closed her journal, and then placed it on the towel rack. "The way that man kisses, I'd stand in line and pay." Marlissa laughed out loud then sighed again, wondering if she'd ever told him that before. She hadn't. As she dried her peach-scented body, Marlissa couldn't recall one time she'd voiced to Kevin how much pleasure she enjoyed from being with him. She also realized that last night was the first time she'd told him she loved him without him telling her first.

"Maybe that was a mistake," she mumbled. "I should have been more affectionate."

Since being freed of her demons, Marlissa realized that she'd taken many things for granted, mainly Kevin. Marlissa realized that in an effort to protect herself, she inflicted hurt on the one true person in her life. Kevin was the one person who didn't take advantage of her in any form. She understood now that, through her behavior, subconsciously, she'd expected him to. She'd expected him to do the same thing the last male she trusted had done.

"I can't change the past, but I will certainly work on the present," Marlissa vowed after wrapping her hair and tying a frontal knot in her hair scarf. She then trotted into the kitchen and poured herself a drink. She'd just placed the crystal glass she'd bought from the Dollar Store down on the table when the doorbell sounded. Her heart nearly jumped through her chest when she recognized his image through the peephole.

"Kevin, what are you doing here?" she asked after yanking the door open.

"I . . . I came to see you," he stuttered, taking note of her attire. She was wearing striped pajamas and a matching robe. "I didn't mean to wake you. I'll call you later." He then turned to leave.

"Kevin, wait, don't leave," she called, and at the same time gripped his arm. "I wasn't asleep, I was just relaxing."

His arm muscles relaxed and he stepped inside. "Enjoying your time alone?" he asked once he was seated on the couch.

Marlissa tilted her head. "How did you know I was alone?"

"Leon told me," Kevin answered matter-of-factly.

"When did you talk to Leon?"

"I saw him this afternoon at the gas station on Telegraph. He said you spend Sunday evenings alone." Kevin looked around the small living area as if trying to find something interesting to talk about. His eyes fell on the crystal glass. "I knew it!" he yelled, shaking his head and pounding his fist against the couch cushions.

"You knew what?" Marlissa didn't know anything.

"That this whole rehabilitation act was just that, an act."

She followed his eyes to the crystal glass. "Kevin, this is peach cider, not alcohol." Marlissa picked up the glass and held it to his nose. "Does this smell like alcohol to you?"

He sniffed, then shook his head from side to side, indicating no for an answer.

Marlissa lowered the glass to his lips. "Now taste it."

Kevin hesitantly, but obediently, took a sip. "That's pretty good."

"So am I," Marlissa said after taking a sip, and then placed the glass back on the table.

"Kevin, I told you before, I'm not the same person I was when we married. I don't practice destructive behavior anymore and I don't lie."

Kevin admitted his error. "Marlissa, I'm sorry. I shouldn't have jumped to conclusions."

Marlissa smiled. "Apology accepted." She leaned back into the corner groove of the couch. "So, what brings you knocking on my door on a Sunday night?"

Kevin leaned back on the opposite end, resting his arm on the back of the couch. "We need to discuss what you said yesterday," Kevin answered, then ran his hand over his fade. That's what he did when he was nervous: he rubbed his head. He'd done that very thing right before he proposed.

"Why are you nervous, Kevin?" Marlissa moved closer to him.

"Marlissa, what you said changes things."

"What changes things? The fact that I don't want a divorce or that I love you?" Kevin rubbed his head again; she wasn't making this easy for him. Marlissa turned his chin so he would face her. "Kevin, I do love you. I'll always love you. I will understand if you continue with the divorce, but I wanted you to know how I really feel."

"Marlissa, I hear you, really I do. But so much has happened, and, I have to be honest with you, I don't trust you."

Marlissa nodded her understanding. "You have every right not to, but can you at least give me a fair chance?"

Kevin's hot gaze burned through her. She could only imagine the debate going on in his mind. Inwardly, she prayed that he believed she'd changed, and would give their marriage another chance.

"Let's work on reacquainting ourselves and being friends first, and see what happens. It has only been two months since you were served. We have four months before the divorce is final."

"Thank you," she whispered, and wiped the lone tear that trickled down her cheek.

"It's going to take some time for me to get used to you being so soft and sensitive," Kevin commented, and casually placed his arm around her.

"Kevin, I have always been soft and sensitive, on the inside anyway. I just didn't know how to let you inside." She rested her head against his shoulder, relishing his essence. Aside from the rhythmic sound of their breathing, the apartment was completely quiet. Marlissa was just about to doze off when Kevin announced it was time for him to leave.

"I have two corneal transplants in the morning." He gently removed his arm and maneuvered to his full height.

"Wouldn't want you to blind anyone on my account." Marlissa stood and straightened the part of his shirt she'd wrinkled.

Kevin handed her his business card. "Here's my cell. The house number is still the same."

"I've been meaning to ask you, how did you get my cell number?" Marlissa inquired.

"Leon gave it to me about a week ago when I saw him at a gas station near the hospital."

Marlissa laughed. "You and Leon are becoming pretty close."

"You could say that." Kevin hesitated before opening the door, like he wanted to say something. Marlissa wondered what was on his mind, but before she could ask, Kevin was gone. His Batman exits were starting to annoy her.

Chapter 9

Starla didn't afford the florist's deliveryman as much as a glance when he entered the accounting office where she worked as a bookkeeper. In the three years she'd worked there, a floral delivery was made, on average, twice a week, but in that time span not one petal had been intended for her. Starla had no reason to expect that today would be any different.

"Starla Scott?"

Starla peeked up from her work and eyed the baby face belonging to the mature voice. "Yes."

"I have a delivery for you."

The bouquet of roses was so close, the soft petals nearly grazed her face, but Starla asked the deliveryman, "Where's the package?" Hopefully, the facial expression of the maybe twenty-something-year-old young man didn't mirror his thoughts. If so, she was sure he thought she belonged in a special education class.

"Ms. Scott, please sign here." The young man extended his pen and clipboard.

Starla, still a little dazed, signed, and before she could thank him, young blood had disappeared. Starla didn't have a chance to smell the red beauties before her coworker, Vangie, ambushed her.

"Girl, what are you doing and whom are you doing it with?" Vangie moved the petals back and hunted for the card. Starla snatched it just in the nick of time and shoved it into her pocket.

"Ms. All-Up-In-My-Business, I'm not doing anything."

"Girl, tell the truth and shame the devil. You know you did *something* to get these." Vangie lowered her voice. "The last time I got a bouquet like this, I almost got arrested for lewd behavior while operating a motor vehicle."

"Vangie, you need Jesus, quick!" Starla said once she stopped laughing.

"Pray for a sista." Although she laughed, Vangie was serious. "Who is he?"

"My husband." Starla blushed.

Vangie's face contorted. "You ain't right!" Vangie slapped her hands on her hips. "You come in here every day, acting like nothing's new, when all along you've been holding back. What kind of friend are you?"

Starla waved Vangie's tantrum off. "Girl, shut up. Leon and I are not together. He's just spending time with the boys." As the words left her mouth, Starla questioned their validity.

"The boys are really going to love these," Vangie said sarcastically, pointing at the roses.

"They sure will," Starla agreed, and Vangie rolled her eyes.

"Real talk, are you and Leon getting back together?"

Starla hunched her shoulders. "I don't know," she answered honestly. Starla attempted to steer the conversation away from her and Leon. "Don't these smell heavenly?" she asked after sniffing the petals.

"Lose the mask; this is me, girl."

Starla rolled her eyes. "I can't stand you."

"But how do you feel about Leon?" Vangie sat down in Starla's chair as if it were her own. "Do you want to reconcile?"

"You know I love my . . . my . . . Girl, Leon has been so good to me lately, I can't think of anything bad to call him." The women shared a laugh. "He's better than the old Leon because now he's saved, but I don't know if I can trust him enough to live as husband and wife again."

Vangie waved her hands in the air. "Explain to me how you trusted Leon when he wasn't saved, but now that he is, you're having a hard time."

"It's hard, Vangie. It hurt so badly when he left and I lost so much, I don't know if I have enough in me to try again. I've been praying, but I'm still not sure."

"Until you figure it out, be careful, if you know what I mean." Vangie narrowed her eyes at Starla, and she knew precisely what Vangie was referring to.

"I don't have any intentions of sleeping with Leon, but if I do, we are married."

"True, but if you're not sure you want to commit to him, sex will only complicate things."

"As always, you're right." Starla grabbed Vangie's arm and pulled her upright. "Now get out of my chair, I have work to do."

Long after Vangie went back to her desk, Starla pulled the card from her pocket and read the printed words:

Meet me at Kincaid's 7:00
L

"Leon, why are you making this so hard?" she grumbled. Leon knew Kincaid's was one of her favorite steak and seafood restaurants. She wondered if he could afford Kincaid's, until she recalled Leon's vow to spend his last dime and breathe pleasing her. And right now Starla was very pleased. She hummed while phoning and arranging for her next-door neighbor to watch the boys for the evening.

Starla prayed fervently the entire ten-minute drive from her townhouse complex to Kincaid's and still didn't have an answer to her dilemma. Was she ready to take another chance on Leon? Or could she walk away and leave her heart with him? She stepped from her Camry and decided the only walking she was prepared to do was inside the restaurant to enjoy a five-star seafood meal.

Once inside the waterfront establishment in Oakland's Jack London Square, Starla expected to see Leon, but that wasn't to be.

"I'm glad you decided to accept my invitation."

Starla spun around to stand face-to-face with Lewis Mason. Flabbergasted, Starla repeatedly opened her mouth to speak, but only one word would come. "Lewis?"

"You are absolutely beautiful this evening," Lewis said in reference to the form-fitting black dress that stopped just above Starla's knees.

"Thank you," Starla managed. She'd anticipated hearing those exact words from her husband.

"Mr. Mason, your table is ready," someone announced from behind.

Lewis extended his arm to Starla and the two followed the host to a corner table with an unobstructed view of the bay. "Your waiter will be with you momentarily."

"Thank you," Lewis replied, but Starla was still trying to figure out how she'd ended up in a romantic dinner setting with Lewis Mason.

"How are you feeling this evening, Starla?" Lewis smiled as if being with Starla this way was exactly what he wanted and was the natural thing to do.

"I . . . I'm confused. Lewis, I didn't know the flowers were from you. I thought I was meeting my husband."

Lewis placed his enormous hands on the table, making sure his two-carat diamond ring and Movado were on parade. "Why would you think that? Surely Leon can't afford long-stem roses and this restaurant with his income."

"Never mind," Starla mumbled, and looked out the window. She'd been so excited about seeing Leon that the thought never occurred to her that Leon had given her his entire paycheck two days ago.

Once the waiter introduced himself and had taken their drink orders, Starla cut to the chase.

"Lewis, what's the meaning of this? I thought you and I were friends."

"We are friends," Lewis said, then leaned back in his chair. "I told you a few days ago I was going to turn up the heat."

"I thought you meant in prayer."

Lewis raised an eyebrow. "I did mean in prayer, but you and I aren't praying for the same thing."

"I'm praying for what direction to take in my marriage. What are you praying for?"

Before Lewis could respond, the waiter returned with their beverages and took their dinner order.

"Lewis, what are you praying for?" Starla repeated once the waiter left.

"Starla, I'm going to lay my cards on the table. I'm praying you will realize that Leon isn't the one for you, and that you will divorce him and marry me." Starla's eyes bucked and her mouth gaped. Lewis continued. "Starla, I have been attracted to you for quite some time, and I feel that you and I would be good together. The boys like me and I can provide a good life along with stability. You and the boys will never want for anything. That's a lot more than Leon Scott can provide."

Starla swallowed a big gulp of water. Lewis had laid his cards on the table, but Starla wished he'd pick them back up and throw the deck out the window into the bay. "Lewis, you're forgetting something: I don't love you, I love Leon."

The declaration didn't ruffle Lewis's feathers one bit. He didn't flinch or adjust his posture. "I know you don't love me, but in time you will. Besides, you married for love the first time and look what that got you: a drunk who left you with nothing. Next time around, try marrying someone who loves you instead." Lewis sipped his Roy Rogers and allowed his words to marinate in Starla's head.

"Lewis, are you trying to tell me that you're in love with me?" Starla finally asked, while at the same time praying he'd deny it.

"Yes, Starla, I believe I am."

Lord, what am I going to do? Starla's mind screamed so loud, she wondered if Lewis heard it. She couldn't run anymore; she had to make a decision, for real now. Either she would continue life with Leon or start a new one with Lewis. Once again, she looked out the window. Whatever her decision, she wasn't going to make it tonight. With her appetite dissipated, Starla wasn't going to eat, either.

"Lewis, I'm sorry, but this is too overwhelming for me. I have to go." Starla pushed her chair back and stood to leave. Lewis stood also.

"Starla, I know it's going to take some time for you to adapt to the idea. Take all the time you need. I'll always be here for you and the boys."

Starla hurried out the door before the tears fell and blurred her vision. Leon had told her those exact words years before, and he left her alone and without a house, with two little boys to raise.

Chapter 10

"Kevin, this doesn't make any sense! I have been calling you for three days and you won't return my calls. I know you're there, you're letting the devil work through that caller ID to avoid my calls. I am still your mother and your pastor, and I know you haven't forgotten what the Word says about obeying your parents. Now, because I am your mother and I'm saved, I have already forgiven you for that outrageous, not to mention unjustified, display of disrespect. Shoot, Kevin, stop acting stubborn like your father and call me, or else I'm coming down to that hospital!"

Kevin calmly pressed the delete message button on his cell phone. His mother had left similar messages on both his home phone and office line. He would have returned her calls if she would only admit that she was wrong for manipulating him into filing for divorce. Yes, he was frustrated with his life and needed to move on, but it was his mother's constant pushing that coerced him. Pastor Jennings relentlessly hounded him about how wrong Marlissa was for him. "She's not saved." "She's mean." "She's disrespectful." She'd say anything to paint a bad picture of Marlissa. Right now, Marlissa was looking pretty good.

The new Marlissa was sweet and thoughtful. Remembering Kevin's early-morning prayer time, Marlissa called him every day and joined him over the phone. The first day, the gesture astonished him to the point that he couldn't pray. Kevin held the line silently and listened to her pray for his spiritual and physical strength, then for guidance and success in the surgeries he was to perform that morning. Of course, she wouldn't let the horns of the altar loose without praying for the complete restoration of their marriage. "That was beautiful. Thank you," was his humble response.

Following Tuesday's prayer session, Kevin wanted to see her. After his last surgery, he dropped by the insurance office to invite her to a movie. The depth of the disappointment he felt at her decline surprised even him.

"I would love to, but I have to work at Macy's. Maybe this weekend?" Marlissa offered.

"Maybe," he said. "I'll call you later." Before he left, Marlissa pacified him with a light hug. Thinking back now, Kevin regretted not giving into the temptation to enjoy the softness of her glossed lips.

Kevin's cell phone rang. He checked the caller ID. Relieved that it wasn't his mother, he answered.

"Hello, Dr. Jennings." It was Marlissa.

"Hey." Kevin's body instantly relaxed at the sound of her voice.

"Is this a bad time? I don't want anything, just wanted to see how the clinic is going."

Marlissa really didn't want anything. Kevin was totally aware that her frequent calls were to demonstrate to him how committed she was to rebuilding their marriage, and that he was important to her. "I hope you're not working too hard."

"I have a full schedule this afternoon, but I'll be fine."

"You're already fine." Marlissa tried her hand at flirting. "Both physically and spiritually, you're the finest man I know."

Kevin interpreted the declaration as a compliment he couldn't receive with so much hanging over them. "Marlissa, I have to run, my patients are waiting. I'll talk to you later." Before she could say good-bye, Kevin disconnected. He sat at his desk and second-guessed the brush-off, but only momentarily.

***

Marlissa waited anxiously for Pastor Drake to continue his Bible Study series on the Fruit of the Spirit. Tonight's fruit was meekness. Marlissa had just propped her notebook on her lap when Kevin's long frame filled the seat next to her. Marlissa's pen, notebook, and jaw all fell at the same time.

"Kevin?"

"Hope you don't mind me intruding, but I wanted to check out Bible Study," Kevin said after replacing the items in her lap.

"I don't mind at all." Marlissa smiled. "Why don't you sit on the end? That'll leave more room for you to stretch your leg."

"Thanks, but this new prosthesis is quite comfortable."

"You're going to love Pastor Drake's Bible Study teachings. He really knows how to break the Word down to where even I can understand it." Marlissa lifted her eyes toward the podium as Pastor Drake began.

Pastor Drake's approach was new to Kevin. Unlike his mother, Pastor Drake didn't prolong time by discussing irrelevant information. Pastor Drake didn't preach; he taught and stayed on point. Pastor Jennings would start off teaching, but before the session was over, she'd be walking across the platform, whooping and hollering about something that had absolutely nothing to do with the topic.

Kevin was blessed by Pastor Drake's teaching, but what touched him most and almost brought him to tears was Marlissa's behavior. It was an awesome sight: her paying attention and taking notes like she was a student in class for the first time. "Thank you, Lord," he whispered. Enjoying church service with Marlissa was something he'd prayed for too many times to count. It was a desire he'd written off as fantasy, but tonight it was his reality. Kevin decided to let his guard down, and seized the moment. As she started on her third page, Kevin casually positioned his arm around Marlissa, and she paused long enough to offer him a smile, then continued writing.

"Come on, I want you to meet Pastor Drake." After the benediction Marlissa grabbed Kevin's arm and started toward the dais, but before they reached Pastor Drake, one of the church mothers he'd seen sitting in the front row blocked their path.

"You must be Kevin," the elderly woman stated. "You had better be, sitting so close to my baby in church. And I saw your arm around her."

"Mother, I—" Kevin didn't finish before another mother approached.

"It's so nice to finally meet you. Marlissa talks about you all the time. But she didn't tell us how handsome you are."

Kevin looked down at Marlissa. She beamed with joy, and he wondered if he'd ever seen her that happy before.

"Daughter, is this who I think it is?" Kevin turned to find Pastor Drake standing directly behind him. Surrounded by the two women and Pastor Drake, Kevin felt like he was being inspected for the FDA's seal of approval. Each bore a smile, but he could tell they were scanning him. Marlissa finally stopped blushing long enough to introduce him to the fruit inspectors.

"Kevin, this is Pastor and First Lady Drake." She then gestured to the petite elderly woman who had begun the interrogation. "This is Leon's mother, Mother Scott." Marlissa then interlocked her arm with Kevin's. "Everyone, this is my husband, Dr. Kevin Jennings."

Kevin politely greeted the aggressive group.

"I understand Pastor Rosalie Jennings is your mother. I haven't seen her in years, how is she?" Pastor Drake inquired.

"She's fine." Kevin's short response didn't seem to alarm Pastor Drake at all.

"How does it feel to be the top eye doctor at Sutter?" Mother Scott asked, then stepped closer and added, "I've been seeing black spots here lately, what do you think it could be?"

Kevin attempted not to laugh too hard at the stranger who moments earlier had reprimanded him for touching his wife and now wanted free medical advice. "Mother, I can't diagnose a problem without a complete eye exam."

"Humph, and you call yourself an expert." Mother Scott shook her head. "I'm going to give you a try anyway because Marlissa says you're the best, and I trust my baby's opinion. Besides, you're saved, so it can't hurt."

This time Kevin laughed out loud and so did everyone else. "Thanks for the vote of confidence, Mother." He handed her a business card. "I'd be glad to see you, just call the clinic and schedule an appointment. Tell them to book you for this Friday."

"Thank you." Kevin had won her over, Mother Scott was blushing.

"Once you get your eyes checked, you can stop misreading the announcements," First Lady Drake teased. "Last Sunday, you announced to the church that a special hearse would be here at six o'clock for anyone needing a ride to Sacramento. What you should have said was there was a special choir rehearsal at six o'clock for the upcoming engagement in Sacramento."

Mother Scott wasn't blushing anymore, now that everyone was laughing at her.

"Don't worry, Mother, I'll make sure you read the announcements correctly from now on." Kevin's words didn't offer much comfort.

"Mother Scott, God knows your heart," Pastor Drake said before First Lady and Mother Scott let loose in the house of the Lord. "Dr. Jennings, I hope you enjoyed Bible Study," he said, turning to Kevin.

"Please, 'Kevin' is fine. I enjoyed it immensely, I'm sure I'll be back."

"I pray that you will." Pastor Drake paused before his next statement. "Restoration Ministries has a marriage clinic that meets on the third Thursday of the month. The two of you might want to sit in on a session."

Marlissa felt Kevin's arm muscles tense, but she continued smiling.

"I'll keep that in mind," Kevin politely responded. "It's been a pleasure meeting you all. I'll see you on Friday," he said to Mother Scott, who was still brooding.

"I didn't know you are so close to your pastor," Kevin said as he and Marlissa exited the vestibule.

"Kevin, I'll always be grateful to the leaders of this church. They took me in when I was sick, wanting to die, and nursed me back to life. They showed me how to love myself when I didn't even like myself."

"They're very protective of you."

"That's because they've invested a lot into me," Marlissa answered, fishing her keys from her purse.

Slowly making their way across the parking lot, Kevin realized he wasn't ready to leave Marlissa's company. She'd just entered the code on the keyless entry pad when he asked, "It's just a little after eight. Do you want to hang out at Starbucks for a while?"

"Sure," she answered quickly.

"You really want to spend some time with me, huh?"

She giggled. "Honey, I'm so excited I could turn cartwheels right here in the parking lot. God is answering my prayers. We can park at my complex and walk from there."

Seeing her giddy over him overwhelmed Kevin. He leaned down and lightly brushed his lips over hers. "I'll follow you." Kevin waited until she was securely inside before heading to his SUV. A second before he turned the ignition, his cell phone vibrated. It was his mother.

"Hello, Mother." Kevin started the vehicle and shifted into drive.

Pastor Jennings didn't bother with pleasantries. "Kevin, where have you been? Why haven't you returned my calls? I could have been dying for all you knew!"

"Mother, it's late. Save the drama and get to the purpose of your call."

"*Kevin Hezekiah Jennings,* have you forgotten that I'm your mother?"

Kevin sighed, and wondered if all female pastors were as dramatic as his mother. "How can I forget when you remind me on a regular basis?"

Pastor Jennings ignored the sarcasm. "Why weren't you at Bible Study last night? It's one thing to be mad at me, but don't take it out on the Lord."

He turned onto Piedmont Avenue. Kevin shook his head, although his mother couldn't see him. It amazed him how his mother thought she could control every aspect of his life, including how he served the Lord. "Mother, I have to go now. I'm busy."

"What are you doing and why aren't you at home?" Pastor Jennings questioned.

"Mother, how do you know I'm not at home? I do answer my cell when I'm at home." Kevin pulled the phone away from his ear, but that didn't stop him from hearing the effects of his mother's temper tantrum.

"Kevin, you know good and well you're not at home! I've been waiting here at your house all evening. Now, where are you?" She was still screaming when Kevin disconnected the call. Before exiting the SUV, he made a note to have his locks changed.

Kevin waited in front of the complex while Marlissa parked her car in the underground garage. He debated if he was doing the right thing by spending time with her. He wasn't sure if he wanted to remain married to her. Taking that into consideration, he didn't think it wise. She had been very clear with her intentions, and he didn't want to mislead her. Watching her approach him just then, he realized the person being misled was him.

For just a moment, he entertained the truth. He enjoyed the new Marlissa, and, yes, he wanted to be her husband again. He didn't trust her with his heart, but he still loved her.

She held out her hand to him. "Ready?"

He didn't answer, just affectionately took her hand in his. The two walked quietly down Piedmont Avenue. On this trip, Marlissa didn't window shop, and Kevin didn't leave her behind.

Seated at the same corner table they'd shared weeks before, Kevin sipped hot apple cider while Marlissa enjoyed her usual chai tea.

Kevin took a sip and placed the cup on the round table. "Marlissa, can you explain something to me?"

Marlissa covered his hand with hers. "Go ahead."

Kevin took mental note of her effort to express affection. "I don't understand how attending one church service, drunk, changed your life. You spent many Sundays and Tuesday nights at church with me and you weren't moved at all. I prayed for you all the time, but the more I prayed, the more you resisted. I would have given anything to see you interested in church like you are now. I guess what I'm asking is, why did you have to leave me to find the Lord?"

Marlissa sipped her tea before answering. "Kevin, I'll be straight with you. I couldn't relate to the God your mother preached about. I didn't understand her God." She paused for him to respond; when he didn't, Marlissa continued. "The God your mother presented was condemning and judgmental. Her God was full of rules and regulations, and He didn't love you unless you followed this long list of rules. You couldn't make any mistakes; you had to be perfect to serve her God. Your mother preached about a loving God, but her God didn't require her to love sinners like me. I was never good enough for her. I'm still not. To be completely honest, I didn't want the God she was selling."

"But I wasn't like that with you," Kevin spoke up. Marlissa heard the depth of his pain, and saw the turbulence as anger and hurt collided together in his eyes. "I was always there for you even after . . . after you rejected me."

Marlissa didn't bother wiping away the tears that moistened her cheeks. She hurt for Kevin and all they had lost. "Kevin, you're right. It's like I told you before: I didn't love myself. Therefore, I couldn't accept the love you offered. I don't know how to make you understand, but my leaving had nothing to do with you. You were a wonderful husband; I was the one all twisted up. It's like you said the first day we met: I was crazy. I *had* to be crazy to leave you." Marlissa smiled and that seemed to lighten his mood. "I'm not crazy anymore, and I know what I want. I want us, Kevin."

Kevin wanted to tell her he wanted the same, but his heart wasn't ready. Instead, he asked, "When can I see you again?" He figured it wasn't the response she wanted, but it was the best he could offer.

"When do you want to see me?"

Kevin finished his cider. "Tomorrow for dinner."

Marlissa pouted. "I'm sorry, but I'm working at Macy's every night this week. This is my only night off." The sound of Marlissa's cell phone startled them both. "Excuse me."

Kevin listened as Marlissa tried to convince the caller she wasn't in any kind of trouble. Giving up, she handed the phone to Kevin. "Will you tell Leon that I am with you?"

He received the phone and leaned back in the chair. "That's right, Leon, she hasn't left my sight all evening. And, by the way, I met your mother this evening. She's a character. I'm going to see her on Friday."

Marlissa leaned back with her arms folded as Kevin and Leon talked on and on about what she considered unnecessary jibber jabber. "I'd better go, someone's getting jealous . . . Thanks for looking out . . . I'll make sure she gets home safely."

Marlissa defended herself after he handed her back the phone and she secured it on the waist clip. "I'm not jealous, but I don't get to spend much time with you. I don't want to share what little time I have."

Kevin smiled and tightened his grip. It pleased him that Marlissa really wanted to spend more time with him. "'Lissa, if I ask you to quit your night job, would you?"

"I haven't heard that in a long time," Marlissa said in reference to Kevin's pet name for her.

"It's been a long time since I've wanted to call you that." Kevin broke the uneasy silence that followed. "Well, would you?"

"Why would you want me to do that?"

"It's like you said, with you working two jobs, that doesn't leave much time for us to work on building a relationship. If it's money you're worried about, I'll make up the difference. But if we're going to give this a serious try, spending time together is extremely critical."

Marlissa thought for a long moment. "What if we don't work out and Leon moves back home?"

"Then I'll assist you in securing a place. I'll even cosign for you."

Marlissa quietly evaluated his proposal. In his subtle way, Kevin was expressing his desire to provide for her. It was never his desire for his wife to work one job; two was completely out of the question. Kevin was also conveying how much he wanted to be with her; he just wasn't ready to totally commit. She had to regain his trust, and this was Kevin's way of testing her level of commitment.

"All right, I'll quit tomorrow morning."

"Does that mean you'll be free for dinner tomorrow?" he asked, squeezing her hand.

"Where do you have in mind?"

"Elephant Bar, then a movie."

"It's a date, Dr. Jennings." Marlissa smiled, then looked down at her watch. "It's past my bedtime, I still have a day job, remember?"

"And I have two surgeries in the morning," Kevin added, rising to his feet.

The walk back to the complex was quiet, but it was a different tranquility than they'd experienced on the walk down. The night sky appeared clearer and the stars more brilliant. This stillness was one of understanding, and, in a small way, acceptance. This round Kevin didn't hold her hand, opting instead to relax his arm around her shoulder.

"I enjoyed being with you tonight," he said once they reached the complex. "I really enjoyed Bible Study, and I even enjoyed meeting your nosey church members." They shared a stiff laugh.

"They just love me, that's all."

So do I, he thought, but didn't voice it.

Marlissa took the initiative and settled the nervous silence that followed. "Can I have a good night kiss?"

Kevin smiled and moved closer to her. "I thought you'd never ask."

"Just for future reference, don't wait for me to ask. Since when does a man need permission to kiss his wife?"

Kevin quickly pushed away the negative memory that rushed to the forefront of his mind. This was the new Marlissa, not the one who rejected him. He lifted her chin, then lowered his lips to hers, and, for the moment, savored the type of contentment a man could only find in his wife. Then, just when he thought the thrill would end, Marlissa parted her lips and sent him spiraling deeper into ecstasy.

"I love you," she whispered once they separated.

"I know." And he did know. Kevin felt the profundity of her emotions in her kiss. "Talk to you in the morning." Tonight he waited until she was securely inside the elevator before heading to his car.

Chapter 11

"Baby, please try to understand my position." Leon's pleading wasn't enough to convince Starla that her husband wasn't hiding something from her. For the third consecutive time, Leon had cancelled his visit with the boys because of his changing work schedule. "I don't make enough money as it is. I can't just tell my employer I'm not coming to work because I want to take my kids to the movies."

"Why did you bother coming back into our lives if you weren't ready to commit to us?" Starla quickly corrected the last word. "I mean, to the boys. It's not fair to them. They look forward to seeing you, Leon."

Starla was being unreasonable. He sighed into the phone. "Starla, please—"

"Please nothing!" Starla screamed so loudly that Leon's ear started ringing. "It's not the boys' fault you drank away our stable home environment and now you have to work two jobs. It's not fair to them that they can't see their father. My boys deserve better than that. They deserve better than you!"

"You're right, baby, it is my fault. Please try to work with me on this. Once the business is restarted, everything will change."

"Tell it to someone who cares!"

Leon stayed glued in the same spot long after Starla slammed the phone down in his ear. He was trying to understand what was happening in his life. Everything was suddenly spinning out of control. Three weeks ago, he and Starla were getting along almost like old times. Lately, for some unforeseen reason, all Leon and Starla could manage was arguing, and she constantly threw his past as a sucker punch. Last week, Starla accused him of drinking again, and today she said he wasn't good enough for *her* boys. "God, I'm doing my best. How can I get her to see that this is only temporary? How can I convince her to have faith in me again? Even the thief crucified with Jesus received another chance." He mumbled the prayer.

Leon started to phone her back, but he knew his wife well enough to know that the sound of his voice would only make matters worse. Besides, Starla needed time to deal with whatever it was that really had her perturbed. Starla was a master at lashing out instead of dealing with the issue at hand. One of their biggest arguments outside of Leon's drinking occurred in Starla's eighth month of pregnancy with their first son, Montel.

Starla had accused Leon of cheating with the checker at the local convenience store all because Leon stopped there almost every day. Never mind that he was purchasing watermelon and ice cream for Starla. It turned out that Starla didn't really want the watermelon or the ice cream. What she wanted was for Leon to attend Lamaze classes with her but was afraid to ask, because of his busy schedule.

Leon clipped his phone to his waist and went back inside the gas station. To encourage himself, Leon hummed one of his favorite songs, Yolanda Adam's "The Battle Is The Lord's."

"Girl, I don't mean to be all up in your business, not all of it anyway, but are you *crazy?*" Vangie asked after Starla slammed down the phone receiver. "Did I just hear you dismiss your husband because he's working?"

Starla pulled back the two braids that had fallen in her face. "This is the third time that trifling, dim-witted husband of mine has cancelled on the boys. They deserve better than what he's giving them."

Vangie pursed her lips. "Oh really? They deserve more than a father who's working two jobs and studying for his contractor's license so he can start his own business and provide a better life for them?" Starla didn't answer. "Girlfriend, you're absolutely right. Your boys deserve much better than that."

"Look, Vangie." Starla's attitude was evident as her neck rolled back and forth. "It's Leon's fault he has to work two jobs in the first place, not mine, and definitely not my boys'. We didn't tell him to drink our lives away."

Vangie shushed her. "Will you lower your voice before we both get fired?" Vangie grabbed her arm and led her over to the corner near the window where their voices wouldn't be easily heard. "All I'm saying is, you can do a lot worst than Leon. True, the man made a major mistake, but at least he's working to rectify his wrongs. So what if he has to work two jobs? It's just for a little while. For goodness' sake, the man practically hands over ever dime to you anyway."

"That still doesn't make it any easier on me." Starla pouted and rolled her eyes.

"Oh," Vangie said, backing out of the corner. "Now we're getting to the meat. This is not about the boys. You're mad because *you* wanted to see him."

Starla confirmed Vangie's assessment by walking quietly back to her desk.

"Girl, ain't nothing wrong with wanting to see your husband, but you might get better results if you told him that instead of attacking him," Vangie said, following close behind.

Starla didn't respond. She couldn't. Expressing to Leon how much she really wanted and needed to see him would commit her to reconciliation. She wasn't ready to do that just yet. A few weeks ago she'd played with the idea, but that was before Lewis stated his position. At first it was a no-brainer: she didn't want Lewis; she loved Leon. But then Leon started canceling his time with them, and the fear of being alone again resurfaced.

"Leon loves you, but there's not one man on this earth who feels good when his woman belittles him." With that said, Vangie walked away.

Leon was in the middle of restocking twenty-ounce plastic bottles of soda when he felt a little hand touch his back. No sooner had he turned around than little Jaylen's arms were around his waist.

"Hey, son." Leon tried to return his hug, but Montel quickly raced to his free arm. "What are you guys doing here?"

The oldest, Montel, took the liberty of being the spokesperson. "Mommy said you couldn't come see us today because you had to work. But we still wanted to see you, Daddy."

"I wanted to see you too. I miss you guys." Leon kissed the boys' foreheads, then looked up at Starla, who was standing back and watching the affectionate exchange. For the first time she realized that she was the one who was a dimwit when it came to how much Leon loved their boys.

"You guys want something to drink?" The boys readily accepted Leon's offer and followed him over to the soda fountain.

"Hey, Dad, can we have chips, too?" Jaylen asked.

"And candy, too?" Montel added.

Starla figured she'd better intervene before the boys talked Leon out of his week's paycheck. "Boys, choose one item. Daddy has to get back to work."

"Okay." The boys pouted, and like the firm, loving father he was, Leon bought the boys drinks and helped them make ice cream cones at the self-serve station.

"Thank you for bringing the boys by," Leon said to Starla after the boys were consumed with their treats.

Starla bit her lower lip, and Leon waited for her to say what was on her mind. "I'm sorry. I didn't mean what I said on the phone."

"Why don't you tell me what's really bothering you?" Leon said, and placed his arm around her.

"I miss you." Starla bundled the words together and Leon grinned from ear to ear.

"You do?"

"I was mad because I wanted to see you," Starla finally admitted.

"Come here." Leon pulled Starla closer to him, and mumbled something in her ear that caused her to giggle uncontrollably.

"Forgive me?"

"Of course I do." Leon held her face to his. "Baby, stop analyzing everything; just trust what you feel, trust me again."

Leon and Starla were so engrossed in the kiss that followed that they didn't hear a customer enter the store. It was the boys' teasing that finally broke the spell.

"Look, Jaylen, Daddy is kissing Mommy."

"Uh-uh, Mommy is kissing Daddy," Jaylen corrected.

"I'll call you later." Leon gave Starla one final peck then rushed to assist the customer.

***

Lewis's eyes remained transfixed on the surveillance camera monitor in his office at the back
of the gas station. He didn't like the open display
of affection that had transpired between Starla
and Leon. In fact, he found it rather nauseating,
but as long as he was Leon's boss and controlled
his schedule, he could live with it.

"God sure does work in mysterious ways," was
what he said a month ago after taking ownership of
the station on Telegraph and recognizing the name
Leon Scott on his list of employees. Scheduling
was something he no longer handled, being the
owner of a major trucking company that ran from
Death Valley to the tip of the Oregon border and
employed over 300 people. But for Leon's benefit,
Lewis scheduled the Telegraph store personally.

With the schedule, Lewis made sure Leon
stayed busy and away from Starla and the boys.
Today it was Starla who'd made the surprise
move. She wasn't supposed to just show up
like that, but she had, and Lewis had to watch
Leon kiss his woman. A minute sooner and
Starla would have seen him stocking the change
machine. Lewis had promised to give her all the
time and space she needed to dispose of Leon,
but Starla had just proven to him that she didn't
know what was best for herself or the boys.

Lewis spent the next hour behind his desk
with his head bowed in prayer.

Chapter 12

As Marlissa waited for the elevator to travel to the fifth floor, she tightened her jacket and gripped the picnic basket. When the doors opened on the third floor, she glanced down at her watch. "Come on, I only have an hour," she pleaded with the silver doors. Marlissa had exerted too much energy into planning this surprise in-office picnic to be disappointed. The mere fact that Marlissa had planned all week for one hour was major progress for her.

Marlissa's inexperience in the romance and creativity departments, and lack of female friends, left her seeking help from her best friend's wife. When Starla came by to visit Leon earlier in the week, Marlissa squeezed on the couch with them with a pen and writing pad in hand.

"What type of message do you want to send?" Starla had asked once Leon retreated to his room. "What do you want to put on his mind?"

"Message?" Marlissa frowned.

"You know, what do you want your surprise to convey to him?"

"Huh?" Marlissa still didn't understand.

"I'll never understand how you ever landed a man like Dr. Kevin Jennings," Starla teased. "Do you want Kevin to get full on the food or full from looking at you?"

Marlissa finally understood. "Girl, don't play! You know I want him drooling so bad that he'll want to take me home with him."

Marlissa and Kevin were making steady progress in their relationship. With her nights now free, they spent most evenings together. Some nights she'd cook for him or watch a DVD with him at her apartment until Leon returned. In the last two weeks, they'd laughed and talked more than in their first year of marriage. Marlissa became more relaxed with expressing her affections. Every day she made it a point to compliment him, and when they were together she initiated the limited physical contact.

Today, Marlissa opted to give Kevin the royal treatment, which included fine china, cloth napkins, handblown crystal goblets, gold candlesticks, and the sounds of Kirk Whalum's saxophone. She hoped Kevin was hungry, because Marlissa had prepared his favorites: roasted garlic and lime chicken, wild rice with steamed broccoli, and, of course for dessert, banana pudding.

Finally, the elevator reached the fifth floor, and Marlissa hurriedly stepped off. Marlissa quickly found Kevin's nurse, who helped her slip into his office undetected.

"Dr. Jennings sure is going to be surprised," the nurse said, then leaned in closer and added, "I like you better than the other one."

Marlissa smiled and thanked the kind middle-aged woman. Once inside the office, Marlissa went right to work. She'd just lit the second candle when the door opened.

At first Kevin thought he'd entered the wrong office, but then he saw her standing beside his desk. He was in the right office, of that he was now certain. The room contained everything he liked, including the woman who was now walking toward him.

"I hope you're hungry, Dr. Jennings," Marlissa said after a soft kiss.

"I hope you didn't wear that dress to work." Kevin commented on the form-fitting tangerine-colored tank dress.

"Do you like it?" Marlissa turned and modeled for him. "You're the first person to see me wear this."

Kevin cleared his throat. "Make sure I'm the *only* person who sees you in that dress."

"Are you flirting with me?"

"I guess I am," Kevin said, realizing this was the first time he'd flirted with her since they'd been "dating."

Marlissa took him by the hand and led him to his desk. "I'll change when I get back to work. Come on, let's eat."

"You remembered," he whispered after she placed the plate in front of him.

"Of course I remember what you like." She winked at him, causing Kevin to drop his fork. "I also got you some of the peach cider you've come to enjoy."

When Marlissa continued to stand, he asked, "Aren't you going to eat?"

"I ate earlier, this is your time," Marlissa answered, and handed him a cloth napkin.

Kevin hesitated and debated which one he preferred on his lap: the napkin or Marlissa. He decided on both. In one swift motion, Kevin swooped Marlissa off her feet and onto his lap.

"Whoa," she squealed, then relaxed as he brought her face to his. After the kiss that left him trying to remember what day it was, Kevin gently stroked her cheeks. He assumed she'd interpreted the desire in his eyes as hunger, because her next statement was, "Let's eat."

Kevin savored his private feast with Marlissa seated on his lap, his favorite part being when Marlissa spoon-fed him the banana pudding and kissed the excess from his mouth.

"I have to get back to the insurance company," she said, regrettably stepping from his lap. Kevin also stood and helped repack the picnic basket. With the packing completed, Marlissa turned to find Kevin holding her coat open.

"Now that you're full, you're in a hurry to get rid of me, huh?" Marlissa mused, stepping into her coat.

"It's not about getting rid of you." Kevin turned her to face him after the coat was secure. "I don't want you showing off my business." He was about to kiss her again when an intruder invaded his office.

The three stood frozen in place, each wondering what the other was doing there and sizing up the enemy. Preparing to protect Marlissa, Kevin moved in front of her, just before the volcano erupted, spewing hot lava and destroying everything in its path.

"What the devil is going on in here?" Pastor Jennings slammed the door so hard, Marlissa flinched.

"Mother, have you lost your mind? This is a hospital. You can't—" Kevin started.

"Don't tell me what I can't do!" She pointed to Marlissa. "What is she doing here?"

"Mother, that's none of your business! Now behave before I call security!"

"If a heathen like her can just walk up in here, so can I!"

"I'll see you later." Marlissa grabbed the basket and practically ran from the office.

Pastor Jennings went to the door and yelled after her. "The only place you'll see my son is at your divorce hearing! Now stay away from him like I told you!" She focused her attention on her son. "Kevin, what's going on around here?"

Kevin was so angry, he couldn't speak. He huffed, then balled his fist and went after his wife. He found her still waiting for the elevator, crying.

"Baby, I am so sorry for that." Kevin tried to hold her, but she wouldn't return his embrace. Giving up, he lifted her chin, forcing her to meet his gaze. "My mother's opinion doesn't matter, only mine. I enjoyed my office picnic, but I found the most pleasure in the company. 'Lissa, you did good today. I appreciate the effort."

Marlissa wiped her face and forced a smile. It wasn't the ending she'd hoped for, but she'd scored a point. The elevator doors opened and Kevin kissed her before going to fight Goliath.

"So, that's why you've missed church two Sundays in a row and why you can't return my calls; you've been hanging out with that drunk!" Pastor Jennings didn't even wait for Kevin to close the door.

"Marlissa is not a drunk anymore, and I have been to church, just not your church," Kevin answered, then sat down behind his desk. He reached into the desk drawer for a red stress-relief ball.

"What do you mean *your* church? That's *our* church."

"Mother, why are you here?" Kevin's patience was about to run out. He rapidly squeezed the ball.

The temper tantrum wasn't working; Pastor Jennings tried a softer approach. "Son, please tell me you're not going to allow yourself to get entangled again with that yoke of bondage. We both know Marlissa is not right for you. Your divorce will be final soon. Let her go so that God can bless you with the one He's chosen for you."

"Let me guess, Reyna?" Kevin smirked. "Mother, if you think Reyna is so great, then you marry her." Kevin stood and walked to the door. With every step he squeezed the ball. "If I divorce Marlissa it will be my decision, not yours. And if I were to remarry, it wouldn't be to Reyna. One of you is enough." Kevin walked out, but she called after him.

"What do you mean, *if* you divorce Marlissa?"

"The devil is a lie!" Pastor Jennings repeated the slogan and prayed all the way back to her church office. "I'm not going to let the devil destroy what I've worked so hard to accomplish."

She picked up the phone and dialed Tyson's cell number. One of the benefits of being Tyson's pastor was having a lawyer at her disposal at all times.

Tyson didn't get the second syllable of "hello" out before Pastor Jennings started digging in. "Tyson, what's going on with Kevin's divorce?"

"Well, hello, Pastor. How are you today?"

"You tell me. What's the status on Kevin's divorce? When is it going to be final?"

Tyson took a deep breath. "Pastor, you know I can't discuss that with you. I suggest you ask your son to tell you what you want to know."

"I did, but he won't tell me," Pastor Jennings admitted.

"Neither will I," Tyson responded in that no-nonsense business tone she hated; although she only hated it when it was directed toward her.

Pastor Jennings exhaled long and slowly. "Tyson, can you talk to me as his friend and not as his lawyer?"

"I'll try," Tyson answered honestly.

"Is Kevin trying to decide if he wants to reconcile with that drunk?"

"Kevin's not trying to decide anything. I believe he knows if he wants to remain married to Marlissa or not." He paused. "Pastor, you do know that Marlissa is saved now?"

"So I hear," she said dryly. "Well, does he want her or not?"

"You'll have to ask Kevin that yourself."

Pastor Jennings gave up. Tyson wasn't giving up any information and that infuriated her. If anyone knew what Kevin was up to, it was Tyson, but he wasn't telling and right now he was wasting her time.

"Good-bye, Tyson." After disconnecting, she paced her office until she heard Reyna come in. Reyna barely had a chance to set her purse on the desk before Pastor Jennings started barking. "Where have you been?"

"I went to the bank and then to the office supply store." Reyna held up the white plastic bag with red letters.

"That's not what I mean. Why haven't you been spending more time with Kevin? While you're running around buying pens and Post-its, Marlissa is posting in his office!"

"What?" Reyna was confused. "I thought you said we should let him cool down for a while."

"Forget what I told you." Pastor Jennings waved her hands in the air. "You need to be more aggressive if you want to be Mrs. Kevin Jennings." She finally sat down. "According to my calculations, his divorce will be final in three months. During that time, you need to stay in his face. Every time he turns around, he should see a reflection of you. When he's not looking at you, he should be speaking to you on the phone. Even if you have to make a CD and send him subliminal messages, get his attention!"

Reyna laughed. "That's a little extreme, don't you think?"

"No, it's not, and while you're at it, stop dressing like a nun. Style your hair and put on some makeup."

"I thought you said modesty was best," Reyna questioned. "You said I should dress like you."

Pastor Jennings rolled her eyes at Reyna. Yes, she'd told Reyna that, but it wasn't working with Kevin just like it hadn't worked with her late husband. Her husband had constantly complained about her plain-Jane, holier-than-thou look, but Pastor Jennings had refused to change. She wouldn't even wear lingerie to bed, favoring long cotton flannel pajamas or a muumuu. That's probably why, for most of their marriage, her late husband kept a mistress. She was usually

someone half Rosalie's age and a lot more liber-
ated when it came to sexuality.

"Reyna, in a battle, sometimes you have to
change your methodology if you want to win.
From what I saw today, we're in a battle and
your opponent is not going to go away quietly."
Rosalie leaned back in her chair. "I've taken you
as far I as I can, the rest is up to you."

Chapter 13

"Did you rock the good doc's world or what?" Leon cheerfully asked upon entering the apartment. Marlissa didn't verbally respond, just shrugged. Leon sat down next to her on the couch; that's when he noticed she was crying.

Leon frowned. "I can't believe he didn't like a surprise like that. I don't know a man alive who wouldn't. You must not have done everything Starla told you to because that woman, man, that woman knows what to do, I tell you."

Marlissa jumped in before Leon gave himself a stroke. "He did like it." She paused. "It was his mother who didn't like me."

"What was his mother doing there?"

Marlissa filled him in on the horrid details. "Leon, sometimes I wonder if all of this is worth it. I'm scared I'll never live down my past and I'll never be good enough to be accepted."

Leon swallowed and waited for her to finish. He knew exactly how she felt. He'd been asking himself the same questions concerning his relationship with Starla.

"What if we're just wasting our time? What if, no matter how hard we try, Starla and Kevin will never forgive us? At least, not to the point where they're willing to trust us again?" Leon remained still while she blew her nose. "Sometimes I think I should just give up, you know, move on. I don't know, start over in another state or something."

After the sniffles, Leon took her by the hand and prayed for the right words that would not only encourage her, but him also. "Brat, the first thing you have to do is stop allowing people like Pastor Jennings to control you and how you feel about yourself."

"What do you mean?"

"This morning, when you left here, you felt good about yourself and about life. Now you're sitting here doubting yourself because of one person's stupidity. Rosalie Jennings may be a pastor, but she's not God. She doesn't control your destiny, you do." Leon paused. "Remember this, anything that we love is worth fighting for. I love Starla and those boys more than anything in the world. I believe with all my heart, I have to, that we'll be reunited. But if that never happens, the time and energy I've invested into showing them how important they are to me is more than worth it. Love is always worth it." Leon smiled as a thought came to him. "Look at it like this: Jesus knew everyone wouldn't receive Him, but the chance to offer salvation to the world was worth the trip to the cross."

Marlissa shrugged. "Since you put it that way."

Leon bowed his head and prayed for them, Starla, and his boys. Finally, he prayed for Pastor Jennings. He asked God to heal her of whatever was causing her to lash out at Marlissa.

The telephone rang. "Can you get that? I need to take a shower before I visit the boys."

Leon headed off to his room and Marlissa answered the phone. It was Kevin calling from the newly installed security gate. She buzzed him into the building, then ran to the bathroom to freshen up.

When she opened the door, Kevin looked down at her and pouted. "What happened to the dress?" She was now wearing sweats.

"We heathens do wear regular clothes." She smiled, but the pain his mother's words had caused was still evident. He stepped inside and closed the door.

"Come here." He pulled her close to him and held her until her body relaxed. "Don't let Mother bother you. You're not a heathen. What you are is beautiful, and in that orange dress, you're *hot*."

"Thank you," she managed between blushing and laughing. Taking his hand, Marlissa led him to the couch, and, like old times, she snuggled against him while he rubbed her shoulder. "Kevin," she said, her voice just above a whisper, "I don't want to come between you and your mother."

He stopped rubbing her shoulder. "'Lissa, what are you saying?"

She raised her head so she could look him in the eyes when she made her next statement. "If staying married to me is going to damage your relationship with your mother . . . I . . . I . . . you know." She looked away.

He turned her face back to his. "My relationship with my mother has been strained since the car accident eighteen years ago. Mother still blames herself because she ran the red light and crashed into an oncoming truck. Since then she's been trying to make it up to me by trying to control every aspect of my life. For the most part, I've been passive, but I'll never allow her to control our relationship. If I did, we wouldn't be married now. I'd be married to Reyna with ten kids." Kevin shook his head at that scenario.

"Do you still want children?"

He didn't hesitate. "Yes."

"Me too."

Kevin's hand glided over her abdomen as he kissed her.

"Hey, brat, I'll call you if I'm not coming home tonight." They parted and stared at Leon, who was dressed and smelled more like he was on his way to church than to see his wife and kids. "Carry on." Before either could say anything, Leon was gone.

"If I didn't like Leon, I wouldn't be able to handle your living arrangement," Kevin finally admitted. "At first I was jealous because Leon is the one who helped you to change. I wanted to be that person. Since I've gotten to know him, I understand that he was just what you needed at that time, and I now respect your friendship."

"I kind of thought you were checking him out, the way you always kept *running* into him."

"Who I should have been checking out is his mother." Kevin shook his head. "Mother Scott is too much. Two weeks in a row, she has been forty-five minutes late for her appointment. Then she wants to debate with me about everything."

"That's Mother." Marlissa laughed out loud.

"I tried to test her peripheral vision and she told me that wasn't important because eyes were made to focus straight ahead, not side to side. Besides, the Lord told her that her side vision was fine. I don't know what I'm going to do with her."

"I hope that doesn't stop you from joining us on Memorial Day."

"If I miss her church picnic, Mother Scott will whip me."

"No, she—" Marlissa thought about it, then nodded her head. "Yes, she will." There was a brief pause. "Pastor Drake called the other day and asked how you and I are doing."

"What did you tell him?"

"I told him we're good." She smiled slightly. "I hope I didn't lie to him."

"You didn't."

Driving home, Kevin dropped the façade and was truthful with himself. He was stuck. Aside from a few snags, mainly his mother, the renewed relationship was working. The communication was wonderful, and in the affection department, Marlissa had had a rebirth. The old Marlissa would have never attempted something like what she'd done today. The woman who briefly shared his bed was too rigid and uncomfortable with her sexuality. The alcohol did soften her a bit, but that cheapened the experience for him.

The progress still wasn't enough for him to lower his guard enough to tell Marlissa those three little words she frequently graced his ear with, or to discuss the divorce. To make matters worse, his desire to be intimate with her was increasing every day. Today with her on his lap he'd almost reached his breaking point, but the fear of her rejecting him kept him in check.

That was the one thing he couldn't get past. How could they live as husband and wife if Marlissa was perturbed by his body? That was the origin of their problems. Marlissa hadn't flipped out until he revealed his body; then both of their worlds began spinning out of control. Kevin refused to live his life in a box, exposing only parts of himself.

He wondered why she'd asked him about kids. Didn't she remember how one-sided and unfulfilling their sex life was? Kevin pushed those thoughts to the back of his mind for now, but real soon they'd have to deal with those unresolved issues.

Chapter 14

Starla shook Leon for the third time without any success. When he was exhausted, a 6.0 earthquake along the San Andreas Fault couldn't raise Leon from his coma-like sleep. Starla wished she had remembered his routine before draining every ounce of his energy. Then again, in her frame of mind it wouldn't have mattered.

Starla had repeatedly vowed she wouldn't sleep with Leon until all of their issues were resolved, but training Marlissa in how to win Kevin's affections unleashed the she-bear in Starla. After tucking the boys in for the night, Leon didn't stand a chance, as if he wanted one. She recalled Vangie's warning, but three years was a long time and Leon was her husband. Despite their present situation, they still loved each other. Six hours ago, Starla didn't see anything wrong with making love to her husband. Starla didn't want to see, she wanted to feel. By his reaction, Leon needed the reunion more than she.

Leon had been honest with her from the beginning. The closest he remembered coming to having sex during their separation was the night he met Marlissa. He submitted to HIV testing just in case in his drunken state he'd had unprotected sex. Starla considered it only fair to tell him about her unplanned date with Lewis. She didn't mention his name, just that he was a man from her church. The bottom line was that they both were starved.

Gazing now at his motionless body and the face exhibiting a smile of satisfaction and contentment, Starla second-guessed her decision to please her flesh.

The circumstances were the same. Leon wanted to renew their vows and start over. Starla still wasn't sure she could do that. The beautiful experience they shared through the night couldn't alleviate her anxiety over trusting Leon with her heart again. Yes, he was doing all the right things for all the right reasons. The boys loved him, and Lord knows she did, but fear is a powerful thing. For Starla, the fear came power-packed with insecurity and abandonment.

At age eight, Starla had sat at the kitchen table practicing multiplication while her parents talked in their bedroom with the door closed. Halfway through the problems, her father stepped into the kitchen and gave her a hug, then kissed her on the forehead. "I love you and I'll see you later," he had said, and left. "Later" ended up being thirteen years; her parents separated that day. The next time Starla saw her father, he was on his deathbed after suffering a heart attack.

Her father's abandonment left Starla insecure, and afraid to love and to be loved. In Starla's view, something must have been terribly wrong with her, if her own father could walk off and leave her without ever looking back. To cope, Starla built a brick wall around her heart and hid deep within the confines. She dealt with everyone as temporary and more superior.

Leon was the only person to see past the pretense and remove the bricks, one at a time. Leon gave her the security and validation she hadn't gotten from her father. Starla considered herself average looking, but Leon made her feel like a beautiful queen. They shared everything and handled every problem together until David's death. For the second time in her life, Starla was abandoned and emotionally scarred by a man she loved. Right now she didn't have the strength or courage to try again.

There was an alternative: Lewis. He'd made it clear; she didn't have to love him. Starla immediately shook that idea and tried waking Leon again.

"Baby, wake up."

This time Leon groaned and reached for her, but Starla grabbed his hands.

"Baby, you have to go before the boys wake up and find you here." She shook him again, but it was her words that caused his eyes to open.

"What?"

"The boys can't see us like this. It'll confuse them."

Leon was wide awake now, but his facial expression said he wished he weren't. "Starla, how would seeing us in the same bed confuse the boys? We're their parents and we are married." Leon held his breath, but Starla said the words anyway.

"But we're not together."

Leon snatched his hand away from her grasp and sat up. "So what was last night, a booty call in reverse?"

"No!" Starla defended herself. "I wanted to be with you. I missed you."

"If you want to be with me, then why aren't we together? Why are you asking me to sneak out like some trick?"

"Leon, please try to understand," Starla pleaded. "I need more time."

Leon jumped out of bed and gathered his clothing. "Funny how you don't need more time when I can't spend time with you because of work or when I'm marking up your neck. A few hours ago you were asking for something more, but it sure wasn't time." Starla looked away. "It seems you only need more time when it comes to what I want. I want us, but apparently you don't."

"That's not true."

"So that whole seduction scene was an illusion, and you're not throwing me out like day-old garbage after making love to me several times?"

"Yes! No! Leon, you're twisting everything!"

"I'm twisting everything?" Leon pointed at her. "You're the one who said we wouldn't make love unless were back together."

"I know, but I'm still not ready."

Leon stepped into his shoes, not bothering to button his shirt. He exhaled deeply and sat down on the side of the bed next to Starla, who was now crying quietly. "Star." His voice was calmer. "I need you to tell me what *your* truth is. Up until now I thought we were on the same wavelength and striving for the same goal. Do you really want our family unit restored?"

Starla sniffled and answered honestly. "Yes, I do."

"Then what are we waiting for? I'm doing everything right by you and the boys; why isn't that enough for you?" Starla didn't respond. "Are you waiting for me to reestablish the business?" When she still didn't respond, he asked, "Do you love me enough to trust me again?"

Starla gripped the sheet and pulled it tightly around her. "I am scared." Leon recognized the raw fear he hadn't seen in years, and gathered Starla into his arms until the trembling stopped and the tears subsided.

"Star, I am sorry for the hell I have put you through, but maybe this will help you finally heal from the wounds imposed on you by your father's disappearance. You have never really dealt with that part of your life, and I acted as a good Band-Aid until I hurt you. Now it's paralyzing you again."

Starla lifted her eyes to meet his. "I know you're right, but can you give me more time?"

Leon brushed her braids away from her face. "Is the fear of trusting me again the only thing holding you back?"

Starla kissed his lips. "Leon, if I wasn't afraid you'd leave me again, I would tell you to move in tomorrow. I am not worried about money, I know you have what it takes to revive Star Construction and make it better than it was. I have total faith in you in that area."

"Thank you, but I want your total trust. I won't stop until I gain it."

Leon placed Starla's head against his body and prayed. Normally, he prayed for their marriage, but this prayer was specifically for his wife's healing.

After Leon left, Starla lay in bed, unable to sleep. She resented Leon for being so quick and accurate in his diagnosis of her real issue. *I love him for it,* she thought. The questions she'd suppressed, compressed, and compacted to the back of her mind, Leon, with very little effort, yanked to the forefront.

Questions like: why hadn't James Howard wanted to be a father to her? Why did he wait until the life had practically left his body before contacting her again? Had he ever missed her? Those questions and many more would forever go unanswered. Starla had tried on several occasions to search for the answers from her mother, but that proved ineffective. The only answer Yvonne would offer was, "He's a dog that returned to his vomit." When Starla asked what she meant by the statement, Yvonne wouldn't respond to the question asked, but instead would remind Starla that they had managed to survive just fine without him.

But Starla hadn't survived, she merely existed. Leon was right. Her love for him was real, but she'd used him to cover the hole left by her father. To her realization, the hole had grown. It had to have if she was even considering marrying someone she didn't love or wasn't in the least bit attracted to.

Starla went to the closet and pulled out the obituary she kept hidden away. She'd read her father's life story so often, she had it memorized.

James Howard, born October 17, 1947, was the third child born to Fletcher and Annie Howard in Sherman, Texas. He received Christ at an early age . . . He leaves to cherish his memories, wife Odessa, and one daughter, Starla Howard of Hayward, California . . . and a host of friends.

As always, when she finished reciting the words, the worn yellow paper was stained with her tears. "Daddy, why did you leave me?" she cried repeatedly without any resolution. She gave up on sleep and fell to her knees alongside her bed, finding solace in the comfort of the Father's presence. She succumbed to sleep that, only minutes before, evaded her. She didn't sleep long before the boys alerted her that it was time for breakfast.

"Mommy, you went to sleep, just like Grandma does when she prays," Montel observed.

Starla was too tired to laugh along with her son about how her mother-in-law prayed herself to sleep. "Mommy's tired. Give me ten minutes and I'll make breakfast." Starla was barely standing on her wobbly legs when Montel, who was an exact replica of Leon, personality included, offered his advice.

"Mommy, next time don't play with Daddy so much and you won't be so tired."

Starla gasped. "What are you talking about?"

"I heard you and Daddy wrestling last night."

Starla ran into her bathroom, too embarrassed to face a six-year-old.

Leon finally emerged from his bedroom to find Marlissa at church, caught up in high praise. Pastor Jamal Bryant was preaching about getting radical and recovering all the stuff the enemy had stolen. Leon stood back, chuckling and watching Marlissa dance around the room and at the same time hollering, "Thank ya!" with her hands raised. She was so loud he wondered how she managed to hear the television. Leon listened to the announcer at the end of the service before attempting to gain Marlissa's attention by placing his arm around her shoulder. "Hey, brat—"

Marlissa didn't afford him the opportunity of completing his sentence. In fast-forward mode, she elbowed him in the groin, then turned and prepared to deliver a powerful kick to the same location. Her foot was halfway to the bull's-eye when she recognized Leon bent over, gasping for air.

"*Leon?*" She slowly lowered her leg. "What are you doing here?"

"Crazy woman, I live here!" Leon managed. "Are you trying to kill me?"

Marlissa helped him to the couch. "I didn't hear you come in last night. You called and said you were staying over at Starla's."

Leon leaned forward. "I did stay with Starla, for a while anyway, but that's another story. Woman, tell me how you can go from dancing in the Spirit to fighting for the kill in two seconds flat?"

Marlissa laughed. "I'm sorry. I thought you were an intruder. Next time you better announce yourself before you get hurt for real."

"I am hurt for real." Leon was smiling, but Marlissa knew he was troubled.

"Things didn't go according to plan, huh?" she asked.

Leon leaned his head back and sighed. "For the most part we made good progress, but there's still major ground to cover. At least now I know how she really feels and what the real problem is."

"Good for you. I wish I knew how Kevin feels about me. I think he still loves me by his actions, but he hasn't verbalized anything yet."

"Why don't you just ask him?"

"That's a thought," was her reply, although she didn't have the courage to follow through.

Chapter 15

Kevin looked at the caller ID and debated answering his cell phone. It was Reyna again. She'd been calling twice a day and had popped up unexpectedly at his office during the week. Unfortunately for Reyna, he had been called in for a surgical consult on a trauma victim. As for her phone calls, Kevin made it a point to keep them short and impersonal, hoping she would get the message, but she didn't. Reyna was persistent in her pursuit.

"Thank you, Jesus," Kevin mumbled when his phone finally stopped ringing and the message indicator tune didn't sound. After adjusting his prosthesis, he finished dressing.

Since he planned to spend the day at the park, Kevin decided on his hunter green and black–and–white Reebok sweat suit. It was a hard decision, because Marlissa had selected the sweat suit for him on one of their shopping trips. He knew she liked it, but she also admired how well he could fill out a pair of jeans. "I can't believe this." He laughed out loud. "I'm trying to impress my wife."

The doorbell sounded right on schedule. Tyson Stokes's anal personality bothered most people, but Kevin appreciated the trait in his best friend. Tyson maintained control in all situations, which was why Kevin invited him to Restoration Ministries' spring picnic. Thinking it was Tyson at the door, he opened the door without checking the peephole.

"Reyna, what are you doing here?"

Reyna wasn't deterred by the disdain in Kevin's voice or the frown on his face. She simply stepped inside like he had invited her in. "Kevin, I came by to see how you're doing. Over the phone you sounded as if something was bothering you, so I came by to check on you." Reyna smiled and ran her fingers along his arm. "Your well-being is my number-one priority."

Kevin considered his next move. The indirect approach hadn't worked with Reyna. He had a feeling a direct approach wouldn't either, but he gave it a try.

"Reyna, it's not something that's bothering me, it's someone."

Reyna appeared to be concerned. "Kevin, is your ex-wife bothering you? Because I can tell her to leave you alone. I—"

Kevin held his hand up, palm open. "Reyna, stop! You sound just like my mother." Kevin took a deep breath and contemplated his next move. "Reyna, please listen to me carefully. Marlissa is not my ex-wife. She's my wife and she's not the one bothering me." He pointed to her. "You are. Your constant phone calls and uninvited visits are annoying me to no end."

Reyna twisted her face, like she was trying to decipher a coded message.

"I'm sorry, for a while I did lead you on, but truthfully, Reyna, I'm not interested in having a relationship with you. I have never been and never will be. Please stop calling and stalking me. And please, stop living the life my mother dictates to you. Find out who you are and what you want."

Reyna's face twisted in the opposite direction, but she didn't speak.

"My mother probably told you not to listen to me, because she thinks I don't know what I want, but she's wrong. Please stop chasing me, and walk away with what pride you have left."

She still didn't respond.

"Reyna, do you understand what I'm telling you?" Before she could answer, the bell sounded again. Kevin went to answer the door. It was Tyson.

"Hey, man." Tyson leaned against the door-frame in khaki slacks and a striped button-down shirt.

"Come in." Kevin stepped aside for Tyson to pass.

Tyson stopped midstride when he saw Reyna. For a split second his mouth gaped, then twisted. "Uh, I didn't know you had company. Do you want me to wait in the car?"

"That won't be necessary. Reyna was just leaving," Kevin answered, but Reyna still didn't respond. Finally, Kevin left her standing there, and returned to his bedroom for his wallet and a splash of Marlissa's favorite cologne.

Tyson was surprised to see Reyna, especially the way she was dressed. The entire time he'd known Reyna, he'd never seen her legs. Today she wore a skirt that stopped just above the knee, and instead of her usual black and browns, Reyna had chosen canary yellow. She also sported a new hairstyle and makeup as well.

"Reyna, take my advice and leave Kevin alone. Chasing after him will only leave you with a broken heart. I know what Pastor Jennings says, but Kevin is a grown man and he knows who he wants. You can't make him want you." Reyna gazed at Tyson. "To be honest, I don't think *you* really want him. I think you want him because Pastor Jennings has fed that desire to you. Learn to hear the voice of God for yourself and live the life He has planned for you. Not what someone has dictated to you."

When Kevin returned, Tyson was standing in the foyer alone. "How did you get her to leave?" Kevin asked.

"I took her by the hand and walked her to the car." Tyson smiled, but both knew that Reyna's obsession wasn't a laughing matter.

"I feel sorry for her," Kevin admitted. "And part of it is my fault, I should have nipped this in the bud a long time ago. To make matters worse, if Marlissa hadn't returned, I could have ruined both of our lives by using her to replace my boo."

Tyson cocked his head. "Your boo? Your relationship with Marlissa must be progressing well."

Kevin smiled. "For the most part things are good. We still have a long way to go, but so far I am satisfied with the progress."

"Do you regret your decision about the divorce?"

Kevin set the alarm before locking the door. "No. I love her."

Marlissa spotted Kevin's SUV the second it entered the parking lot at Lake Chabot. Acting like she hadn't seen him in years, Marlissa ran across the picnic area and through the parking lot, and grabbed his neck before he was completely out of the vehicle.

"Hey, handsome." She complimented him on his sweat suit after kissing him. "I missed you."

"You're doing wonders for my ego, you just saw me last night." The two kissed again.

"Looks like you've gotten over your fear of pit bulls," Tyson said, walking around the SUV with a half smile.

Marlissa released Kevin and hugged Tyson. "They turned out to be toothless Chihuahuas. Just like you are when you're not wearing a suit and carrying a briefcase."

"What are you guys talking about?" Kevin wanted to know.

"That's our little secret," Tyson answered, and whispered in Marlissa's ear. "I'm glad you took my advice."

Marlissa smiled at both Kevin and Tyson. "Thanks so much for coming to my church picnic. It really means a lot to me."

"No problem." Kevin smiled, but she didn't kiss him again.

Mother Scott's voice traveled across the picnic area and through the parking lot. "Kevin!"

"Lord, help me," Kevin prayed, holding Marlissa's hand, maneuvering around parked cars. Tyson followed.

Before they made it to Mother Scott, little Montel approached. "Auntie Marlissa, is that your boyfriend?"

"Montel!" Starla grabbed her outspoken son by the hand. "I'm sorry, girl, this boy says whatever comes to mind."

"Just like his daddy," Leon added, walking up and greeting Kevin and Tyson.

Mother Scott couldn't wait any longer; she made her way through the crowded picnic area to her favorite doctor. "Hey, Kevin, I knew you would make it. Come on, let me introduce you around." She then noticed Tyson. "Who are you?"

"Mother, this is my friend, Tyson Stokes," Kevin answered.

Mother Scott narrowed her eyes at Tyson. "Are you a doctor too?"

"No, Mother, I'm an attorney."

In one smooth motion, Mother Scott squeezed between them and interlocked an arm around Kevin and Tyson. "Come on, I want you all to meet some people." She called over her shoulder. "Marlissa, make them a plate. Be sure to give them some of the potato salad in the red bowl, that's the one I made."

"Where is she going?" Marlissa asked Leon.

"In five minutes my mother will have the entire congregation lined up for free medical and legal advice."

"I don't doubt it." Marlissa watched for a moment, then did as she was told and went to fix Kevin and Tyson something to eat.

Leon knew his mother well. Mother Scott proudly introduced Kevin and Tyson to every member in the church and the visitors, making sure to announce they were a doctor and a lawyer. To the single women, she also added that Kevin was Marlissa's husband. Most of the congregation had figured as much by Kevin's frequent visits to Restoration Ministries, but Mother Scott made sure they understood he was off-limits.

"Hello, Kevin." First Lady Drake walked up.

Mother Scott was still mad about First Lady teasing her. "I can call him Kevin because we're family, but to you he's Dr. Jennings," Mother Scott said, then rolled her eyes.

"Marlissa is my baby too. Now stop rolling your eyes before your one good eye rolls out of its socket."

"Drake, you better stop talking about me. I have a lawyer now, and Tyson would represent me for free just in case I find myself on trial for murder."

Tyson laughed. "I like these people already."

"Don't take us seriously, we love each other to death; we're prayer partners, you know," First Lady Drake assured Tyson.

"These two prayer warriors can pray the devil out of anybody. I am living proof," Marlissa commented, finally joining them with plates in tow.

"Thank you." Tyson relieved her of the smaller of the two plates. Marlissa then squeezed next to Kevin.

"If we weren't in public I'd sit you on my lap," Kevin mumbled before feeding her a spoonful of Mother Scott's potato salad. "You know you're wearing that dress." He was referring to the lime green dress that subtly accented her figure. Marlissa was too busy blushing to notice that Pastor Drake had approached the picnic table.

"Hello, Kevin, Marlissa," Pastor Drake greeted them.

Kevin almost didn't recognize the pastor now that he was dressed in a sweat suit similar to his own, and a baseball cap. Today Pastor Drake didn't resemble a pastor at all; out here he dressed like any other man. *Interesting,* Kevin thought. Pastor Jennings didn't leave the house for a trip to the grocery store unless she was adorned in a suit of some kind. "You have to always look the part." That's what she said the one time the church went horseback riding. Pastor Jennings showed up wearing a long-sleeved blouse and ankle-length skirt, complete with two-inch heels. She did tie a red scarf around her neck for the occasion.

"Hello, Pastor Drake," they answered, then introduced Tyson.

"I hope you're enjoying yourself." Pastor Drake's question was directed to Kevin. He didn't need to ask Marlissa if she was having fun, since she was still blushing from Kevin's flirtations.

"I am." Kevin smiled, then turned to his wife. "The food is good and the company is exceptional."

"I bet it is!" Pastor roared. "You do know that there are over one hundred individuals besides Marlissa out here, don't you?"

"Yes, but she's the one I . . ." Kevin regained control of his emotions before he spilled his feelings in public. "She's the reason I'm here."

Tyson didn't miss the almost slip, and Kevin suspected Pastor Drake didn't either. They both stared at him with expectancy. Apparently, Marlissa did, because she was still blushing.

Pastor Drake invited Tyson and Kevin to join him in a game of dominos against the deacons and they quickly accepted the challenge. Marlissa went to find Starla and Mother Scott.

"I'm so sorry about Montel," Starla said. "I didn't mean to embarrass you."

"I was only embarrassed because I didn't know how to answer his question," Marlissa admitted.

"Why not? They way the two of you are carrying on, papa will be begging mama to come home soon," Starla teased.

"I could say the same thing about you." Marlissa arched her eyebrows.

Starla's hands flew to her hips. "What has that big-mouthed husband of mine told you?"

"Nothing." Marlissa paused and Starla blew a sigh of relief. "But Montel said he can hear his mommy and daddy wrestling at nighttime."

"Ugh! That boy!" Starla fumed.

"Don't be mad at him. You and Leon shouldn't be *wrestling* anyway."

"Mother, we are married," Starla reminded her mother-in-law.

"Then stop playing and act like it. Married people are supposed to live together. If you can't get along under the same roof, you shouldn't be wrestling in them sheets." Mother Scott let her unsolicited opinion sink in before adding, "Now, baby, that's your and Leon's business. I ain't going to stick my nose in it, but you might want to train that big-mouthed grandson of mine that what happens at home stays at home." She turned to Marlissa. "I like the good doctor, but you make sure you get the ring and the house back before you start wrestling."

"You have nothing to worry about, Mother," Marlissa answered quickly before Mother Scott went off on a tangent. "The good doctor won't step into the ring unless he's committed." She grabbed Starla by the arm. "Come on, let's check on the boys." They trotted off before Mother Scott could form her next sentence.

"Thanks, girl," Starla said once they were out of earshot.

"I missed you." Kevin approached Marlissa from behind and wrapped his arms around her waist. Marlissa spun around before he could kiss her cheek. Her eyes were laced with fear.

"I'm sorry, didn't mean to scare you." Reading the fear in her eyes, Kevin took two steps back.

"I didn't hear you come up." Marlissa relaxed, but Kevin was still apprehensive. He waited for her to approach him before shaking the memories from the past that instantly flashed before his eyes.

"Where's Tyson?" she asked, looking over his shoulder.

"He's fishing with Leon and some other guys." Lake Chabot was known for its trout and catfish, as well as its panoramic views of the Bay Area. Kevin slowly came back to the present. "Want to go for a walk with me?" Marlissa's answer was to interlock her arm with his, and they slowly began walking.

They didn't talk; it wasn't necessary. The trees rustling in the soft breeze and the birds chirping on the branches above their heads spoke for them. Nature expressed their sentiments. A quarter mile into the trail, Kevin held her hand, but not before kissing it. Marlissa, now more assertive than she ever imagined possible, took Kevin's hand and led him to a rock big enough for the two of them. Once he was seated, Marlissa proceeded to kiss him senseless.

"Where did that come from?" Kevin looked as though he was dazed.

"Here," Marlissa answered, placing his hand over her heart. "I love you, Kevin."

Kevin pressed her as close to him as humanly possible. He moved his mouth to say the words, but Marlissa jumped backward. Kevin's cell phone was vibrating.

"I'm sorry." He checked the number. Without answering the call, Kevin replaced the phone on his clip and reached for Marlissa. "Where were we?"

Instead of receiving his affections, she asked, "Was that Reyna?"

Kevin had never lied to Marlissa and he wasn't going to start now. "Yes."

Marlissa exhaled deeply, then chose her words carefully. "Kevin, earlier you accused me of being jealous of Reyna. Should I be?"

"No."

"Really? Then why does she call you and visit you? Are you in a relationship with her?"

"No."

"Were you?" she persisted. "She's not chasing you without cause."

Kevin closed his eyes; it was his turn to exhale. Marlissa took that as his answer, and turned her back to him. "Did you sleep with her or anyone else?"

"No." Kevin turned her to face him and took her hands in his, but Marlissa refused eye contact, opting to watch two squirrels chase each other around a nearby tree stump. "Honestly, I did entertain the idea of a relationship with Reyna, even marriage. But that was only because I was trying to fill the void you left in my life."

The statement caught Marlissa off guard. "Are you trying to say it's *my* fault Reyna thinks she's going to be the next Mrs. Jennings?"

"What I am saying is I was hurting and missing you. Yes, I did lead her on, but I have since made it clear to her that I am not interested in her, period. Unfortunately, neither she nor my mother believes me. I hope you do."

Marlissa repositioned herself between his legs and placed her arms around his neck. "I believe you." She sealed her answer with a kiss so intoxicating that Kevin could have sworn he was drunk. "Do you believe I am a different person now?"

"Oh yeah." He attempted another kiss, but his phone vibrated again, and he assumed it was Reyna. "What!" he answered without checking the caller ID.

"Y'all have been gone a long time." It was Mother Scott. "Come on back here before y'all start a wrestling match."

Kevin stared into the phone. "Huh?"

"You heard what I said. Get back here now." The line went dead.

"I don't know who is worse, Mother Scott or my mother," Kevin declared after relaying Mother Scott's message to Marlissa.

"Trust me, your mother is on a whole different level," Marlissa replied without bothering to explain the message to Kevin. He didn't understand until they returned to the picnic area and Mother Scott walked up to him and inspected the lower part of his pants. Tyson and Leon came just in time to hear Kevin ask, "Mother, what are you checking for?" He was truly puzzled by her peculiar behavior.

"Grass stains," Mother answered, then went on to inspect Marlissa's hair.

Kevin couldn't help but laugh along with everyone else, but now he also had a new revelation. Mother Scott may have been in the early stages of glaucoma, but her spiritual vision was 20/20.

"Can I see you tonight?" Kevin asked Marlissa while they walked back to his SUV. "We need to talk."

"Okay." Marlissa was excited. Kevin had spent the day with her and still wanted more. "Do you want to come by the apartment or meet at Starbucks?"

Kevin electronically unlocked the door for Tyson. Before climbing inside, Tyson hugged Marlissa. "I enjoyed myself today; thanks for inviting me. You're right. I do need to lighten up, but just a little." Just that quick, Tyson was serious again. "Take care of my boy."

Marlissa returned her attention to Kevin. "Where do you want to meet?"

"At the house. We can watch the fireworks from the A's game out on the deck."

Marlissa swallowed hard. "Are you sure?"

"Yes. You still know where it is, don't you?"

"Of course," she whispered. Marlissa didn't know what to make of Kevin inviting her into the home they once shared. Her apprehension nearly made him want to withdraw the invitation.

"I'll see you in an hour." Kevin lightly kissed her cheek, then joined Tyson inside the SUV.

Chapter 16

"The boys are sound asleep," Leon announced upon returning to the living area of Starla's townhouse. Knowing that the boys would be asleep before reaching the freeway, Leon came home with Starla to assist her with carrying the boys into the house. He offered to bathe them and tuck them in while she rested. Starla readily accepted and remained on the couch in deep thought. It was time to stop straddling the fence and make a decision.

"I'm leaving now." Leon kissed her cheek, then started for the door.

Starla reached for him and urged him to sit down next to her.

Leon assumed something was on her mind; she'd been acting strange ever since leaving the park. The second he sat down, Starla cuddled next to him. Whatever was on her mind was major, of that Leon was certain. Leon kissed her forehead and waited for his wife to speak.

"I liked the way we were today," she began. "You, me, the boys; we were a family again. I miss that."

"Me too." Leon brushed her braids off her face.

"I've enjoyed attending church as a family these past weeks. Actually, I think I like your church better than mine. I just love watching you dance in the Spirit."

"I like watching you dance, too." Leon smiled.

"I've been thinking about what's most important to me and I have made some decisions about my life. There are some loose ends I need to tie up in order to move forward with our marriage."

Leon closed his eyes and held his breath, then waited for her next statement.

"It's time you gave Marlissa your thirty-day notice to vacate. It's time for you to come home."

Leon exhaled and gripped Starla tightly. "Are you sure?"

Starla raised her head to his. "Yes. I love you and I want our family back. The boys need their father and I need my husband. I need my friend."

"Why thirty days? I can move in tomorrow."

Starla laughed, then kissed him. "I figured you would say that, but I have some things I need to take care of, and so do you. When you do return home, I don't want any obstacles in our way."

"I can take care of everything I need to right here with you and the boys," Leon insisted.

"You have your licensing exam next week and you need a quiet place to study. You won't get that here with two boys running around and with me jumping your bones. I don't want anything to interfere with you reviving Star Construction. You're well on your way with that new truck you purchased."

What she said made sense, but Leon needed more assurance. He'd waited and prayed too long for this moment. "And what are you going to be doing in the meantime?"

Starla paused before answering, as if she were trying to conjure up the nerve. "I am going to visit my father's widow. I am hoping to find some answers to why my father deserted me. I may even try to get some answers from my mother again."

Leon held her and kissed her face. "Star, I am so proud of you for having the courage to move past your pain. I love you more for giving me another chance." Starla rested once again against his chest. "Do you want me to go with you?" he offered.

"Thank you, but I have to do this on my own, and if I don't do it now, I will never move on."

"Star, I will always be here for you. You know you're—"

Starla helped him finish the sentence. "The star that lights my path."

"I don't know why I still fall for that corny line." Starla laughed.

"Because you know it's the truth." Leon kissed her again.

"Honey." Starla was serious again. "I need you tonight. Can you stay here with me? All of this has left me vulnerable and I am scared."

Leon stood, and then lifted her from the couch. After carrying her upstairs to the bedroom, Leon ran Starla a hot bubble bath. Afterward, he gave her a massage, then held her until she fell asleep.

Marlissa slowly climbed the stairs leading to the front door of the 6,000 square-foot home on Moraga Avenue. If she were still a resident of the flat, Marlissa would have used the garage door opener and parked inside the three-car garage, then entered through the gourmet kitchen. She would then grab a piece of fruit from the wire basket stationed on the mauve granite countertop. From there she would travel through a maze of polished hardwood floors, past a brass chandelier centered perfectly above a mahogany table that seated eight, earth-toned walls lined with original art crowned by vaulted ceilings, and a home office, which doubled as a library. Finally, passing through the double oak doors, she would end her journey on the king-sized cherry wood four poster bed centered perfectly in the master bedroom suite. Before indulging in the comfort of the down comforter, she would stop in her walk-in closet and return her shoes to the appropriate shelf. If she was in the mood, a hot spa treatment was at her disposal in the sunken Jacuzzi tub. Or, if in a hurry, the oversized shower worked just fine.

That was then. Today, she was a guest, and like any guest would do, Marlissa pressed the doorbell and waited to be invited in.

"Hold on, I'll let you in the garage," were the first words out of Kevin's mouth when he saw her standing on his porch.

"Okay." Marlissa walked back to her car, suddenly nervous about being back at the place she once called home. Once she parked securely inside the garage, Kevin opened her door and assisted her.

Marlissa gestured toward the black Mercedes S500. "When did you buy another car?"

"About a year ago," he answered nonchalantly. "I only drive it on special occasions."

"It's nice." Marlissa half smiled.

Kevin sensed her uneasiness and invited her inside.

Much to her delight, not much inside had changed. There were the obvious signs of the lack of a woman's presence, like mail and magazines strewn around the kitchen countertop. In place of fruit, the wire bowl was loaded with packaged cookies and peanuts. However, the rest of the house was immaculate, at least the part she could see. But then Kevin was always neat.

Kevin observed her mannerisms carefully. Marlissa was nervous about being in their home. She kept her arms folded and avoided eye contact. His defenses immediately shot up.

"Are you afraid of being here with me?" Kevin's tone was firmer than he meant for it to be.

Marlissa discounted his hostility. "No, it's just that it's been so long since the last time I was here . . . I, well, I didn't think . . . I really love . . ." Marlissa couldn't form a complete thought or sentence. She gave up trying and surrendered to her emotions.

Pleased that he wasn't the cause of her anxiety, Kevin set aside his self-preservation shield and embraced her.

"What I was trying to convey was that I miss our home," Marlissa voiced once she settled down.

"Look around, nothing has changed. A part of you is in every room of this house. If the walls could talk, they'd say 'Welcome home.'" He smiled.

"What about the owner? What would he say?"

Her voice was so soft, Kevin barely heard her. He wished he hadn't. Marlissa was moving too fast for him. Kevin couldn't answer that before they had a chance to talk. "He'd say, 'have a seat on the deck, the fireworks will start soon.'" He stepped away from her. "I'll bring out some cider."

Marlissa forced a smile and obeyed. Midway through the living room her joy returned. Their wedding picture was still in its place, right above the fireplace. "He still cares," she mumbled.

Marlissa was audibly counting the lights outlining the Bay Bridge when Kevin joined her on the wooden bench, carrying a bottle of peach cider, one glass, and a blanket. A major selling point for them both had been the view from the backyard. The hill location offered unobstructed views of every major bridge in the Bay Area, Oakland and San Francisco skylines, plus the great Pacific Ocean. The couple had planned to make many memories out there underneath the star-studded sky, but never did.

"This has been a long time coming," he said when he stood beside her.

Marlissa relieved him of the glass and cider, then waited for him to sit next to her. "You know what they say, better late than never." He didn't respond. "I guess you're drinking from the bottle," she said after he wrapped the blanket around them.

"No, I'm drinking from here." This time it was Marlissa who was rendered helpless by his kiss. "I owed you that one from the rock earlier."

"I like the way you pay up." Marlissa used her hand to fan herself.

Kevin leaned away from her. Now he was the one moving too fast. He handed her the glass then poured the cider. Marlissa had just offered him a sip when the kaleidoscope of color and what sounded like thunder began. She rested her head against his shoulder, and Kevin pulled the blanket tighter, bringing Marlissa even closer.

The intimate venue almost proved to be too much for Kevin's defenses. Not even halfway through the pyrotechnic show, he was totally consumed by her. The fragrance of her hair, the warmth of her body so close to his, and the kiss they shared earlier: it was perfect. Too perfect; he almost forgot the reason he wanted to talk to her in the first place. Reality came crashing down when Marlissa began massaging his partial limb.

"It's been a long day and your muscles must be tired." Kevin knew her intentions were good, but right now he couldn't receive her affections. He gently removed her hand and held it for the duration of the show.

Long after the finale of the fireworks, they sat there drinking in the serenity along with the sounds of night, neither knowing what to say. Marlissa made the first move.

"That was nice." She stood and stretched. "Thanks for inviting me home."

Kevin wasn't ready for her to leave, and he wasn't ready to have the talk, either. He quickly searched his mind for any excuse to keep her around. "Want to watch a little of *A Walk to Remember?*"

Marlissa looked at her watch. It was after ten o'clock and well past Kevin's bedtime, considering he had to perform surgery in the morning. "Sure, you know that's my favorite."

"Come on, we still have to talk."

Once again they cuddled underneath the blanket, this time in the sunken den, but they didn't talk. Within minutes, they fell asleep.

Marlissa awakened to find herself alone on the couch. Once her vision focused, she scanned the den for Kevin and called out his name. Next, she checked the kitchen and living room: nothing. Looking down at her watch, she realized it was after midnight. *Kevin must have gone to bed.* Marlissa grabbed her purse then headed to the door to let herself out, but couldn't remember the code to deactivate and reset the alarm. "Shoot," she pouted. "Now I have to wake him up."

Marlissa started down the hall and around the corner. She slowly stepped inside her old bedroom just as Kevin hopped from the bathroom, wearing nothing but the steam from the shower and his crutch.

"Oops." Marlissa made sure she got an eyeful before covering her eyes. *Lord, thank you for that vision!* "I'm sorry. I . . . I assumed you were sleeping." She peeked through her parted fingers and was treated to the sight of him walking away. *Thank ya! I'm going to sleep good tonight.* "I don't know the code to the alarm. I wasn't trying to . . . you know."

"It's the same," Kevin said upon returning, wearing black pajama shorts.

"I didn't know that." Marlissa never considered that he'd still kept the day he proposed as the code. She still had her eyes covered, and this time Kevin didn't disguise his agitation.

"Marlissa, I didn't plan for you to find me like this, but since you did, we can finally get everything out in the open like two adults."

Marlissa removed her hands and attempted to hold his gaze, but his enormous and well-developed upper body kept getting in the way. *Lord, please let this blessing have my name on it.* "What's on your mind?"

"Marlissa, since you've been back, you've been all over me. You say the right things and you do the right things. You constantly convey how much you love me, and that's good, but you're forgetting one important thing." Kevin's voice carried more stability than she thought he felt.

Marlissa was puzzled. "What?"

Kevin struggled to articulate the feelings he'd held in for way too long. "You're disgusted by my body."

Marlissa giggled out loud. "Where did you get a stupid idea like that from?"

"From you," he answered dryly.

Marlissa continued laughing. "If only you could read my mind right now. Whew!"

"I don't need to read your mind because the memories are still fresh."

It was then that she realized he was serious, and she stopped laughing. "Kevin, what memories are you talking about?"

With the assistance of his crutch, Kevin walked over to the bed and sat down. He inhaled and exhaled several times, trying to maintain his courage. Finally, he just let it all out.

"You haven't been the same since seeing my body without the prosthesis on our wedding night. I traumatized you to the point that you started drinking."

Marlissa walked over and stood next to him. "Honey, I don't know what you're talking about."

It was embarrassing enough for him to talk about it, but Marlissa's naiveté infuriated him. "Don't protect my feelings by denying it happened!" He pounded his fist on the bed. "You took one look at me and ran away, screaming. When the manager brought you back, you were wasted, and stayed that way most of our marriage. You had to be drunk to make love to me the first time and the few uneventful times after that. You wouldn't look at me. You covered your eyes just like you did a few minutes ago."

The pain etched on Kevin's face was authentic, the quiver in his voice genuine. He believed what he was saying. His perception was his total reality of what had gone wrong with their marriage. Marlissa sat down next to him. Placing her hand on his shoulder, she spoke softly. "Do you really believe your disfigurement is the reason I started drinking? Do you honestly think I left you because of your body?"

"It's not a matter of thinking it, your actions proved it." Marlissa looked away. "Marlissa," he sighed. "Some things can't be fixed. Maybe our marriage is one of those things. I can't change my body."

Marlissa's head fell along with her shoulders. Kevin knew she was crying, but he couldn't console her now that his wounds were exposed. A part of him wanted her to confirm his feelings and leave. But the other part, the part that loved her, was terrified of the possibility.

Marlissa stopped sniffling and held his hand. "Kevin, I love your body. I have always loved your body. Your body is beautiful to me just the way it is, every inch of it." She kissed his fingers. "You have to believe me."

Taking his fingers back, Kevin was unmoved. "I want to, but the evidence proves differently."

Instead of retreating, she positioned herself on the bed with her back against the pillows alongside him. She wasn't giving up.

"Kevin, I know it's late and you have surgery in the morning, but I need to tell you something I should have told you a long time ago. It may take awhile, but please, bear with me. I promise, it'll explain a lot."

Both his heart and curiosity got the best of him. He rested his back against the headboard. "I'm listening."

Marlissa switched positions, then removed her shoes and sat Indian style with her hands folded. She kept her head bowed so long that Kevin asked if she was praying. She was.

"As you know," she finally began, using the cherry wood armoire as a focal point. "My grandmother raised me after my mother died. My grandmother was good to me; for the most part I didn't lack anything and she instilled good morals and values in me. She was also very strict. My grandmother didn't allow me to date or even talk to boys over the phone until I was fifteen. I couldn't even walk to the store with a boy. One Sunday, a boy from the church she sent me to walked me home. I didn't think he liked me beyond friendship, but it didn't matter to Grandma. She didn't send me to church after that."

Kevin folded his arms and wondered down what lane this story would take him.

"I had my first real boyfriend at sixteen. His name was Darius. I was a sophomore, he was a senior. I felt special having an older boyfriend, considering I was totally inexperienced when it came to boys. I was so naive I didn't know what was meant by 'do you have any fries to go with that shake.'" Marlissa chuckled.

"That's pretty bad." Kevin nodded.

"Anyway," she continued, still focusing on the armoire. "It was obvious that Darius had a lot more experience than I had. I just didn't know how much experience. He was the varsity quarterback and on his way to Grambling State on a full scholarship. Since I had to hide our relationship from Grandma, we didn't talk on the phone. I'd meet him around the corner from the house and he would drive me to and from school. At school we didn't communicate though. Darius said he didn't want people in his business and asked that I keep our relationship a secret. Having a secret affair with one of the most popular boys in school really made me feel special. I thought I was in love."

Kevin became concerned when he noticed Marlissa rubbing her hands vigorously and the faraway look in her eyes. Mentally, Marlissa was someplace else, somewhere very painful, but she kept talking to the armoire.

"One morning after he picked me up, Darius said he forgot an English assignment that was due that morning. It was a Wednesday. He asked if I would mind returning to his house for a quick minute. I said I didn't. When we got there, he asked if I wanted to come in and I said yes. Maybe if I'd had more experience I would have noticed something was wrong, but I didn't. If I wasn't so in love, I would have asked why the sign on the door read, 'Welcome to the Johnstons.' Darius's last name was Townsend. I went into the house, just smiling and laughing at his jokes. Darius was funny," she added matter-of-factly. "Once inside, I stopped laughing."

Marlissa had stopped rubbing her hands. She now twisted the ends of the down comforter. Kevin shook off the thought of what he logically assumed happened next. There was a happy ending to this story, there had to be. Marlissa was still a virgin when they met.

"Four of Darius's friends, who I had never seen before, were inside. I wasn't afraid of them because Darius was still holding my hand. That's how much I trusted him. The house was filled with this strange smell. I didn't know it was marijuana until I saw one of the guys pass the little white roll to Darius. Up until that moment I didn't know Darius smoked anything. I still wasn't scared, though."

Marlissa closed her eyes and took a long, deep breath. She moaned while moving her head from side to side. In her hands, the end of the down comforter was now ripped and its contents spilled out. Kevin knew then that what she was about to say next was far worse than what he had imagined. He couldn't stand seeing her this way; it was too painful for him.

"'Lissa, stop. I get the picture."

She didn't hear him. "When they picked me up and carried me into somebody's room and tied me to the bed, that's when I got scared. It all happened so fast. One minute I was standing next to Darius, the next minute I was hollering and screaming for help. I must have screamed real loud because then they gagged me with a shirt or something." Marlissa held conversation with the armoire again. "When Darius stood over me, for some stupid reason, I thought he was going help me. I was his girl; he wasn't just going to sit back quietly and let his boys take what I was saving for him. The Darius I loved wouldn't allow that to happen. He did speak up. His exact words were, 'Since I picked her, I get to bust first.'"

Kevin groaned, but she was in too deep to hear him.

"My guess is that I wasn't the first one. Darius and his boys systematically raped me. They called it running a train." Marlissa looked perplexed. "Maybe that's why they kept making those train noises. Anyway, after Darius shamelessly stole my virginity, I spent the entire school day being treated like a human garbage can." Her voice fell to just above a whisper. "Five people, four of whom I didn't even know, penetrated my every opening, sometimes simultaneously. I didn't know you could use your mouth to have sex. I don't remember everything; for a while I blacked out. I do remember praying and begging God to make them stop, but it didn't work. I didn't pray anymore after that."

Kevin didn't have any tissue nearby and he didn't want to leave her trembling body alone. He removed a pillowcase and used it to wipe her face.

"When they were done, Darius dropped me off at the usual corner like always, but not before threatening me not to tell. The next day I saw him at school kissing another girl. He never spoke to me again."

"I never told my grandmother or anyone else. Who could I tell? I wasn't supposed to have a boyfriend anyway. I aimlessly walked into the house at the normal time as if nothing had happened. Grandma was out shopping so I didn't have to face her. I took a bath three times that evening and twice in the morning. It would be a week before the pain and swelling completely went away. Thankfully, I didn't get pregnant. I did contract an STD that I was secretly treated for at a free local clinic."

For the first time she discerned Kevin's arm around her. "I'm almost done," she said, noting the distress that veiled his face.

"For years I tried hard to bury those memories. I tried to convince myself that they didn't exist, that it was all a bad dream. A horror film

I'd seen on the big screen. I even told myself that I was still a virgin. But the memories wouldn't go away. The visions, the laughter, the smell, and that awful pain, none of it would go away. I started drinking as a way to help me forget." Looking him in the eyes, she told him the truth. "Kevin, I was drinking long before I met you. In fact, the day we met I was rushing to buy some vodka that was on sale. That's how I ran into your cart. I was going to buy some other items, but that was my main staple."

Kevin looked perplexed. "You didn't drink while we dated."

"I stopped drinking because there was something about you that intrigued me. I sobered up so I could get to know you, and then I stayed sober because when I was with you, I didn't hurt as much. You always made me feel safe. That's why I liked to cuddle so much. Being with you pushed my fears away and made me want to love and be loved. Thank you," she said, then kissed his cheek.

"When I accepted your marriage proposal, I really thought I was over my demons. But that night when you stood over me, everything came rushing back. Yes, I did trip out, but, Kevin, it had nothing to do with you or your body. I was in the room with you, but I was screaming at

Darius and four nameless faces. The few times we were intimate were very difficult for me. And, yes, I did use alcohol to help me relax enough to be intimate with you, but I only closed my eyes to block out visions of the past, not you. You have to believe that."

For Marlissa it felt like an eternity waiting for Kevin to respond. "Why didn't you tell me this before?" he finally replied.

"It was too painful, and, besides, I had lied to you about being a virgin. You said you were saving yourself for your wife. I was afraid you wouldn't want me if you knew how many males had penetrated me. I was damaged goods. With your mother relentlessly preaching against women who weren't pure and holy, women like me, I assumed you felt the same. Plus, I really thought I was over it."

Marlissa answered his next question before he could ask. "Kevin, I left because I was hurting you and I couldn't stop it. I couldn't handle my demons, so I reverted to what was familiar, alcohol. I was too weak to fight and I couldn't stop hurting you. I hated myself for that, so I gave up and left. I gave up the fight and on myself. You deserved so much better than what I was capable of giving you. I love you too much to ever hurt you. I know that sounds crazy, but it's the truth."

Kevin pulled Marlissa as close to him as humanly possible, and held her for a long time. He listened to her cries while rubbing her back. "Do I still make you feel safe?" he asked as he wiped her face.

"Always."

He kissed her tenderly, and then turned out the light.

Chapter 17

"Brat, get up!" Leon banged on Marlissa's door on the way to his room. "Hurry up, woman, I got a praise report."

"Me too," Marlissa announced, stepping into the apartment.

Leon shook his head. "Hold on, neither one of us stayed here last night?" Leon asked excitedly.

"Apparently not." Marlissa dropped her purse on the couch.

The friends stood grinning at each other, waiting for what they hoped was good news.

"Since I am the oldest, I will go first," Leon decided, and didn't allow time for Marlissa to disagree. "Consider yourself notified: in thirty days I'm going home to mama!" he bellowed while shaking his key ring. Marlissa screamed and hugged Leon, then the two performed a praise victory dance complete with speaking in tongues.

"I am so happy for the two of you." She listened to him explain about Starla wanting to find some answers to her past. "I'll be praying for her."

"Now, why are you looking so serene at seven o'clock in the morning?" Leon folded his arms and leaned against the wall. "Spill it, brat."

"I got a new key too," Marlissa beamed. "He didn't ask me to move back in, but he gave me a key so I can get in anytime I want." She went on to tell Leon about the fireworks and the misunderstanding.

"It's about time you told him the truth. I bet you feel a lot better."

"I do feel better," Marlissa admitted. "If I'd known he felt that way, I would have told him sooner. What's strange is that I thought the truth would pull him away from me, but after I told him, we were closer than ever."

Leon raised an eyebrow. "Just how much closer were you?"

Marlissa rolled her eyes. "No closer than you and Starla."

"I ain't mad at'cha." Leon turned serious. "Are you going to be able to handle this place by yourself?"

"If not, I'll just have to move into that big house with my fine husband," she teased.

"How soon do you think that will be?" Leon was concerned about her being alone.

"I think very soon. Last night we made major progress. He didn't say it, but I know Kevin loves me. It was written all over his face and I felt it in the way he made—"

Leon waved his hands in the air. "Hold up! That's too much information."

"Mr. Don't Know Nothing At All, I was going to say the way he made me feel safe after I poured my past out to him." Marlissa knelt in front of the couch. "For your information, Kevin and I didn't hold any championship wrestling matches last night. We cuddled."

"Oh, he's the *sensitive* type," Leon said, kneeling beside her.

Marlissa rolled her eyes once again. "No, he's *my* type."

"I am happy for you, brat, for both of us." Leon checked his watch. "We'd better hurry before we're late for work."

"A few extra minutes won't hurt. We owe God that." Marlissa reached for Leon's hand and began praying.

Kevin held his sterile, gloved hands out in front of him and prayed once again. He always said at least one prayer for a successful outcome before each surgery. Now, standing above the anesthetized patient, Kevin was on his third prayer. He'd performed at least a hundred corneal transplants; it was one of his specialties. But never had he picked up a surgical instrument after being up for twenty-four hours straight, and never had his mind been so preoccupied before a surgery.

In the past, Kevin had always been able to put his personal life on the back burner once he scrubbed. He couldn't do that today. Kevin was more than physically tired; he was mentally drained. Marlissa's revelations had taken him on an emotional roller coaster ride that was still taking him through loops and upside-down sharp turns hours later.

Long after Marlissa had fallen asleep in his arms, Kevin lay there holding her and praying for her. At times, he shed silent tears thinking about the barbaric abuse she'd endured at such a young age. When the alarm sounded at 5:00 a.m., he still wasn't ready to leave her. She looked so peaceful entwined with the now-ruined comforter. Her dark brown tresses were splayed out on the pillow, and the residue of dried drool stained her face, but Marlissa was beautiful. Kevin couldn't remember if he had ever seen her so tranquil. Marlissa tossed and turned all night, every night, when they previously shared the same bed. Last night Marlissa barely moved at all, but then Kevin was holding her so tightly, she probably couldn't move if she wanted to.

He didn't wake Marlissa until it was time for him to leave, wanting her to rest as long as possible. Figuring Marlissa didn't want to miss work, he reluctantly stirred her.

"'Lissa, I'm leaving now," he whispered into her ear before kissing her on the forehead.

"What time is it?" She stretched, but didn't open her eyes.

"Six." Kevin took her hand and something shiny glared. It was a key. She opened her eyes wider. "That's a new key. I had the locks changed a few weeks ago."

"I'll leave it in the mailbox." Marlissa squeezed her hand shut and looked inquisitively at Kevin.

"Keep it," he replied quickly, then added, "use it often."

Marlissa didn't ask questions and Kevin didn't offer clarification. Each accepted the moment for what it was: a step in the right direction.

"I left some money for you to buy a new comforter and a day at the spa. You used to enjoy that." Kevin brushed the back of his hand across her cheek.

"Thank you, sweetheart." She wrapped her arms around his neck. "I would kiss you, but one whiff of this morning breath and you may fall out under the power."

"Save it for me." Kevin gazed at her like he wanted to say something, but didn't. Following a quick word of prayer, he left.

Now, as he awaited the signal from the anesthesiologist, so many things made sense to him. The reason she accused him of being a rapist that first day. Why she found it hard to trust him in the beginning. The way she always jumped and appeared frightened whenever he touched her from behind. Why she resisted him so much.

Marlissa was a new woman, a woman he could now understand. She was ready and willing to love him. Presently, he wanted nothing more than to love her back; he just wasn't ready to tell her that.

"Dr. Jennings, we're ready," the anesthesiologist announced.

Kevin prayed one more time before accepting the surgical instrument.

Chapter 18

Starla had read the ten digits so many times she could recite them backward. Ten years ago, when her father's widow gave her the number, Starla had promised to use it. She hadn't meant for it to take so long. At both the funeral and repast, Starla heard story after story and even more praises for Deacon James Howard. Up until then she didn't know her father had attended church. He didn't when he lived with her. Starla couldn't remember her father ever mentioning God; he didn't even pray over his food.

The warm stories everyone shared made her feel proud, then angry. The fuzzy memories Starla had seemed irrelevant. The tall, cinnamon-complexioned man with wavy black hair she remembered wasn't the same mild-mannered, respected deacon everyone raved about. The James Howard she knew was boisterous and full of energy. He was exciting, adventurous, and the most loving person she knew. Not one day went by that he didn't come home and kiss her before he kissed her mother. When he brought flowers home for Yvonne, he also presented some to Starla. Identical to the James Howard these strangers described, the father she knew was always a man of his word.

If her dad promised to take her somewhere, they went. If he vowed to buy her a new doll on Friday, after receiving his paycheck from his job at a uniform delivery company, James would do just that. The only time James didn't keep his word was when he threatened to spank her. To Starla's contentment, James could never bring himself to hurt his only child.

"Why did you leave?" Starla asked the worn piece of paper again, and, as always, there wasn't a response. Starla bowed her head in prayer.

Father, please grant me the strength to follow through with this. Prepare my heart to handle whatever information I discover. And, God, give me the strength to forgive my father for leaving me and my mother.

Starla took a deep breath and removed the cordless phone from its base. She'd just finished with the area code when the doorbell sounded.

"Mommy, somebody's at the door!" Montel yelled from the living room.

Starla replaced the unit and headed downstairs, pondering who was on the other side of the door intruding on private time. Leon had begun training the boys to "take care" of their mother, so before Starla opened the door, the boys stood on each side of her.

"Lewis, what are you doing here?"

This time it was Jaylen who had diarrhea of the mouth. He pointed to the roses in Lewis's hand. "My daddy already gave her some."

"Jaylen!" Starla scolded.

"Oh. Really?" Lewis asked the unsuspecting three-year-old, but big brother Montel answered.

"And he's moving back home, so you can't come here anymore."

"Montel, Jaylen, go to your room, now!" Starla pointed toward the staircase. The boys slowly walked away, each intermittently looking back at Lewis. "Ugh, them Scott genes," she mumbled before directing her attention to Lewis. "Lewis, come in and have a seat."

"Are you sure it's okay with your security guards?" Lewis teased.

"Positive," Starla assured him.

"These were for you." He handed her the yellow roses.

"Thank you, Lewis, but the boys are correct. Leon and I have reconciled."

Lewis leisurely placed the scented beauties on the coffee table and sat on the loveseat. "Is that why you haven't returned my calls or attended church these past weeks?"

Starla sat across from him on the couch. "I have been attending services with Leon. As for your calls, I don't think it's appropriate for us to spend time together on the phone or otherwise, considering your proposition."

Lewis remained cool. "Starla, I thought you agreed to seriously consider my proposal. I thought you wanted a stable environment for you and the boys."

Starla leaned forward, placing her elbows on her knees. "Lewis, I know you don't understand and I don't expect you to. I earnestly considered your proposal and all the things you could offer me and the boys. When it comes to possessions, you win hands down. But I love Leon, nothing can ever change that. I'd rather struggle with him than live a life of luxury with someone I don't love."

"What about your boys? Is it fair to make them struggle?" Starla could tell he was losing his cool by the way his voice inflected.

"Lewis, my boys are fine. They love and adore their father, just as much as I do." Starla sighed. "Leon loves his family so much, he'd give his life for us without hesitation. You can't replace that kind of love with material possessions."

"Yet Leon replaced it with alcohol without hesitation," Lewis reminded her. "He loved you so much that he left you unprotected and homeless for a bottle."

A vision of her father flashed before her, and Starla blinked back tears. "Lewis, what you're saying is the truth; there's nothing I can say to change those facts. However, those facts don't change how I feel." Starla stood, indicating the conversation was over.

"Maybe you should pray about this some more," he suggested, and stood.

Starla smiled. "I have prayed. That's how I know this is right."

Lewis moved closer. "I prayed too, and that's how I know you and I are meant to be." In one maneuver, Lewis pressed her to him and kissed her. Starla wasn't able to push him away before the boys grabbed Lewis's legs. Jaylen punched him in the groin and Montel latched on to his thigh with his teeth. Neither of them had heard the boys creep back down the stairs.

"Ouch!" Lewis released Starla and pushed the boys off of him.

Recognizing the fear in her babies, Starla finished the job they started. "Don't you ever put your hands on me or my boys! Now get out!" she ordered after kneeing Lewis in the groin.

Lewis, bent over and gasping for air, slowly made his way to the door. "St . . . Starla, wait. We need to talk."

"I'm going to tell my daddy!" Montel screamed after dumping Lewis's flowers into the garbage.

"Montel, hush! Lewis, out!" Starla ordered.

"Starla, you know I would never hurt you or the boys," Lewis grunted through clenched teeth.

"Lewis, all I know is that there is no way I'd ever choose you over my husband. I don't know what god you've been praying to, but it certainly isn't the true and living God. Please don't call me or come here again," Starla ordered before she slammed the door in his face. No sooner had she locked the door than the boys ran to her. "Are you all right?" she asked after hugging each of them.

"Yes. I can't wait to tell Daddy you know how to fight." Montel grinned. Starla laughed and Jaylen picked up the cordless handset.

"Jaylen, what are you doing?" Starla asked.

"I'm calling Daddy."

Starla promptly snatched the phone from her youngest protector and replaced it on the base. "Boys, have a seat. I'm going to teach you a game called 'let's keep Daddy out of jail.' Then I have a very important call to make."

Chapter 19

Marlissa took total advantage of having the insurance office all to herself. The reprieve was temporary; Mr. Atkins was scheduled to return in an hour. There would be just enough time for her to eat a bagged lunch, use the restroom, and call Starla for another lesson. Marlissa started on her turkey sandwich first.

Thus far, every one of Starla's lessons had yielded success. Kevin nearly fell off balance upon coming home two nights ago and finding new bedding and a hot, candlelit bubble bath waiting for him. Marlissa considered Starla's suggestion that she join Kevin, but that would have been a bit too aggressive. Kevin enjoyed his treat in the master bath alone.

"I could get used to this," Kevin said with his head lying in her lap as she massaged his temples later after dinner. Marlissa assumed he was referring to the motion of her fingers. Kevin switched positions on the couch and gathered Marlissa to him, and in no time fell asleep.

Marlissa bit into the caramel rice cake and giggled out loud. In place of a day at the spa, she went grocery shopping with the money Kevin had given her. Out of habit, when he returned home, Kevin reached into the wire basket for a snack as he sorted through the mail. His face twisted when he realized the chips and peanuts were gone. The only items in the fruit basket were fruit. He opened the cookie jar and grunted. His favorite round snacks had been replaced with much bigger and tasteless assorted rice cakes. Kevin didn't argue with Marlissa about monitoring his sugar intake. "Just keep me supplied with this sugar," he had said, and then kissed her.

Marlissa didn't have a problem with that at all. In fact, she wanted to give him much more than sugar. She just didn't know how to bring up the subject of sex without asking him to commit to reconciliation. Since telling him about her violation, Kevin seemed to have softened a lot. He constantly held her when they were together, which was often. Too often, Marlissa thought, for them to still be in limbo. Marlissa spent so much time with him that she hadn't had time to look for a one-bedroom apartment.

They ate dinner together and went to church and Bible Study together. Marlissa spent the night a couple of times tucked underneath his arms. It seemed as though Kevin didn't want her out of his presence, but he never once mentioned the divorce or her moving back in. Kevin didn't voice his feelings toward her, either, but she felt them every time he held her and kissed her.

Marlissa, too absorbed with thoughts of Kevin, wasn't aware that she no longer had the office all to herself. She practically choked upon hearing her name.

"Marlissa."

Marlissa stared at the woman standing in front of her. With only inches separating them, she cautiously greeted her adversary with a nod in place of the customary smile and handshake. "Hello, Pastor Jennings. Mr. Atkins isn't in at this time. Come back later this afternoon. I'm sure he'll be able to squeeze you in."

Pastor Jennings leaned over the desk, making the space between them even smaller. "I didn't come here to discuss insurance. I came here to see you." Marlissa flinched and Pastor Jennings smiled. "Are you intimidated?"

Marlissa took a deep breath and tried to draw in as much oxygen as possible before Pastor Jennings's negative energy took over. "What can I do for you?" she asked, knowing the answer.

Pastor Jennings planted her fist on the desk and knocked over Marlissa's nameplate. "Stay away from my son. Divorce him like a good girl, and run along to find someone else's life to ruin." Pastor Jennings didn't smile or blink.

Marlissa didn't understand why, after all this time, Pastor Jennings's words still pierced her. She was used to the venom, but today she refused to allow her mother-in-law the privilege of controlling her emotions. Marlissa abruptly stood. The action caused Pastor Jennings to pull back.

"Pastor Jennings, I am not ruining *my* husband's life. If Kevin and I divorce, it will be *our* decision, not yours!"

It took a moment for Pastor Jennings to organize her next statement; she hadn't anticipated Marlissa standing up to her.

"You are ruining his life. Kevin barely communicates with me now and he hasn't been to church in weeks." She glared at her. "You're seducing and enticing him away from God," Pastor Jennings delivered through clenched teeth.

"Pastor Jennings." Marlissa paused. "And I use the title loosely. I haven't enticed Kevin into anything. By choice, Kevin sits next to me every Sunday at service and every Wednesday night at Bible Study. We pray and read the Bible together." This time Marlissa leaned into Pastor Jennings's space. "If Kevin's not speaking to you, it could be because you're always trying to run his life."

Pastor Jennings took a step back. "I am his mother. I have a right to protect him! I—"

Marlissa cut her off. "Just what are you protecting him from? What do you think I'm going to do to him?"

"The same thing worldly women like you always do. Manipulate him with your body then use him until all his money and dignity are gone. Just like before."

Marlissa folded her arms. "You have me mixed up with someone else. I admit I hurt Kevin in the past, but I never used him. I love him way too much for that."

"Marlissa, there's a big difference between love and lust." Pastor Jennings smirked. "Kevin will soon learn the difference, and you'll be out with the trash where you belong."

All of a sudden Marlissa felt empowered. A bravado she'd never experienced before ignited in her belly and permeated throughout her being. She walked around the desk and stood toe-to-toe with Pastor Jennings. "I know the difference better than you think, but I don't have to prove that to you. I don't have to validate your off-base opinions of me, but what I will do is remind you of the facts." Marlissa held up her forefinger. "First, I am not a 'worldly' woman, as you put it. I am a child of God." Marlissa added another finger. "Second, I am not Kevin's woman, I am his wife. I don't have to manipulate him with my body; he can have it anytime he wants." Marlissa added one last finger. "I love Kevin and I intend to remain Mrs. Kevin Jennings until the day I die. My goal is to be *everything* he needs and I don't care what you or anyone else thinks about it." Marlissa walked to the office door and held it open. "Have a good day, mother-in-law."

Pastor Jennings was appalled. "I know you're not throwing me out!"

"No, Pastor Jennings, I am hoping you will act like a church lady and leave gracefully."

Pastor Jennings stomped past Marlissa, mumbling something incomprehensible. After closing the door, Marlissa shook her head. If she didn't know any better, she would have sworn she heard Pastor Jennings curse.

Marlissa didn't have a chance to sit down before her cell phone rang. It was Kevin. "Hey, gorgeous."

"What's wrong? Your voice is lacking its usual spunk."

"Nothing, now." Marlissa decided against burdening Kevin with the details about his mother's visit. "How did the surgeries go?"

"God did it again, but I need intercession for this afternoon's clinic. Mother Scott has an appointment." Kevin laughed. "And you know she's going to be late and throw me off schedule."

"Where do you want to meet for dinner?"

"Baby, I forgot to tell you, I'm meeting with Tyson and Leon this evening."

Marlissa smacked her lips. "Now I have to take a back seat to Tyson and Leon?"

"Marlissa Jennings, you will never ride in the back seat as long as I'm driving."

What does that mean? she wondered, but asked instead, "Do I have to save you a seat at Bible Study?"

"You don't have to, but it will save me the hassle of physically tossing someone out of my spot." Kevin chuckled, but she knew he was very serious.

"You would physically inflict harm in the house of God just to be close to me?" Marlissa mused.

The commotion outside his office door distracted him. "Oh, Lord," Kevin mumbled upon recognizing Reyna's and Mother Scott's voices. "Marlissa, something's come up. I'll see you tonight."

"Is everything all right?" It was Marlissa's turn to be concerned.

"I hope so, but pray anyway." Before Marlissa could ask what to pray for, the line went dead.

***

Kevin opened his office door and couldn't believe his eyes. Mother Scott was an hour early for her appointment, and Reyna, who didn't have an appointment, was dressed in a mini-skirt holding a picnic basket. He didn't bother with a greeting.

"Lower your voices. This is a hospital and my place of business," Kevin scolded. "Now get in here before I call security and have both of you thrown out."

The women scowled at one another as they walked past Kevin, but didn't say a word until they were safely inside Kevin's office.

"Would someone like to tell me what's going on?" he barked after closing the door behind them.

"That's what I would like to know!" Mother Scott took the lead. "I came here on time for once and find you've been cheating on my baby. I know the Lord told me to get over here for a reason."

"What?" As usual, Kevin couldn't follow Mother Scott's train of thought.

"Kevin, don't listen to her!" Reyna jumped in. "I was just bringing you lunch."

"Reyna, I told you—"

"You're offering a lot more than lunch in that outfit," Mother Scott continued as if Kevin hadn't said a word. "And when I greeted you on the elevator, you said you were meeting your fiancé for lunch. Don't try to change the story now."

"I don't need to explain anything to you. It isn't any of your business who I spend my time with!"

"Reyna!" Kevin attempted to jump in, but failed again.

"If I take that basket and beat you upside the head with it, I bet you'll start explaining."

Kevin took the basket from Reyna, just in case Mother Scott made good on the threat.

"Kevin, tell me the truth right now. Are you cheating on Marlissa with this woman? Is she your fiancée or not?" Mother Scott demanded.

Reyna pointed in her face. "I told you our relationship is none of your business!"

"Enough!" Kevin slammed the basket on the desk. "Both of you sit down now and don't say another word." Kevin watched as both women moved their mouths to speak, then decided to refrain. Mother Scott and Reyna slowly crept to the two chairs facing Kevin's desk, but neither wanted to be the one to sit down first.

"Now!" Kevin's roar caused the two foes to promptly plop into the seats.

Kevin remained standing, and massaged his forehead. "Reyna, this is the last time I am going to tell you not to come here uninvited. The next time you show up, I'm going to call security. This is also the last time I'm going to explain to you that I am not interested in a relationship with you. Not now, not in the future, not even in the afterlife." Mother Scott chuckled at that comment. Kevin grimaced at her, and then continued. "Reyna, do you understand what I am saying to you?"

"But your mother said—"

"Reyna, forget what my mother said and listen to me," Kevin said, pointing at himself.

Mother Scott grunted. "Child, you don't need an eye doctor, you need one of those doctors who do those brain scans in that big machine. Your light is on but there's still a vacancy sign hanging out front."

"Mother Scott, that's enough," Kevin warned. "A minute ago you were acting just as childish as she was." He smirked. "A prayer warrior, threatening to beat her with a picnic basket."

"I was just trying to look out for my baby."

Kevin couldn't believe that Mother Scott had the audacity to roll her eyes at him. "Mother, you have nothing to worry about." Kevin directed his next statement to them both. "Under no circumstances will I tolerate this display of juvenile, not to mention non-Christian, behavior that I just witnessed in my place of business. In addition to reporting you to security, Mother Scott, I will also stop seeing you as a patient if this happens again. Do you both understand?"

"Yes," they mumbled almost in unison.

"Good-bye, Reyna." Kevin stood and handed her back the basket. Before starting for the door, he turned to Mother Scott. "You stay here. I'll see you during lunch, because if I let you go, you will return an hour later than your scheduled time."

Mother Scott rolled her eyes again. "I ain't worried about no scheduled time. I follow the time the Lord gives me."

Kevin started to respond, but figured, *What's the use?*

Chapter 20

"Man, I can't believe my eyes." Tyson chuckled. "I never thought I would see Kevin Hezekiah Jennings standing over a hot stove. I thought the only thing you knew how to make was cold cereal."

Kevin was too busy concentrating on the cookbook and stirring the cream sauce to pay Tyson much attention. Tyson leaned on the counter and Kevin exploded.

"Man, be careful! It's taken me all day to get those rolls to rise and you're about to smash them."

Tyson jumped back with his hands raised. "Sorry, man, I didn't see them." Kevin grunted at his friend and moved the dough to a safe location. "Man, Marlissa has you *jacked up*."

Kevin relaxed at the sound of Marlissa's name, even smiled. "That's my baby."

"It's good to see you happy again." Tyson frowned when he pulled a rice cake from the cookie jar. "Ugh, whose bright idea was this?"

"Marlissa said I need to watch my sugar intake."

"What else does she have you watching, the cooking channel?" Tyson put the rice cake back.

"Man, forget you." Kevin discarded his friend's musing. "If I want to cook my wife a special dinner, that's none of your business." Kevin checked the oven temperature before placing the salmon inside.

"I guess that means you've discussed the divorce with her?" Tyson said, sampling a crab-stuffed mushroom.

"Those are not for you!" Kevin scolded, then asked, "How is it?"

Tyson laughed at his boy, and then took another one. "Not bad. So how did she take the news?"

Kevin rescued the mushrooms before Tyson devoured them. "I haven't discussed it with her yet."

"What? Why not?"

Kevin shrugged. "I don't know if the time is right."

Tyson threw his hands in the air. "Man, you're standing in here in an apron and mittens looking like Yan Can Cook on steroids and you don't know if the time is right?" Tyson shook his head. "You're crazy."

"Hey, man, don't you have somewhere to go or some people to harass or something?" Kevin charged.

"Hey, doc, don't you have a wife you need to talk to?"

Kevin exhaled deeply. "I don't need a lawyer, I can handle my wife by myself."

"Fine, but if you don't talk to your wife soon, you *will* need a friend to talk to."

That was an hour ago and Kevin had long since admitted that Tyson was right; he did need to have a talk with Marlissa about the divorce. Kevin really didn't understand his reluctance. Their rekindled relationship had blossomed into a love affair that, at moments, stirred him to a point where nothing and no one mattered to him. Marlissa filled his dreams and most of his conscious thoughts. On more than one occasion Kevin had reprimanded himself for daydreaming, trying to recall her scent, her smile, or her touch while examining patients.

Touch: now that was a much-needed addition to their relationship. During their marriage Kevin had spent many days literally starved for the touch of the woman he loved. In the beginning he would voice his need, but Marlissa refused to make the effort, so he stopped. Presently, Marlissa could give lessons on the art of sensual touch. Kevin didn't know if she was aware, but on several occasions her soft touches had rendered him senseless. And her kisses . . .

"Get a grip," Kevin reminded himself, and pressed the play button on the CD changer.

He heard the garage door at the precise moment he lit the third candle on the formal dining room table. Marlissa had just unbuttoned her coat when he stepped into the kitchen.

"Hey, beautiful," he said, followed by a hug.

Marlissa thought the hug was tighter and the kiss a little more intense than normal. "I hope you're not expecting any other visitors tonight."

"Of course. I am an only child and I don't like to share." Kevin still held her.

"Good." Marlissa stepped back and removed her coat.

"Get a grip," Kevin mumbled. Marlissa was wearing that tangerine tank dress, his favorite. Kevin promptly received her coat and hung it in the coat closet. "Have a seat in the dining room. Dinner will be served shortly," he instructed, then swiftly disappeared.

Marlissa followed Kevin's instructions and walked to the dining room. The display before her left her awestruck. "Honey, did you do all this?" she called over her shoulder.

Kevin approached from behind, but instead of jumping, Marlissa relaxed into his embrace. Kevin expressed appreciation by nibbling on her neck, something he hadn't done in a long time. "Yes, I cooked and set the table," he answered between bites. "I made your favorites, stuffed mushrooms, baked salmon, asparagus, baked potato."

Marlissa didn't hear the menu; she was too busy praying he would give her a hickey.

"First, I want you to open this." Kevin had to tell her twice before she was able to comprehend what he'd said and open her eyes. A white box lay in her chair.

Kevin's arms remained around her and his lips against her neck as Marlissa opened the tall box.

"Kevin," Marlissa gasped. "Thank you." It was the angel she'd admired in the store window on Piedmont Avenue six weeks before when Kevin first unexpectedly showed up at the apartment. "When did you get this?"

"That day after I left you in Starbucks."

Marlissa suddenly spun around. "I didn't know you cared back then," she whispered as tears pooled in her eyes.

Kevin removed the angel from her hands and placed it on the mahogany table. "'Lissa, I never stopped caring about you." He wiped her cheek, and then reassured her with a kiss that escalated them to a level of passion they'd never experienced. If not for the need for oxygen, they would have continued the voyage. Kevin struggled to regain control. "We should eat now."

Marlissa recognized the distraction for what it was and agreed. "Do you need some help?"

"No. I think you should stay in here."

Marlissa reached for him, but this time it was Kevin who retreated. "I'll be right back."

Inside the kitchen Kevin was so distracted by his desire for Marlissa that he absentmindedly tried to remove the bread from the oven without an oven mitt. "Ouch!" Kevin shook his hand then ran some cold water to alleviate the burning sensation. While the pain subsided, he battled with his desire to touch Marlissa. Convinced his willpower would win, Keven rejoined Marlissa in the dining room.

"Honey, I can't believe you did all of this for me," she said as she watched him spread the feast in front of her. "You must have been in the kitchen all day." Marlissa meant the compliment, but mainly wanted to redirect her thoughts. At the moment, food was the furthest thing from her mind.

"I don't mind, you're worth it."

As usual they enjoyed dinner nibbling from each other's plate. Seated next to Marlissa at the table, the candlelight, soft music, and the tangerine dress proved to be too much for Kevin to handle. Watching Marlissa eat stimulated Kevin almost to the point of pushing him over the edge. He soon gave up on feeding her and surrendered to the silent beckoning of her lips. Food was long forgotten as each feasted without interruption.

"This is getting out of hand," Kevin whispered when Marlissa maneuvered to sit on his lap.

If he would just use his hands, Marlissa thought, kissing his neck.

"Kevin, why don't you touch me?" she whispered back. "I know I appeared nervous before, but I like the way you used to touch me."

Kevin pulled back and regained control of his breathing. "I like touching you, but if my hands start roaming your body, I won't be able to stop."

"Okay." She blushed, but his face was stone serious. Marlissa had a way to relieve his anxiety. "Let's dance." She took Kevin's hand and led him into the living room.

Dancing to the melodic sounds of Brian McKnight and Luther Vandross, the sensual kissing continued, but it wasn't enough for Marlissa.

Frustrated, she reached behind her and covered his hands with hers. Kevin assumed she was trying to break away, and motioned to step backward. His breath caught when she glided his hands to a part of her he hadn't touched in a very long time. Marlissa buried her head in his chest while he caressed.

"'Lissa," he said, his breath labored, "you should leave now."

"Why?" she asked, and at the same time pressed closer into him. "I thought you like when I spend the night."

Kevin stopped his expedition and cupped her face. "Baby, if you stay here tonight, you'll end up in my bed, but we won't be sleeping. And we won't cuddle until the sun comes up."

"Oh," was the only word Marlissa could verbalize.

Expressions of both relief and disappointment washed over Kevin's face as he watched Marlissa walk away from him and back to the dining room table where she blew out the candles. His eyes bulged and his mouth gaped as he watched her remove her shoes, then unzip and step out of her dress, leaving it in a heap on the floor next to her shoes.

"Come on," she beckoned, then started for the bedroom.

Kevin made it to the bedroom to find that Marlissa had already pulled the bedding back, and waited for him to join her on the four poster, king-sized bed.

Kevin stood in the doorway warring with his emotions and his flesh. Making love to Marlissa was definitely something he wanted to do, maybe even needed to do. How was this going to affect their relationship? What if she had a flashback? What if she didn't like it? All those questions flooded his mind, but when Marlissa removed her undergarments and reached out to him, Kevin decided there was only one way to find out.

"Are you sure this is what you want?" he asked, positioning himself next to her on the pillow top mattress. For an answer, she unbuttoned and removed his shirt.

"Leave the light on. I need to see you," Marlissa said, grabbing Kevin's hand when he reached for the lamp after removing his prosthesis. That was all Kevin needed to hear.

Kevin glanced down at the woman snuggled against him and thanked God this beautiful, passionate woman was his wife. If not, he would be in serious trouble. After this episode he had to be with Marlissa all the days of his natural life. He gained new respect for her; watching her at times fighting to overcome visions of the past. It was then he would speak tenderly, helping her to relax and surrender to him. Kevin had waited so long for her to respond to him, yet her abandonment unraveled him. One thing was certain: he loved Marlissa more than ever. Feeling her body shift in his arms, Kevin closed his eyes.

Grinning from ear to ear, Marlissa felt like a new woman; like she had just come alive. The tears still flowed in a steady stream, but she wasn't sad at all. Making love to Kevin, to her husband, the man she loved more than anything, was liberating. At moments it was difficult, but Kevin's gentleness and care took her mind and body to heights she couldn't have imagined in her best dream. She chuckled to herself, reminiscing about how vocal and active she had been. *I can't believe that was me.* She laughed silently. Yellow-orange rays sprayed the room and caused Marlissa to blush. Kevin had said they wouldn't cuddle until sunrise. She raised her head and whispered, "I love you." Assuming Kevin was asleep, Marlissa rested against him, then drifted off to sleep.

***

"'Lissa, wake up." Kevin shook her. "We're going to be late for church."

"Church?" Marlissa had completely forgotten it was Sunday morning. It couldn't be time for church; she'd only dozed off three hours ago. After stretching, she casually scanned her surroundings and smiled. It was not a dream; she and Kevin had made love in their house and in their bed.

"You do remember what church is?" Kevin teased, brushing her curls back.

"Of course I do, but I wouldn't be mad if we stayed right here." This morning, Marlissa didn't give morning breath a second thought, and neither did Kevin. They kissed until Kevin finally pulled back.

"I would love to, but I need to see a doctor."

Marlissa sat up with concerned etched all over her face. "Baby, what's the matter?"

"I think you may have busted my eardrum with all that screaming you did last night," Kevin said with a straight face.

"Forget you." Marlissa threw a pillow at him when he continued making fun of her.

He mimicked her voice. "Kevin, Kevin, oh, Kevin!"

Totally embarrassed, Marlissa gathered the sheet around her and started for the bathroom.

"Come back here, wild woman." Kevin, without much effort, lifted her and laid her back on the bed. "I love hearing you scream my name, don't ever stop. It does wonders for my ego."

After the kiss, Marlissa had a comeback for him. "I'll keep screaming if you keep roaring like you're the king of the jungle."

Kevin laughed out loud. "You've got jokes, huh? I'll have you know that I am the king."

"I'll second that motion." Marlissa didn't ask him how the latest turn of events affected their relationship. Instead, she accepted his invitation to join him for a shower.

Chapter 21

Kevin and Marlissa made it to Sunday morning service just in time to hear the choir render a spirited version of "The Blessing of Abraham." From an unknown source, Marlissa found enough energy to stand and receive her inheritance. Figuring that she hadn't achieved liberation all by herself, Marlissa pulled on Kevin's hand until he was standing beside her and praising God with her.

Pastor Drake mounted the podium, and the congregation stood to read the scripture displayed on the mounted wall monitor. Marlissa caught a glimpse of Leon and Starla with their boys one row over. They looked like the perfect family. The sight warmed her. She leaned into Kevin, and his arm naturally rested on her shoulder. Everything was working out. After last night, she was certain her future as Mrs. Kevin Jennings was secure.

The bubbling-over joy lost some of its momentum when out of her peripheral vision Marlissa spotted Mother Scott glaring at her. Marlissa ignored her and enjoyed worshipping God with her husband.

"Hey, girl." Starla greeted Marlissa with a hug after service. "You look happy. One can only wonder why."

"I am happy, but I am not going to tell you why." Marlissa blushed.

"You just had to jump into the ring, didn't you?" They hadn't seen Mother Scott approach.

"Mother, I—" Marlissa stammered.

With her mouth twisted, Mother Scott planted her fist on her tiny waist. "Don't try to deny it. With my one good eye, I can tell you done had a championship bout."

Starla didn't help at all. "Girl, your *happiness* is showing all over your face. Even the pitch in your 'Thank ya' was higher."

Marlissa's face flushed when Starla asked what had worked: the dress or the bubble bath. "Starla, not in front of Mother!" Marlissa scolded.

Starla smacked her lips. "Where do you think I get all this experienced knowledge from?"

"Mother?" Marlissa gasped, and gazed at Mother Scott in amazement.

Mother Scott rolled her eyes. "Don't look at me like that. I wasn't happily married for thirty years and had four babies by praying and reading the

Bible alone." The women were still laughing when Kevin and Leon joined them.

"What's so funny?" Leon asked.

"You'll see later," Mother Scott answered Leon, and then turned to Kevin. "And so will you."

The men were still lost and the women still giggling when Pastor Drake approached the group.

"Good word this morning, Pastor," Marlissa greeted him.

"Thank you, Sister Marlissa. I'm glad you made it in time to hear it."

Pastor Drake's response left Marlissa speechless. Suddenly she wondered if the whole congregation knew how she had spent her night and part of the morning. Then she decided she didn't care. Kevin was legally her husband.

Pastor Drake watched the interaction between Kevin and Marlissa with a careful eye. Now, as during service, they were in constant physical contact with one another, making it obvious to everyone that their relationship had escalated.

"Looks like the four of you are ready for the marriage clinic?" Pastor Drake included Leon and Starla.

"I am going to join the church first," Starla answered, but Kevin just slightly grinned and nodded.

"We'll think about it," Marlissa responded.

"I'll keep praying for you," Pastor Drake said before watching them walk away.

As she walked to the car, Marlissa disregarded the gnawing feeling in her stomach that had surfaced upon feeling Kevin's body instantly tense the second Pastor Drake mentioned the marriage clinic. "That ain't nothing but the devil," she mumbled.

The Kevin she knew would not have made love to her unless he loved her. Not once last night or this morning had Kevin voiced the sentiment, but Marlissa was convinced he loved her. He had to. She buckled her seat belt and decided she wouldn't pressure him. She would wait for him to open up. He'd revealed his heart to her once before and she'd broken it. Now she owed him time.

Chapter 22

Starla massaged Leon's shoulders as he sat at the computer with his eyes transfixed on the monitor. Leon wasn't supposed to move back home for another week, but Leon had never been a good observer of time, especially when it came to being away from his family. Starla didn't mind. They carried on like newlyweds and the boys couldn't have been happier.

"Baby, relax," Starla reassured him. "I know you passed your exam." In seconds, the results of Leon's state contractor's license exam would be displayed on the screen.

"Star, you don't know how much I want this for us. Really, I need this," Leon revealed.

Starla did understand. Leon needed to make retribution for all the heartache he had caused, and regain his wife's total trust. He needed to keep the vows he'd made to her.

"I know, baby." Starla hugged him from behind and kissed his cheek. "And I believe in you."

Leon sighed heavily, then nervously typed in the identifying information. No sooner had the reporting window opened than Starla screamed, "I knew you could do it!"

With closed eyes, Leon whispered a word of thanks, and then stood and spun Starla around. "We're on our way!" The weight of the world lifted as he danced an updated version of the bump with Starla.

The celebration aroused the boys' curiosity. Leon and Starla were still dancing when Montel intruded. "Mommy, why are you laughing and crying?"

"Baby, I am happy," Starla explained.

"We're both happy," Leon yelled.

The boys giggled uncontrollably as Leon lifted them simultaneously and spun them around. "I feel like celebrating," Leon announced.

"Daddy, can we go to Chuck E. Cheese's? I want to be happy too."

Looking into Jaylen's expectant eyes, Leon couldn't refuse his son. "Yes, and we can go to the movies, too." He set the boys down and watched them trot off.

"Daddy, I'm glad you're home," Montel called over his shoulder.

"Me too," Jaylen added.

Leon's heart swelled with joy. His prayers were being answered one at a time. The hell and darkness of the past three years was finally being lifted. The shame of abandoning his family and the guilt of David's death was slowly being erased. His family loved and needed him again.

Starla rubbed his left bicep. "I am happy you're home too." Leon sat on the desk and Starla stood in front of him, holding his head close to her bosom. Leon relaxed his arms around her waist. Before she felt Leon's tears soak her tee, Starla knew he was shedding tears of joy.

He looked up with thick puddles in his eyes. "When you come back from Modesto, we're going to have our own private celebration." Starla had finally made arrangements to visit with her father's widow to get some answers about why he'd deserted her.

Starla's eyes lit up at the thought. "Really?"

"Yes. I'll have Mama come stay with the boys, and you and I are going to Calistoga for a few days."

"Thank you!" Starla kissed Leon's face and hugged him to her again. She had wanted to indulge in a mud bath treatment for a long time, but she could no longer afford the luxury. Thinking about the cost of the Napa Valley getaway dulled her enthusiasm. That, and the fact the somehow Leon had purchased a new work truck. "Honey, Calistoga is a bit expensive; maybe we should find somewhere closer to home."

Leon rose to his full height. "Star, I am well aware of how much a few days in Calistoga cost and I can handle it."

"But, honey, now we have the truck payments and we need business licenses and supplies, and advertisements and—"

Leon covered her mouth with his right hand. "Baby, trust me. I got this." Only after Starla nodded did Leon remove his hand. Leon pulled out his wallet. "Here's some money for your trip. I had your oil changed and the tires checked yesterday, so you shouldn't have any problems. Buy something for me while you're in Modesto. I'm sure there's a Victoria's Secret somewhere down there in the valley."

Starla's eyes moistened again. "Thank you."

"Star, are you sure you don't need me to go with you?"

Starla shook her head, then kissed his cheek. "Just be here to love me when I return."

As she drove down Highway 99, Starla replayed in her mind the telephone conversation with her father's widow. Odessa had been surprisingly friendly toward her, practically begging her to come for a visit. One of her comments still had Starla puzzled. "James would have loved for you to see where he lived," was what Odessa had said.

If James Howard had wanted Starla to see where he lived, he would have come back for her. Ten years and he never came back. Starla accepted the hard, naked truth: James Howard didn't want her or her mother. James was self-centered and cruel like her mother claimed, but deep inside she loved her father. If James Howard was alive to beg her forgiveness, Starla would have gladly given it.

As she exited onto Hatch Road, Starla began praying for the courage to continue the journey back in time. She had an overwhelming urge to cross the ramp and speed as fast as she could back to the Bay Area, but twenty years of pain and wonder forced her to the blue and white house on Lyndstom Avenue. She sat quietly listening to the idle engine until the screen door opened.

"Starla, is that you?" a woman called from the porch.

Odessa didn't look much older than Starla remembered. Her hair was sprinkled with salt and she had picked up a few pounds, but other than that, Odessa Howard was the same. She stood just one inch taller than Starla. Today Starla thought the same thing about Odessa she had ten years ago: she bore a strong resemblance to Starla's mother.

She sucked in every ounce of courage, exited the vehicle, and then started down the cement walkway.

"Yes, Mrs. Howard, it's me." The two shared a brief hug.

"Baby, call me Odessa. I've remarried; my last name is Jones now." Odessa placed her arm around Starla's shoulder. "Where are your boys?"

"They're with my husband. I thought it best to come alone," Starla answered.

"That's too bad. I would've loved to see James's grandchildren. He would be so happy to finally have some boys in the family."

Is that why he left me, because I wasn't a boy? Starla asked herself. "I have pictures," she said aloud.

"Baby, come on inside before we have a heat stroke out here."

Starla slowly took in her surroundings before following Odessa inside. It was this average-looking house with the big yard containing fruit trees and a hammock that her father had left her for. Maybe the big oak had provided him more pleasure than she and her mother could have, or maybe he'd found solace on the gazebo. Starla momentarily shut her eyes as to imprint the scenery permanently in her mind.

Inside the house, Odessa introduced Starla to her new husband. Starla thought the gentleman looked familiar. She'd definitely seen him somewhere before, but where? Odessa answered her unspoken question.

"Starla, this is my husband, Hiawatha Jones. He's a deacon at the church." Odessa then turned to her husband. "Hiawatha, this is James's daughter, Starla."

Starla now remembered. Deacon Jones had spoken at her father's funeral. He extended his hand and the two exchanged pleasantries. Deacon Jones then excused himself to give the women some privacy. Odessa invited Starla to the kitchen table.

"Can I get you something cold to drink?" Odessa offered.

Starla accepted a bottled water, more to calm her nerves than to quench her thirst.

"Starla, you look so much like James it's scary," Odessa observed. "Lord, I wish James was here. You don't know how many days he prayed for this very thing, having you in his home."

Starla took a swig of water. "Odessa, I came here today because I need to get some answers about my father. I hope you can help me. I've tried talking to my mother, but she refuses to offer any assistance. I need to know why my father left my mother and me." Starla swallowed in an effort to steady her voice. "I need to know what was so wrong with me that my loving father would up and leave, and not try to contact us until he was dying and too feeble to be a father to me. Why did he no longer desire to be a husband to my mother?"

Starla didn't understand Odessa's stunned facial expression, but continued. "Can you explain to me how you can speak of my father as if he cared about me, when it's obvious he didn't?"

"Starla, how could you possibly think James didn't care about you? You were his only child. James adored you."

"Then why did he leave his wife and child?"

For a while Odessa was speechless. She reached for Starla's hand, then withdrew before contact. She wrung her hands before resting them in the praying position. "Oh, Starla, I can't believe that after all this time, you don't know the truth. Your mother hasn't told you."

Starla stopped in the midst of searching her purse for tissue. "What truth?"

"I am so sorry you've had to bear this burden all by yourself for all these years."

"Odessa, what are you talking about?" Starla persisted.

"Starla, your father and mother weren't married. James was my husband for twenty-six years."

"No," Starla said, shaking her head. The numbers didn't add up.

"James and I went through some turbulent times in the beginning. That's when he began having an affair with your mother. When Yvonne became pregnant with you, James left me. We were separated for nine years, but we never divorced. During that time he lived with you and your mother. Then, one day, he said the Lord dealt with him and he couldn't continue living in sin with Yvonne anymore. James turned his life over to the Lord and begged me to let him come back home." Odessa read the disbelief on Starla's face. "It's true, Starla."

"Is that why Mama never used Daddy's last name?"

"Could be. Yvonne was so angry at James she refused to allow him to have any contact with you. She didn't refuse his monthly child support payments, though."

That sounds like Mama, Starla thought.

"James begged her. I even tried reasoning with Yvonne to let James see you, but she flat-out refused. Yvonne was a woman scorned. If she couldn't have James, he couldn't have you. She vowed to take you out of state. At first we thought she was just talking, but then she left for a while. After that we took her threats seriously."

Starla nodded, remembering the time she and her mother lived in Seattle for a year. This time Starla didn't stop the tears from flowing.

"James was so depressed at times over the situation he had created. I felt sorry to the extent that I offered him a divorce so he could be with you, but he refused." Odessa placed her hand on Starla's shoulder. "Those last ten years with James were good years, but, Starla, trust me, James hated every day he couldn't be with you."

Starla's thick tears had blinded her vision when Odessa handed her a napkin.

"Your birthdays were the hardest for him. James would lie out in that hammock all day, nearly getting sunburned, just thinking about you. Sometimes James would hide out in your neighborhood hoping to catch a glimpse of you. On a few occasions he managed to sneak some pictures with one of those disposable cameras."

Starla closed her eyes and attempted to recall ever seeing her father in the neighborhood. She couldn't recall spotting the gray Ford truck once.

"I have a niece who attended Hayward High with you: Evangeline Morris."

Starla's eyes bulged. "Vangie is your niece?"

Odessa smiled. "She's my brother's daughter."

"I can't believe it! I've known Vangie for years. We work together and she's never mentioned my father."

"That's because she doesn't know James was your father," Odessa explained.

Starla rubbed her forehead. "I don't understand."

"James and I were visiting my brother one day when Vangie showed us pictures of her playing with the volleyball team. James nearly broke down crying when he saw you in the first row holding the ball. From then on, James kept track of you through Vangie. Unknowingly, she supplied him with pictures of you and your prom date and your senior yearbook picture. You should have seen how James beamed with pride looking at your pictures. James even caught a few of your games without your mother detecting his presence."

The information was too much for Starla to digest. "I don't believe it. I've spent so many years resenting my father, it's hard for me to receive what you're saying. I mean, you're basically telling me the reason I've suffered all these years is my mother's stubbornness."

Odessa patted her hand. "Starla, I know this must be hard for you to accept, but it's the truth."

Starla wasn't convinced. "I don't believe you. I think you're lying to protect your dead husband," she said bluntly.

"Wait here, I'll prove it to you." Odessa left Starla sitting at the kitchen table.

It was then that Starla allowed herself to consider that just maybe Odessa was telling the truth. Yvonne Griffin was indeed stubborn and sometimes outright spiteful. When Odessa called out of the blue with news of her father's heart attack, Yvonne told Starla not to go to the hospital. "That no-good man left us, why should you go running to see him just because he's sick?" Yvonne had said. Starla could still remember the moment she shared the news of her father's passing with her mother. Yvonne had smiled.

Odessa returned with a cardboard box, with black bold letters spelling "Starla Howard" on it. "James kept every little token he could steal of you," she explained.

Starla gripped her chest as her worst fear became a reality right before her eyes. Odessa displayed picture after picture of her. Some were blurred shots of her walking to school or in her front yard. Her volleyball schedules along with shots of her in motion were numerous and clearer. The photo of her wearing a black cap and gown had been enlarged, and so had the picture she and Vangie had taken together on graduation day. On the back of each photo, James had scribed the words "my baby girl" and the date. The last thing Odessa retrieved from the box was a thick sealed envelope with Starla's name on it.

"James wrote this letter the week before his heart attack. I think he knew he wasn't going to be around much longer. Honestly, Starla, I think James died of a broken heart."

Starla, too emotional to agree or disagree, didn't say anything.

"Starla, I don't know what's in here, but I think you should be the one to open it. More of your questions might get answered."

Starla's hands shook violently as she took the envelope and placed it into her purse. What did her father have to say to her from the grave?

"You can take this stuff with you, if you want," Odessa offered.

Starla still couldn't speak. She just nodded, then watched as Odessa repacked the box and sealed it.

"Baby, I know this is a lot for you to digest. Learning your father loved you after believing he didn't care for you all this time has got to hurt. But, Starla, please don't hold this against Yvonne."

"My mother lied to me," Starla said, shaking her head.

"I know she did, but you have to forgive her the same way I had to forgive her and your father. What Yvonne did was wrong, but she wasn't trying to hurt you. Yvonne was trying to get back at James for taking nine years of her life."

When Starla's head fell onto the table, Odessa began praying. She prayed so hard and fervently, Hiawatha came in from the porch and joined in.

"Thank you so much," Starla said when she hugged Odessa an hour later. "I wish I had come here a long time ago."

"You came when you were ready," Odessa said, walking her out to the car. "You should bring the boys by sometime."

"I will," Starla promised.

Thirty minutes into the drive home, Starla couldn't resist any longer. She took the Patterson Pass exit and parked at the ARCO gas station. She then removed the envelope from her purse and slowly examined the contents. She read the handwritten letter on the faded paper first.

Dear Baby Girl,

If you're reading this letter, then I am no longer around. You probably won't notice because I haven't been in your life for so long. For that I am so sorry. You had to pay for my sin, but, Starla, I don't regret for one minute fathering you. I do regret every minute I am not able to be a father to you. I have always loved you, Baby Girl, and always will.

From afar I have watched you evolve into a beautiful young woman. I pray that one day God sends you a man who will respect you and cherish you for the queen you are. I pray that God will bless you with sons who will honor you and daughters who will admire you. Most of all, I pray that you will find it in your heart to forgive me for not being there to validate you and teach you about men. Starla, you are a star, and don't you ever forget it.

Baby Girl, I love you always,
Daddy

P.S. You were always on my mind. I have been saving these for you as an inheritance. Buy something nice for yourself.

Starla continued crying, but composed herself enough to count out 120 one hundred–dollar savings bonds, dated for each month her father was separated from her.

"Oh, Daddy!" she wailed out loud. "I'm so sorry for hating you." She was still crying when her cell phone rang. It was Leon.

"Baby, are you all right?"

Starla heaved and stuttered to the point that Leon couldn't understand her.

"Starla, where are you?" With much effort, Starla managed to give her location. "Stay there!" Leon ordered.

Starla couldn't move if she wanted to. Sobs from deep within tore her apart, leaving her gasping for air. It was as if every tear she'd held in from missing her father gushed out all at once. She cried so long and hard, she lost track of time. In between gasps she heard Leon knocking on her window. She hadn't seen him and Marlissa pull up in his truck. Once she opened the door, Leon held her until she settled.

"Baby, what happened?" Leon asked.

Starla still couldn't speak, but gave the letter to Leon, then lay against his chest as he read silently. When he finished, Leon motioned for Marlissa to drive Starla's car.

"Star, let's go home." Leon then carried her to his truck.

Chapter 23

Lewis studied Leon's every move through the surveillance camera, trying to decide how to approach him. He had been camped outside Starla's complex yesterday and witnessed Leon carrying her inside. Lewis couldn't stand not knowing what was going on with Starla. It was bad enough that Starla no longer attended his church, but now she also refused to accept the flowers he'd had delivered to her job.

This morning he took a chance by blocking his number and calling her cell phone. His heart sank when he got her voice mail. To satisfy his need for her, Lewis called three times just to hear her voice tell him to leave a message at the beep.

The longer Lewis observed Leon, the angrier he got. Leon looked happy, too happy for Lewis. He'd noticed Leon smiling more and had heard him whistling on a few occasions, but what puzzled him most was Leon's new attitude. Leon didn't appear dependent on this job anymore, which loosened Lewis's control over him. Last week Leon had informed him he would no longer work the morning shift. When Lewis asked why, the only reason Leon would give was "personal reasons."

Lewis spat profanities the day Leon pulled into the parking lot in that new truck. It disgusted him to know that Starla would risk going into deeper debt just so Leon could have something to ride in. On the outstide, where Lewis stood, Leon wasn't worthy of bus tokens, let alone a brand new truck. Lewis couldn't fathom what demon had possessed his Starla into thinking she would be satisfied with that drunk over him.

Visions of Leon and Starla kissing in the store weeks earlier flashed before him again and caused Lewis to slam his fist on the desk. Lewis bowed his head. "Father, show me how to prove to Starla that I am the one she needs, not that has-been." Leon's knock on the door disturbed his meditation.

"Mr. Mason, I am leaving now," Leon informed his boss.

Lewis went fishing. "Leon, is everything all right at home? You seem a little preoccupied today." Lewis was naive to the fact that Leon didn't like to mix his work and his personal life together, especially with people he didn't know well enough to divulge his business to.

"Mr. Mason, everything is fine."

Leon turned to leave, but Lewis continued. "Is your wife doing better?"

Leon's gaze hardened. "What makes you think something is wrong with my wife? I never said she was sick."

Lewis shifted in his seat, but remained cool. "Leon, you know as well as I, nothing can clutter a man's mind like his woman can."

Leon's face softened, but he didn't smile. "I guess you're right, Mr. Mason, but things couldn't be better with Starla and the boys."

"You're a lucky man, Leon." Lewis forced a smile. "You've been blessed with a wonderful family. I know men who would love to have exactly what you have."

There was something in Lewis's tone, or maybe it was the emptiness in his eyes. Whatever it was, Leon didn't acknowledge Lewis's compliment. "Good evening, Mr. Mason."

The cordless phone rested in the crook of her neck as Marlissa measured ingredients with her free hands. Kevin was due home soon and she wanted dinner ready for him.

"Are you sure you don't need me to give you half of the rent for this month?" Leon asked. "I feel bad about leaving you to foot the lease alone."

Marlissa shifted the phone to her left ear.
"You can't afford that with your wife and kids.
Besides, I don't need the money. My husband
provides me with everything I need." She added
a little sassiness to her voice to let Leon know
that she was referencing more than money.

"Whatever, brat. So when are you moving
out?"

Marlissa's feistiness quickly dissipated. Today, she wasn't any closer to the answer to that
question than she was a month ago. *Where did
the time go?* she wondered.

For the past month, she and Kevin had practically been living together. The only time Marlissa
went to her apartment was on weekends for the
sole purpose of exchanging clothing. Marlissa
didn't plan the turn of events, they just sort of
evolved on their own. Kevin expressed how much
he enjoyed having her around, and after the
revival of their sex life, Marlissa was more than
happy to stay in close proximity.

They experienced almost everything together
as a couple, from praying to grocery shopping.
They continued to attend church and Bible Study
regularly and ate out once a week. In the morn-
ings they prayed together and at night they played
together, enjoying long bubble baths and steamy
showers. Marlissa cooked his meals and saw

to the house being in order when Dr. Jennings returned home from long days of surgeries and clinic patients. Marlissa now not only possessed her own house key, but keys to Kevin's SUV and the Mercedes, which quickly became her vehicle of choice. Kevin had also given her access to his money by allowing her free use of his bank check card.

Kevin found Marlissa's opinion necessary for everything from what shirt and tie ensemble to wear to what he should eat for lunch. One day he went as far as to call from Macy's to ask if he should buy boxers or briefs. "Neither," Marlissa had said once she finished laughing. He promptly disconnected and rushed home. However, not once did Kevin mention stopping the divorce proceedings.

Kevin constantly told her how happy he was and how much he loved having her back, but Kevin never said if he still loved her.

Marlissa often second-guessed her decision to be intimate with him while their future still hung in limbo. Kevin's attention and response to her helped keep those thoughts on the back burner, though. For her, his actions spoke the volumes his mouth wouldn't utter. He loved her. He had to, or else he was just using her to fulfill his sexual needs. Marlissa didn't receive the latter because she believed she knew Kevin. The man she loved was kind and considerate. If he were using her, until the judge signed off they were still husband and wife, and physical intimacy was still a benefit.

"I'm not sure, but I have started packing," she finally answered. That was the truth. Either way Marlissa would have to move soon.

Leon didn't miss the sudden deflation in her voice. "Marlissa, you and Kevin are getting back together, aren't you?"

Marlissa activated her faith, calling those things that be not as though they were. "Of course, it's just a matter of time." She heard the garage door. "Hey, bro, the good doctor's home and I need some healing."

Leon yelled into the phone. "How many times do I have to tell you, *that's too much information!*"

Marlissa replaced the cordless phone on the base. She was still laughing at her friend when Kevin entered the kitchen, carrying his briefcase.

"Hey, gorgeous." Before she could stop stirring the custard for his favorite banana pudding, Kevin had entwined his arms around her from behind. Relishing that she no longer jumped or flinched at his touch, Kevin commenced kissing her cheek, then neck.

"You better stop before I scorch dessert."

"You did say I needed to watch my sugar intake." He resumed assaulting her senses.

Still giggling, Marlissa removed the double boiler from the heat, and turned to face her husband. "Do you still want this kind of sugar?"

When Marlissa finished kissing him, there was a look in Kevin's eyes she'd never seen before. The intense expression was raw and primitive. Marlissa thought something was wrong until Kevin suddenly blinked then smiled.

"'Lissa, we need to talk." Releasing his grip, Kevin stepped back, picked up his briefcase, and placed it on the counter.

Marlissa could have sworn her stomach had just done a somersault with a triple-toe loop. This was the moment she'd been waiting for, she just knew it. Kevin was ready to discuss the divorce. *Talk about the power of confession.* She grinned. Marlissa thought she would explode with anticipation watching Kevin open the briefcase.

"We need to discuss this," he said, then handed her the envelope.

Marlissa opened the envelope and at the same time wondered what type of divorce papers came in a gold square envelope. Her heart sank along with her hopes. It was an invitation to the Sutter Foundation's Annual Gala.

Marlissa cleared her throat, mostly to calm her emotions. She met Kevin's excited gaze. "What's there to discuss?"

Kevin was oblivious to her discontentment. "I think I should attend since I am being honored."

"I agree, you should go." Marlissa set the envelope on the counter, then searched the cabinets for nothing in particular.

Kevin reached for her hands. "I want us to attend as a couple."

"Really? You want me to accompany you?" Marlissa's optimism returned; she'd never been to a hospital function.

"Of course, I want the woman in my life right beside me. I must warn you, though, my mother will probably attend."

"That's fine." Marlissa still hadn't told him about her last confrontation with Pastor Jennings. It didn't matter; she wasn't afraid of her anymore.

"I hope that means you'll join me, because I picked up a little somethin'-somethin' for you."

Happy again, Marlissa giggled. "What?"

"Wait here."

Kevin returned from the garage carrying two boxes. "I thought you could wear this to the gala."

Marlissa tore the wrapping off the smaller box. "Um, honey, I thought you didn't want your business hanging out in the streets." Marlissa grinned and held up the skimpy piece of plum-colored lace and satin.

"That's for me," Kevin answered, then playfully snatched the lingerie from her. "This is for the gala."

She eagerly accepted the larger box from him and ripped it open with more vigor. "It's beautiful, I love it!" Marlissa screamed, and raised the double V-neck beaded black dress. "It's the right size, too."

"Is that all I get?" Kevin asked after the peck on his cheek.

"For now it is." While returning the dress to the box, Marlissa recalled a training session she'd had with Starla. "Why don't you set the table while I put these away?"

"You didn't answer me, will you join me?"

Marlissa cocked her head to the side and smacked her lips. "Dr. Jennings, you're crazy if you think I'm going allow you to leave this house without me." She grabbed the boxes. "I am not going to sit at home while women gnaw at my husband all night."

Kevin's laughter permeated the room as he watched her storm away, fussing at the air. He almost choked on a cherry tomato when she rejoined him. Marlissa had traded in her shirt and blouse for the plum-colored lingerie he'd purchased.

Mentally, Kevin wanted to join Marlissa in the shower, but physically he was totally exhausted. He leaned against the headboard with a Kool-Aid grin and reflected on how he'd spent dinnertime.

"Woman, you are wild!" he yelled in the direction of the bathroom. He didn't think Marlissa would hear him over the shower, but she did.

"You made me this way," she yelled back.

Mentally counting the months since his and Marlissa's reunion, Kevin knew his time of testing and procrastinating was running short. Despite knowing that he needed to come clean with his intentions, fear prevented him from telling Marlissa the truth.

Their current relationship was everything he wanted. Without much effort, he'd allowed himself to become one with Marlissa to the point where he couldn't sleep at night unless he felt her body heat and inhaled her scent. His primary desire, aside from pleasing God, was to please Marlissa in every possible way. Kevin needed her like he needed oxygen and water. The fear of her leaving him again frightened him more than dying. It wasn't fair to drag her along, but she'd broken his heart once before. His heart couldn't stand another jolt. He loved her too much, but didn't trust her with that information.

"Now are you ready to eat dinner?"

Kevin was so absorbed in his thoughts that he hadn't heard the shower stop running. Marlissa stood next to the bed, wearing his robe.

"You do remember what food is, don't you?" Marlissa mused when he offered her that blank stare for an answer once again.

Suddenly, he blinked, and then smiled. "Of course I do. Can you hand me my shorts?"

"Sure." Marlissa leaned against the doorframe and watched him secure his shorts. Kevin rubbed his fade. Something was bothering him. Before she could inquire, Kevin opened up.

"'Lissa, are you happy with our progress?"

She plopped down next to him and giggled. "Didn't you hear a few minutes ago how happy I am?"

He didn't respond in kind to her humor. Somehow, he had to make her understand how vital the answer to that question was for him. "Marlissa, I am serious. I need to know if you're really happy with *me*, not just with the sex."

The heat from his intense gaze caused her laughter to cease. Kevin was attempting to open up, maybe share his feelings with her. Marlissa took advantage of the opportunity. "Honey, I've never been happier. The only time I feel complete is when I am with you." Marlissa fanned his cheeks with her fingertips. "Kevin, are you happy? I too need to know if this is really working for you."

Kevin nodded and covered her hands with his. "Yes. I love the way we are now." Marlissa allowed herself to exhale. "You make this house feel like a home. I can't begin to tell you what you do for me." Kevin drew her face so close to his, their noses touched. "You are so beautiful." The deep passion he tried his best to keep reserved seeped through with every kiss he planted on her face.

"I love you, Kevin."

He tightened his caress. "'Lissa, I—" The sudden piercing and blaring sound of the burglar alarm caused them both to fall backward onto the bed. In the seconds it took for Kevin to get his bearings, Marlissa had jumped up and run out of the room.

"Marlissa, get back here!" Kevin yelled after her. This time she didn't listen to him, or maybe she couldn't hear him over the noise. Kevin maneuvered into his prosthesis and prayed for her safety.

The lights were off and Kevin couldn't see anything or any movement in the living room or dining room. "Marlissa!" he called, but the sound from the alarm drowned his voice. He first saw the shadows in his peripheral vision. Kevin abruptly turned toward the sliding glass door and gripped with both hands the Louisville Slugger he kept underneath his bed. He didn't want to mistakenly hit Marlissa; he turned on the den light before launching his counterattack.

"Oh my God," he gasped. Marlissa was literally beating the life out of the intruder. She swung left and right combinations like a championship prize fighter. "Marlissa!" Kevin yelled just as she went into motion for a karate kick that sent the intruder flying across the room and landing face first into the thirty-gallon fish tank.

Kevin quickly raced into the kitchen to quiet the alarm before Marlissa committed murder.

"Marlissa!" he yelled, returning to the den just as she was about to ram the intruder's head into the sliding glass door.

Marlissa must have been in her fight zone, because she didn't notice that the lights were on or that the high-pitched siren had ceased. She definitely didn't hear the squealing coming from her wet victim.

"Marlissa, let her go!" Kevin pried the badly beaten and wet Reyna away from Marlissa, and sat her on the couch.

"Reyna?" Marlissa still hadn't come out of the zone yet. The name sounded familiar to her, but it didn't fully register in her memory bank.

"Is anything broken?" Kevin quickly assessed Reyna as she sang a chorus of "ouch oh ouch."

"I don't know." Reyna whimpered, then cried, "Oh, my face."

"The swelling will eventually go down and your face will be discolored for a while, but you'll live. Now would you like to tell me what you're doing here?"

"Reyna?" Marlissa's thinking faculties returned, and, upon realizing it was Reyna she had beaten, Marlissa smirked, then quickly repented for being happy about it.

With the one eye she could still see out of, Reyna scanned the room for a stall tactic to keep from explaining her unannounced presence. It was then that she noticed that Marlissa was wearing Kevin's robe and he wasn't wearing a shirt. The thunderbolts running through Reyna's head grew fiercer at the realization of what she'd interrupted.

"Reyna, you better tell me what you're doing here before the police arrive," Kevin warned.

Reyna attempted to smack her lips, but winced from the pain. Marlissa had busted her lip.

"You better talk before I let Marlissa loose again." To give validity to his threat, Marlissa stood next to Kevin and pounded her fist into her palm.

"Okay! I was coming over to pay you a surprise visit, but the key your mother gave me didn't fit the front door. So I went around back and climbed onto the deck in hopes of gaining access through the patio door. I took a chance that it was unlocked. I guess I tripped the alarm when I opened the door."

"Reyna, you broke into my house? Are you crazy?" Kevin thought about the question for a quick second. "Don't answer that."

"Kevin," Reyna whined. "I wanted to see you. I was worried about you."

"Then why didn't you ring the doorbell?" Marlissa jumped in.

Reyna didn't have an answer. She couldn't tell Kevin in front of Marlissa that she had planned to seduce him.

The doorbell sounded.

"Reyna, I have warned you over and over about showing up uninvited. I have asked you to leave me alone, but you don't seem to understand English. Maybe a night in jail will help." Kevin went to let the police in.

"Kevin!" Reyna tried to yell, but her jaw hurt too badly. The sound came out more like a squeal.

"Officers, this young lady climbed onto the deck out back and broke into our home. Luckily my wife was able to apprehend her before she stole anything."

The first officer yanked Reyna up by the arm. "Come on, young lady, let's go."

Every attempted scream and protest increased Reyna's pain. She couldn't even jerk away from the officers without wincing. "Kevin, how can you do this to me? You can't let them take me to jail!"

The second officer nodded to Kevin on his way out. "Dr. Jennings, you can come down to the station tomorrow and make a statement."

The second he locked the door, Kevin bent over with laughter. Marlissa leaned against the archway and joined in.

"Woman, remind me never to make you mad. Miss Tyson Ali Frazier De La Hoya."

"Leave me alone." She playfully hit his arm and he picked her up. "I had to learn how to fight after what happened to me."

He nodded his understanding. "Don't get me wrong, I like a woman who knows how to handle herself, but around here it's my job to protect you, not the other way around."

Marlissa cocked her head. "Dr. Jennings, are you reprimanding me?"

"Yes, I am," he answered bluntly. "The next time I tell you to stay put, you stay put."

Marlissa wanted to rebut, but decided against it. "You should punish me for being disobedient."

"Trust me, I will." He flicked off the lights and started down the hall.

They passed by the laundry room and Marlissa recalled another conversation with Starla. "Honey, stop. I have an idea."

Chapter 24

As Kevin reclined, he studied the old brown couch and wondered when it had transformed into its present condition. He remembered the day his mother added the once regal leather piece to her office. In the early days, Pastor Jennings protected the leather almost to the point of worshipping it. When parishioners came for counseling sessions, Pastor Jennings would provide them a folding chair to sit on. "I'm just being a good steward over what God has blessed me with," she said when responding to complaints about her lack of hospitality. That was years ago; now the leather sofa had been used and abused many times over. Permanent stains decorated the sofa and there was a rip across the left arm.

Kevin visually inspected his mother's entire office under critical scrutiny, and for the first time found the experience enlightening. Everything in there was old, worn, and outdated. The traditional depiction of the olive-complexioned, long-wavy-haired, light-eyed Jesus even looked old and tired. The wooden frames that housed Pastor Jennings's self-declarations of qualifications and self-appointed promotions appeared to be off-centered and dusty. The once vibrant rose-colored carpet was now covered with patch-work plastic runner pieces. The wooden desk could have used a good polishing. The high wingback chair was in excellent shape for its age. Rosalie had the factory cover it in plastic before the delivery at least ten years ago. Kevin sniffed. The office smelled old and stale.

He studied the desk photo of Pastor Rosalie Jennings in her white cassock with a Bible tucked underneath her arm, and realized for the first time that all the pictures he owned of his mother contained a Bible of some sort. Whatever the occasion, Pastor Jennings always posed with a Bible. In the picture taken at his graduation of the two of them, his mother held her Bible alongside Kevin's degree. If she was sitting, the Bible rested in her lap. The majority of full body shots displayed the Bible tucked underneath her right hand. For headshots, Rosalie poised a pocket Bible against her cheek.

His thoughts drifted back in time to arguments between his parents. Kevin's father had constantly complained that Rosalie was too involved with God and the church. She was seldom at home, opting to spend most of her time down at the church or with church members. "That Bible don't pay your bills, I do! You would do good to remember that and spend some time at home." Kevin remembered his father barking those lines too many times to count. "That Bible is not the whole world." Reminiscing helped Kevin discern for the first time that the church *was* Rosalie's world. Aside from leading the church and trying to run Kevin's life, Pastor Jennings didn't have a life of her own.

"That's why she wants total control of everything," he mumbled. "She doesn't have any worth outside of the church." Meditating on that reality made him feel sad for his mother. What would she do without the church? What kind of life would she live? Who would she be once she wasn't identified as Pastor Rosalie Jennings? Kevin admitted right then and there that more than likely his mother would die without having a church of some kind to control.

Over the past five years, the church membership had steadily declined, mainly because Pastor Jennings concentrated more on church traditions than on the Bible. She preached more against women wearing pants and makeup than she did about sin. The choir was only allowed to sing old, traditional songs, and she detested praise dancing with a passion. The one tradition she insisted was a misinterpretation of the Word was, of course, the belief that God didn't call women to preach or pastor.

Due to her misguided belief and teachings, 70 percent of the small congregation was over age fifty. The youth department consisted of the older members' young grandchildren, and they were limited to holiday speeches and singing songs about Father Abraham. The longer Kevin dwelled on the realizations of his mother and the environment of the church she pastored, the more he understood that his reason for remaining a member didn't go beyond the fact that Pastor Rosalie Jennings was his mother. Melancholy took over Kevin and he bowed his head in prayer. Kevin didn't finish his prayer before Pastor Jennings flung the door open and launched her tantrum.

"Kevin Hezekiah Jennings, have you lost your mind? How dare you make Reyna spend the night in jail?"

"Pastor Rosalie Jennings, have you lost your mind? How dare you give Reyna what you thought was a key to my house?" Kevin stood in front of her desk with his arms folded. "You should be ashamed of yourself, sending Reyna into the home of a married man."

"Why did you change the locks?" Pastor Jennings totally discarded the inappropriateness of her actions. "And where is my key?" She held out her hand in expectation.

Kevin shook his head slowly from side to side, then returned to his seat and sighed. "Mother, I changed the locks because I didn't want you coming by unannounced anymore. I am not going to give you another key."

Pastor Jennings was livid. "Kevin, I am your mother! I have a right to . . ." She abruptly stopped and glared at her son. "Does Marlissa have a key?"

Kevin answered his mother without pretense or reservation. "Yes, and keys to my vehicles, as well."

Pastor Jennings's nostrils flared and her breathing quickened. "Kevin, why can that woman have access to everything you have and I can't? I am your mother. I gave birth to you and made you what you are today, not her!"

Kevin kept his tone stern and forceful. "Mother, you're forgetting an important fact. Marlissa is my wife and everything I have is hers. True, you gave me life, and I thank you for that, but that doesn't afford you the right to run my life. You can't force me to want Reyna. I don't want Reyna." Kevin paused to let those words sink in. "Reyna and I will never be a couple, so stop trying to make us one."

Pastor Jennings huffed and puffed until all the steam ran out. Deflated, she walked around to her high wingback chair and plopped down. Her eyes roamed around her office as if seeing it for the first time. The desk, the couch, the pictures of herself all seemed foreign to her. And the man sitting in front of her had to be from a faraway country because he spoke a foreign language.

"Kevin," she began somberly. "You don't understand what I am trying to accomplish." She paused. "I am trying to make sure this church is around long after I am gone. Why can't you help me continue the work of the ministry?" she questioned with the sincerest expression.

"Mother, how many times do I have to tell you that I am not a preacher, or pastor, nor do I desire to become one? It's not my calling."

Pastor Jennings interlocked her fingers, then leaned forward. "I know it's not you're calling, but I have trained Reyna well. If the two of you marry, she can run the church for you. That way the church can remain in the family."

Kevin was still shaking his head long after he stood and walked over to the window. For a while he just gazed out the window, focusing on nothing in particular. It was bad enough his mother wanted control of the church while she was alive, but from the grave too?

"Well what do you know," he said, finally turning around. "The truth finally comes out. You're not genuinely concerned about my happiness and you really don't care about Reyna's well-being. This is all about control, plain and simple."

"Kevin, that's not true. You're always analyzing everything. You're an ophthalmologist for goodness' sake, not a psychologist!"

Kevin never thought he would see the day his mother would stoop to rolling her eyes and smacking her lips. "It is true. It has always been about control. I am just now identifying it, but it's definitely control. That's why you avoided spending time with Dad. He wouldn't allow you to control him, so you camped out at church where you had total control."

"I stayed away from your father because he wasn't saved, not because I wanted control!" Pastor Jennings was yelling again, a sure indication Kevin had hit the nail on the head.

"Was Dad saved when you used his money to pull the church out of debt?" If Kevin were in arm's reach, his face would be on fire again, of that he was sure. "No, he wasn't. I know because I was there." Kevin paused briefly before making his next statement. "Mother, there is no easy way to tell you this, but if Reyna pastors this church, it won't be because I'm her husband. I won't be here. I'm moving my membership to Restoration Ministries effective this Sunday."

Pastor Jennings was floored. She knew Kevin had been distant, but the idea of him leaving her leadership never crossed her mind. "You're leaving the church over that woman?"

"I'm not leaving the church." He sighed. "I am moving my membership to the church where my spirit is being fed. I truly enjoy the worship services to the point where I look forward to going. I haven't been excited about coming here in a long time. Pastor Drake's Bible Study is awesome and I'm learning a lot about what true Christianity is and what it's not. There's a sense of family there and true fellowship. I don't feel that here. They have strong ministries in place and it's active for all ages. Mother, all we have here is you."

All the truths spoken didn't matter; Pastor Jennings focused on one thing. "You're choosing that woman over me. You're not going to divorce her, are you?"

"Mother, you should try to get to know Marlissa. She really has changed."

"If she's changed so much, then why is she making you change churches? She's just trying to keep you away from me," she charged.

"Marlissa is not making me do anything. I haven't shared my plans with her yet. I am making this move because this is what's best for me."

Pastor Jennings whined, "Kevin. I am what's best for you, I am your mother."

"You are my mother, that will never change, but you are no longer my pastor. It's better this way. I need to grow, and you need to find out who you are outside of church."

She gasped again as the truth rang out, but she wasn't ready to accept it yet. "I know who I am. I am saved and sanctified."

Kevin started for door. Reaching for the knob, he said, "Mother, learn to listen. The word was *who* you are, not *what* you are. You should do a self-examination. Are you really saved and sanctified or have you grown accustomed to reciting the words? Manipulating Reyna for your benefit and plotting my divorce is not something a saved and sanctified person would practice." Kevin made it out a second before the stapler banged against the door.

Reyna lifted her swollen head from the headrest and timidly rubbed her enlarged eyes, then tried to figure out her location. She had slept the entire ride home from the police station. The big red Walgreens sign came into focus, and Reyna realized she was in the retail drugstore's parking lot. After reading the time on the console, Reyna inspected her clothing. Getting beaten senseless by Marlissa the night before left her vision too blurred to notice that her $200 dress had been ripped and ruined. Reyna patted the top of her head and cringed. Anxious to see the damage firsthand, Reyna released the visor and screamed, "Aw!" Her fresh curls had transformed into a matted mess. This went far beyond a bad hair day, thanks to the head dunk inside the fish tank.

Her hair reaction was cut short once she beheld her reflection. The image was too much. Her face was three different shades of purple. Although the right eye was nearly shut, it was twice the size of the left one, which was open. With both jaws swollen, her nose appeared off center. Her once thin lips had tripled in size, and traces of dry blood trickled down her chin. The vision coupled with the aches that racked her body broke her down. Reyna covered her ravaged face and cried deep sobs. "How in the world did this happen to me?"

Reyna had been asking that question and many others all through the night. It was as if she experienced a reality check behind those cold bars and on the linoleum floor. Why did she think it was appropriate to seduce a married man? What possessed her to scale the deck in a $200 dress? Why was she chasing Kevin anyway? What made her believe they had a future together after Kevin blatantly told her otherwise? All those questions taunted her through the night. Then this morning she asked, why had Pastor Jennings refused to come get her out of jail?

Pastor Jennings had been Reyna's one phone call, but she was more concerned with knowing if Kevin knew she had given Reyna his house key than she was about Reyna being arrested. Once Reyna admitted she had told him, Pastor Jennings went on to scold her for making a mess of everything. "Call me when you get out," Pastor Jennings had snapped, then hung up. At first Reyna thought she was being sarcastic, but by 3:00 a.m. Reyna was resolved to the fact that Pastor Jennings wasn't coming.

"Here."

Reyna cried so hard she didn't see Tyson walking toward the car, nor had she heard him open the door of his BMW. Reyna grabbed tissues from Tyson without looking at him. "Thank you," she offered once her face was clean, but she was too ashamed to hold her head up and glance in his direction.

Tyson didn't press her. "No problem. I picked up some ice packs and some medicine for the aches and pain."

When he turned down her street, Reyna said, "I am sorry to inconvenience you. I didn't know Pastor Jennings would send you to bail me out."

Tyson parked and killed the engine before turning to her. Reyna still wouldn't allow him to see her face, shielding it with her hand.

"Reyna, I haven't spoken with Pastor Jennings since I started visiting Restoration Ministries over a month ago. Kevin called this morning and told me what happened. He is the one who sent me to make sure everything was in order. He's not pressing charges, but he is hoping that now you'll leave him alone."

Reyna winced, but not from the pain. The realization that Pastor Jennings didn't care enough about her to send help penetrated her gut deeper than Marlissa's karate kick.

Tyson walked around to the passenger's side, but before assisting Reyna out of the vehicle, he offered her some words of advice. "Reyna, I think some time away from people, Pastor Jennings included, and alone with God will open your eyes to what's really going on with your life. I think you should pray about your relationship with Pastor Jennings. You should also associate yourself with other Christians. Trust me, Reyna, there's nothing like experiencing the real liberty that comes from the believing in Jesus Christ. I'm so glad I met Pastor Drake at that picnic and accepted his invitation to visit the church. I've learned so much to help me grow in such a short period of time."

Tyson's words resounded in Reyna's head all day. He was just as right today as he had been on Memorial Day. She didn't know who she was or what made her happy. Reyna had walked in Pastor Jennings's shadow for so long, she couldn't even think for herself. Reyna had taken the slogan, "What would Jesus do?" and changed it to "What would Pastor Jennings do?"

Before turning in for the night, Reyna checked for voice messages. Pastor Jennings still hadn't called.

Chapter 25

From the archway, Kevin observed the back of Marlissa's head. For the third consecutive night she had left him alone in bed during the middle of the night, preferring the cushions of the sofa over the firmness of his body. Marlissa didn't know that Kevin had knitted himself to her so that he literally couldn't sleep without her next to him. Marlissa had unknowingly robbed him of what he needed to be alert for the task awaiting him in the operating room in just three short hours. That's not what worried him, though. Kevin was more concerned about why Marlissa was slowing withdrawing from him, and if she would eventually run away again.

The first night Kevin didn't think much of her change of venue. Marlissa had returned to bed in just under an hour and resumed her position under his arm. Last night she stayed away longer, almost two hours, but upon returning she offered Kevin her back. Tonight it had been three hours, and, based on the blanket covering her, Kevin guessed he would spend the rest of the dark hours alone. He was so terrified of being rejected again; tonight he used their playtime to try to convey a message to her.

Kevin methodically and deliberately loved every inch of her. Using all of his skills, Kevin attempted to permanently sear her senses with him to the point where she needed him like she needed oxygen. He wanted to plant a need in her that only he could feed. When she shuddered in tears, he thought he had succeeded.

Using his crutch, Kevin walked over to the couch and hovered above her. He'd assumed she was sleeping, but Marlissa was wide awake, staring at the blank big-screen TV.

"'Lissa, are you all right?"

Slowly she sat upright, and offered him a slight smile before answering, "I will be."

"Why are you out here?" Kevin sat down next to her and placed his arm around her shoulder, then kissed her on the forehead.

"Couldn't sleep," Marlissa answered honestly. Their earlier playtime had left her too emotionally spent to the point where she didn't know if she would ever be able to sleep again. She had connected with Kevin so intimately that she completely surrendered the essence of herself to him. The tears she shed afterward weren't the usual tears of fulfillment. Tonight Marlissa's raw emotions wouldn't allow her to deny the truth any longer: she loved Kevin too much to let him go. If the reconciliation wasn't successful, mentally she wouldn't survive.

Thoughts of life without Kevin were what had drawn her into the den and compelled her to sit and stare at nothing for the past three nights. Marlissa was trying to prepare for the inevitable. By the calendar, the divorce should have been final in the next week or so, and Kevin didn't seem concerned at all. The only thing to pique his interest was the gala scheduled for the following evening.

"Do you want to talk about it?"

Marlissa shook her head from side to side. "Not now, you need some rest."

Kevin gazed down at her intensely, wishing he could read her mind. Was she plotting her getaway? Had her feelings for him changed? Was she tired of him? Had he made a mistake by getting involved with her again? Those questions and more bombarded his mind and caused his chest muscles to constrict.

"Mind if I stay here with you?" His vulnerability wouldn't allow him to be alone. He had to be next to her, to feel her and make sure she didn't completely slip away from him.

Marlissa's answer was to lay her head against his chest. With Kevin's strong arms securely wrapped around her body, Marlissa stopped fretting long enough to fall asleep. Only after Kevin was positive sleep had overtaken her did he allow himself to drift off without loosening his hold on her.

Chapter 26

It was a miracle that Marlissa applied the liquid eyeliner without smearing it and giving an illusion of having a black eye. She didn't recall being this nervous on her wedding day. For her, tonight's gala was just as important. It was the first time she and Kevin would be seen together outside of casual dinners and church. It was the first time they would be addressed publicly in a professional setting as Dr. and Mrs. Jennings, and, with Kevin receiving an award, Marlissa wanted to look perfect. She'd spent Saturday morning receiving head-to-toe body treatments, primping and primming for the occasion. Marlissa enjoyed a facial, manicure, and pedicure, and suffered through a painful eyebrow waxing. At the hair salon, she decided at the last minute to wear her hair pinned up, leaving a few loose curls dangling. Everything was in order; now all she had to do was apply her makeup correctly.

As she outlined her lips and filled in the lip color, Marlissa sat at the vanity and quietly admired her work before she inserted the diamond tear-drop earrings Kevin had given her for her birthday two weeks ago. She then headed to the walk-in closet for the four-inch black beaded slingbacks that matched perfectly with her dress; a treat from Kevin on a shopping trip to Nordstrom. Moments later, while she admired the finished product in the full-length mirror, Kevin walked up from behind and kissed her neck.

"You're beautiful," he whispered. "What can I do to win you?"

Marlissa blushed and inspected his giant muscular frame through the mirrored glass. The black Georgio Armani tuxedo with gold cummerbund was tailored perfectly for his large, well-developed upper torso. "Thanks, gorgeous, but please don't kiss me like that again."

Kevin's defenses immediately shot up, and possessively his arm went around her waist as his lips found her neck again. "What? You gave me permission to kiss you anytime I want, remember?"

Marlissa moaned before verbally responding. "You do have permission, but if you keep doing that, we won't make it to the gala. It took me over twenty minutes to find the right shade to cover your other markings." She'd finally gotten those hickies she desired.

Kevin responded by moving his hands slowly down the sides of her body. "We can be late, it's not like we don't have reserved seating."

Marlissa decided to burst his ego. "True, but you wouldn't look right arriving in a wheelchair and stuttering." Kevin ceased his hand movements and frowned. Marlissa answered his next question before he could voice it. "When I get through with you, not only will you be unable to walk, you won't know your own name. When you accept the award, the only words coming from your mouth will be 'my sweet 'Lissa.'" Marlissa imitated his roar.

Kevin forged shock. "I can't believe you said all that with a straight face. Your ego is bigger than mine."

"That's because I am telling the truth and you know it." Smiling, Marlissa turned to face him. "Say my name."

He pressed her into him. "Frontward or backward? English or Spanish?"

"Too many decisions," Marlissa whispered, suddenly becoming lost in the seduction his voice promised. "Just kiss me."

After a delectable feast, Kevin pulled back. "'Lissa, thank you for sharing this moment with me. Your presence really means a lot to me."

Marlissa wanted him to say more, but he didn't and she wasn't going to push him, not tonight. But very soon he would have to level with her.

"Anytime." She smiled, and then headed back to the bathroom to refresh her lipstick. It was while painting her bottom lip that Marlissa caught a glimpse of her bare left ring finger. She blinked back tears as thoughts of her wedding band flashed before her. The two-carat marquis cut diamond would go perfectly with her outfit, or any outfit for that matter. But she didn't own it anymore; she had left it behind along with the house keys the day she left. "I'll probably never wear that ring again," she mumbled, and placed the lipstick into her black beaded purse. Tonight was Kevin's night and Marlissa loved him enough to allow him to enjoy the moment, but tomorrow she would learn exactly where she stood with him.

"Shall we?" Kevin asked from the doorway with his arm extended.

"Lead the way."

Marlissa gasped and wondered if Cinderella felt this much excitement on her way to the ball. The white majestic Claremont Resort & Spa tucked away in the Berkeley hills was literally a former castle transformed into a grand hotel. The world-class resort amenities included tennis courts, a 20,000 square-foot state-of-the-art spa, and 279 plush guest rooms. World travelers and the Bay Area's elite paid nearly $2,000 per night for the royal treatment. Marlissa, like thousands of regular Bay Area residents, had passed the resort hundreds of times wishing for a glimpse inside. Tonight she wouldn't have to wish.

No sooner had Kevin set the gear shift into park than the valet opened the door to the Mercedes. Kevin thought the early summer night was perfect. Not because the sunset sprayed the sky with yellow and burnt orange rays, nor did he attribute the seventy-degree weather to the magnificence. It was all Marlissa; she was simply beautiful. Admiring the provocative shoes as her shapely long legs stepped from the vehicle, Kevin felt an urge to kiss her.

"You're the most beautiful woman here," Kevin said, after he kissed her hand.

Marlissa giggled. "How do you know that? We haven't gone inside yet."

"Marlissa Jennings, you're the most beautiful woman anywhere and everywhere all the time."

"You're mackin' *real* hard tonight." Marlissa continued giggling as they made their way to the entrance.

Marlissa gasped once again when she stepped through the Victorian double doors. The Claremont was grander than she had imagined. She was immediately drawn to the brilliance above her. Endless rows of crystal chandeliers protruded from the high vaulted ceilings. The luminosity radiated off the cream marble flooring with such opulence, Marlissa felt like taking her shoes off. Near life-sized Victorian paintings telling the resort's history covered the walls. Her inspection was interrupted when the concierge greeted them.

"Good evening, sir." The concierge addressed Kevin in what Marlissa considered a fake French accent. "How may I direct you?"

Marlissa waited anxiously as the concierge searched the guest list after Kevin handed him his ticket.

"I know you're not nervous," Kevin whispered in Marlissa's ear upon feeling her tremble.

"Just a little bit," she admitted.

Before he could respond, a second gentleman approached. "Good evening, Dr. Jennings. If you and your guest will follow me, I'll escort you to your table."

Guest? Marlissa thought, but didn't verbally respond. After all, the gentleman wasn't speaking to her. He was speaking to her husband.

"Thank you." Kevin nodded.

The two of them walked arm in arm into the grand ballroom. Marlissa held her head high and smiled contently as they made their way to the center table at the front of the room, amid smiles and waves from colleagues. Marlissa didn't know anyone, but since Kevin waved, she waved also, not wanting to appear snobbish.

Marlissa's anxiety eased when she saw that Tyson was already seated at Kevin's table. At least she knew someone there other than Kevin and Pastor Jennings. If Pastor Jennings bothered to show, she wouldn't show her true colors in front of Tyson.

"You look good," Marlissa said to Tyson after he and Kevin exchanged greetings.

"Not as good as you," Tyson whispered before giving her a hug.

"Watch yourself," Kevin warned.

"It's good seeing you guys together like this," Tyson said seriously, and then jokingly said to Kevin, "Man, I don't think I have seen you this clean since your wedding."

"Man, I don't think I have seen you this dressed up since yesterday," Kevin replied, referring to the fact that Tyson's wardrobe consisted mainly of tailored suits.

Tyson dismissed the couple's laughter with the wave of his hand at his friends. "Do you think your mother's going to show?"

"I don't know," Kevin answered honestly. "She hasn't spoken to me since I told her I was leaving her church."

Marlissa instinctively placed her hand on top of Kevin's. Kevin didn't talk about it much, but she knew his strained relationship with his mother was taking its toll on him.

"Dr. Jennings, congratulations." Everyone turned to look at an elderly Caucasian couple who arrived at the table.

"Good evening, Dr. Stullman, Mrs. Stullman." Kevin stood and reached across the table to shake their hands. Kevin turned back to Marlissa and her stomach somersaulted. "Marlissa, Dr. Stullman is the medical director at Sutter, and this is his wife, Gloria." The couple smiled at Marlissa and Kevin completed the introductions. "This is my date, Marlissa."

Date? Marlissa's head reflexively jerked toward Kevin, but he was looking straight ahead and didn't notice. Marlissa quickly gathered her emotions and greeted the Stullmans.

Without missing a beat, Kevin introduced Tyson, who shook Dr. Stullman's hand with a grave look on his face.

Once Kevin was seated again and the Stullmans were gone, he continued chatting as if
everything was normal.

Marlissa tried to ignore the gnawing in her
stomach, and pasted a smile on as more people
approached the table. *That was an honest mistake*, she told herself.

One by one, doctors and administrators, along
with their wives or significant others, offered
Kevin congratulatory remarks and handshakes.
Marlissa continually held her smile in place despite the tightening knot in her stomach. Kevin
was too caught up in the euphoria of the moment
to notice the color slowly leaving Marlissa's face.

"Who is this lovely lady?" seemed to be the
question of the evening.

Kevin repeatedly answered without hesitation,
"My date," or "Marlissa." The worst came when
Marlissa took the liberty of introducing herself
as Marlissa Jennings to a middle-aged African
American gentleman. She quietly excused herself
from the table when the surgeon made a comment to Kevin about how beautiful his sister was
and Kevin didn't bother to correct him.

Tyson shook his head and mumbled, "Dummy."

Marlissa didn't know the bathroom location
and didn't care. All she wanted to do was get out
of there. At the moment she didn't care if she

ever stepped foot inside the Claremont again. In a matter of minutes the white castle had turned into a black dungeon and held her prisoner. It was inside the old walls that she was able to finally see the truth for what it was. The reason Kevin hadn't told her he loved her was because he didn't love her anymore. He loved her catering to his every need and sharing his bed, but in public, she was just a date. He had demoted her from the status of wife down to date. She would have much rather been called a girlfriend; at least that carried some form of commitment. "Is that what we've been doing all this time, dating?" Marlissa grumbled as she reached for the exit door.

Once outside, Marlissa's body trembled as reality slapped her in the face. Her marriage was over, never to be restored. She'd wasted her time and had given her body to a man who didn't love her in return. She'd squandered her time and energy on a man who couldn't or wouldn't forgive her. Outside of the bedroom, she wasn't good enough for the good doctor. Now more than ever, Marlissa wanted a drink.

Inside, Kevin continued greeting his colleagues, but his mind was elsewhere, wondering where Marlissa had vanished to. Occasionally, his eyes scanned the crowded room, but to no avail.

"You never found the right time to have that conversation with Marlissa, did you?" Tyson asked the second they were alone.

Kevin hunched his shoulders and smirked. "Not tonight, man. I want to enjoy this evening."

"No problem," Tyson said, and then finished off his iced tea. "Kev, you're my boy. You're an excellent doctor, but when it comes to dealing with your wife, you are four quarters short of a dollar." Tyson stood on his feet. "I hope tonight feels like heaven to you. I have a strong feeling you're going to learn firsthand what the term 'hell on earth' means tomorrow." As another well-wisher approached the table, Tyson went to find Marlissa. He found her outside pacing with her arms folded.

"You should come back inside."

Marlissa stopped pacing. "Tyson, will you drive me home?"

"Now, Marlissa," Tyson held his hands up as if to calm her, "I know you're upset, and you should be, but leaving won't help anything," Tyson reasoned. "You should really come back inside."

"Why?" Marlissa screamed.

"You're his wife."

Marlissa pointed to the double doors. "Those people in there don't know that! They don't have any idea Kevin is married to me. You heard him just as clearly as I did, I'm just his date and his sister." Marlissa's voice broke. "He doesn't care about me anymore."

Tyson handed her his handkerchief and waited for Marlissa to clean her face and blow her nose. "Marlissa." Tyson's tone was soft. "Please come back inside. If not for Kevin, then do it for me. The second Kevin gets into the car you can wring his neck, but please don't leave him here alone. It's bad enough that his mother isn't coming, you and I are all he has." Marlissa didn't respond. Tyson continued. "Just for the record, Kevin does care."

Marlissa walked in circles, debating Tyson's request. Could she go back inside and act like nothing was wrong? Right now she hated herself for loving Kevin so much, and despised him for not returning her love.

"Tyson, when will the divorce be final?"

Tyson closed his eyes. His lips moved, but no words materialized.

"This is not the time for prayer!" Marlissa exclaimed. "Tell me when I should expect my freedom papers."

"I'll pull the file and contact you on Monday, but only if you come back inside."

Marlissa paced some more before she agreed to Tyson's pleas. "Where's the bathroom?"

Tyson held the door open for her, and then followed her inside. "Are you going to follow me inside?" she questioned when they reached the restroom sign.

Tyson offered a stiff smirk. "No need, I'll wait out here. I don't want to take a chance on you performing a disappearing act."

Marlissa rolled her eyes at his imitation of a watchman on the wall.

Dinner was being served when Tyson and Marlissa returned to the table, but Kevin wasn't eating. Tyson's words had stung him and, quite frankly, frightened him. His heart rate slowly settled back to normal when Tyson and Marlissa returned. Marlissa reclaimed her seat next to him, but he wouldn't make eye contact with Tyson.

"Where did you go?" Kevin asked Marlissa.

"Outside." Marlissa placed the gold cloth napkin in her lap and started on her salad.

"Are you all right?"

"I needed some air."

"I hope you feel better." Kevin kissed her cheek and she flashed him a quick smile then continued eating. Kevin knew then that something was very wrong. Her beautiful smile was void of its usual radiance, its usual warmth. What presented itself now was cold and rehearsed. Finally, Kevin looked over at Tyson, who had placed four quarters on the table to remind him of his lack of common sense. Kevin narrowed his eyes at his friend, and then attempted to eat his salad.

Marlissa felt Kevin's gaze burning her skin. She could hear the stress in his breathing. Marlissa glimpsed out of the corner of her eye. Kevin subconsciously rubbed his freshly cut fade. The hot anger waned to lukewarm against her compassion. Marlissa felt sorry for him, and placed a hand on his leg to alleviate his fears. Immediately his hand covered hers and rendered gentle strokes.

As always, Kevin shared his prime rib with her and Marlissa shared her grilled salmon with him, although now she transferred the meat onto his plate instead of feeding him. There were moments when the urge to break down threatened to overtake her, but she held on, determined to play the role of the supportive wife, date, girlfriend, or whatever she was supposed to be, even if it was only for the night.

Marlissa clapped for every word of praise directed toward her husband. Then, like a good woman, she laughed at every joke. When the hospital administrator and medical director presented Kevin with Sutter Hospital's Physician of the Year Award for his outstanding work in corneal transplants and repair, Marlissa was the first to stand and applaud.

"Congratulations, Dr. Jennings," Marlissa whispered in his ear when he hugged her before accepting the award. Marlissa's heart swelled with both pride and sorrow as she listened to Kevin humbly orate his acceptance speech. "I am going to miss him," she mumbled during the final applause.

Kevin and Marlissa walked into the house quietly, each going in a different direction. Kevin went to the kitchen for something to drink. Marlissa went to the bedroom. Kevin remained in the kitchen, praying long after he finished his apple juice, praying that what he feared the most was not about to come upon him. Tyson's words and Marlissa's sudden change in attitude haunted him all the way home. He finally admitted to himself that Tyson was right; he had handled the situation all wrong. He should have leveled with Marlissa a long time ago. He'd yielded to fear and now payday had arrived.

Kevin somberly walked to his bedroom and plopped down on his bed. He had just removed his tie and cummerbund when Marlissa stepped from the bathroom carrying her travel bag. "Where are you going?" he asked, although he knew.

"Home," she answered, without bothering to face him.

"We're at home."

Marlissa continued to remove her clothing from the drawers. "No, Kevin, this is your home. My home is a two-bedroom apartment on Piedmont Avenue, for now anyway." Before heading back to the bathroom for her toiletries, she added, "Dates go home at the end of the evening."

Kevin lowered his head and rubbed his temples. "So that's what this is about. You're upset because I introduced you as my date?"

Kevin's blasé attitude infuriated Marlissa, and she lost her reserve. "What do you think? Is that what we have been doing here, dating?" Marlissa screamed as she yanked clothes off hangers.

"Marlissa!"

"I am a little rusty, maybe you can explain this to me. Since when did cooking, cleaning, waiting on you hand and foot, and giving you free access to my body become a part of dating?"

"Baby, I'm sorry. I—"

"Yes, you are sorry," she interrupted. "Just tell me this, why did you lead me on if you didn't have any intentions of reconciling? And why on earth did you make love to me when you don't love me?"

Kevin walked over to her and attempted to stop her from packing. He reached for her forearms. "Marlissa, please!"

"Please what?" She yanked away from him. "Do you know how cheap you made me feel tonight?" Kevin looked confused. "Kevin, you used me just like Darius did. The only difference is that you paid for it!"

Those words knocked the wind out of Kevin. "Marlissa, that's not the same thing. We're married."

"Really?" Marlissa's voice dripped with sarcasm. "Here behind closed doors we're married, but in public, around your prestigious colleagues, I am your date or an occasional sister!" She glared at him. "In most states you could go to jail for doing to your sister what you have been doing to me!" The travel bag was full and Marlissa was angry at herself for being stupid enough to think she had a chance to redeem herself. She was angry at herself for causing the problems that put her in this situation in the first place. Angry because she didn't follow Mother Scott's advice, and had yielded to him without a commitment. But what disgusted her most was she had allowed another man to make a fool of her.

"Kevin, you and Darius are one in the same. He filled my head with all kinds of wonderful crap, then joined his friends in abusing me. You did the same thing. The only difference is, you didn't take it by force. I freely gave myself to you because I trusted you. I thought you had integrity."

By the time Kevin collected his thoughts and found his voice, Marlissa had left the bedroom. "Marlissa, please don't leave. I am not like Darius. We need to talk."

Marlissa stopped abruptly and shook her head. "No, we don't. Your actions tonight spoke volumes. Tonight you expressed what's really in your heart, and it's not me." She looked around the room and tried to erase all the memories. "I'll be back for the rest of my stuff later. Don't worry about the money for an apartment, I don't want your money. I don't want anything from you but the one thing I can't let go of." Marlissa turned to leave, but then stopped again just before she opened the door leading to the garage. "Kevin, you are just like your mother. You can't handle the humanity in people. You expect people to be perfect, and when they don't live up to your high standards, you don't know how to forgive and move on. You only love when it's convenient for you. I took the same vows you did and if the situation were reversed, I would have forgiven you. I wouldn't hold your past against you, and under no circumstances would I have led you on and used you the way you used me. You should rejoin your mother's church. You and Pastor Jennings are made for each other." This time she didn't turn back.

Chapter 27

Marlissa lost track of time sitting in the parking lot of the twenty-four-hour Quik Stop. The clock on the console of her Lexus read 11:58 p.m., but that was before the last round of crying and wailing. That was before her head began throbbing and her facial muscles began flinching involuntarily. The clock now read 12:46 a.m. It was after midnight in her life in every sense. The darkness and demons that had tormented her in the past had quickly returned, invading her mind and spirit with a vengeance. For the first time in over a year, Marlissa wanted a drink. She needed a drink. Just one drink would numb the pain and torture of Kevin's rejection.

She craved alcohol to the point where she licked her lips and imagined that the familiar fragrance had filled the car. She moaned, longing for the temporary comfort her old, warm liquid friends could give. "I need this," was what she'd told herself when she pulled into the parking lot over an hour ago, but she still couldn't bring herself to open the car door. If Marlissa went inside, she would do more than throw away months of sobriety. She would give Kevin power over her life and prove Pastor Jennings's judgments about her to be true. All that mattered, but what kept her confined to the security of her vehicle, was the knowledge that one drink could harm the unborn child she carried; the child Kevin would never know about.

"I can't do this." She sniffled as fresh tears formed. "God, please help me."

Without consideration of the time, Marlissa grabbed her cell phone and called the one person she trusted to see her fragility.

"What's the matter?" Leon didn't waste time with pleasantries. If Marlissa called this late, something was definitely wrong. Marlissa attempted to tell him, but her sobs distorted her words. All Leon could make out were the words "Kevin" and "divorce."

"Where are you?"

"At the Quik Stop near the apartment," she managed to enunciate clearly.

"Marlissa," Leon asked guardedly, "did you go inside?"

"No." She heard Leon exhale. "But I want to. I really want to. I want the pain to stop. Just one drink is all I need."

Leon immediately started praying. Marlissa could hear Starla in the background praying with him.

"Tell her to get over here," she heard Starla say at the close of the prayer. "She shouldn't be alone tonight, not like this."

Marlissa cried again, this time grateful for friends like Leon and Starla. "Okay," she answered before Leon could make the offer.

Leon stayed on the phone with her until the headlights from her Lexus were visible from his living room window. He then went out to meet her.

"I am glad you didn't get out of the car this time of night dressed like that," Leon said after she stepped from the car. She was still wearing the dress Kevin had bought her. In her haste to leave, she'd forgotten to change. Visions of the evening's earlier events flashed, and Marlissa fell back against the car and broke down again.

Leon carried her inside and placed her on the couch. Once Marlissa settled down, Starla handed her the cup of hot instant chai tea she'd made while Leon comforted Marlissa. Allowing Marlissa to take the lead, Leon and Starla remained silent.

"I am so sorry for disturbing you guys, but I couldn't help it," Marlissa said after a few sips.

"That's what friends are for," Starla replied. "Do you want to tell us what happened tonight?"

"Not the gory details." Marlissa took another sip. "Kevin and I aren't reconciling. I'm not sure exactly when, but in a few days I'll be a single woman."

The announcement stunned Starla. "I can't believe it. Why?" Leon didn't say anything.

"Kevin doesn't love me." Marlissa sniffled.

"Of course he does." Starla refused to believe any different. "It's written all over his face. Trust me, you hold that man's heart."

"No. Kevin doesn't love me," Marlissa said sadly, shaking her head.

Leon finally spoke. "Did he tell you that?"

Marlissa wiped her face. "Not verbally, but his actions were crystal clear. Funny how your hindsight vision is twenty-twenty."

"What are you going to do?" Starla asked.

Marlissa attempted to answer, but her emotions got the best of her again. Both Leon and Starla put their arms around her. "My life is a mess!"

Leon shushed her. "We don't have to figure it out tonight, we have tomorrow and the day after and the day after that."

***

Sunday morning, Marlissa awakened to the smell of bacon and eggs. Normally she found the scent tantalizing, but today it was nauseating. She held on as long as she could before the smell caused her to sprint to the bathroom.

"Mommy, Auntie Marlissa is sick!" Montel yelled over the retching.

Starla raced from the kitchen and found Marlissa on her knees with her face in the toilet bowl.

"Is she going to die?" Jaylen asked, hearing her gasp for air.

"No, Jaylen, she's not going to die. She's just not feeling well today." Starla sent the boys to the kitchen for breakfast, then attended to Marlissa. Leon had already left the house.

"Thank you," Marlissa managed after she placed the cold towel from Starla over her face. "Sorry, I messed up your rug."

"That's what the washing machine is for."

Starla's words were meant to be calming, but that one sentence set Marlissa up for another wild ride on her emotional rollercoaster. After being with Kevin, the household appliance held a dual meaning for her. "My life is a mess," she bawled.

"It won't always hurt this much. Trust me, I know." Starla rubbed the back of Marlissa's head.

"You don't understand," Marlissa insisted. "My life really is a mess. I need a second job. I have to find another apartment. I don't have a husband. And I'm pregnant!"

Starla ceased rubbing. "You're what?"

"I'm a step away from being single and homeless. I'm going to have my baby all alone!" Marlissa wailed. "We're going to have to live in a shelter or in my car!"

Starla stood up. "Marlissa, you're putting *way* too much on it. No matter what happens with your marriage, Kevin is not going to allow the mother of his child to go homeless. He's not going allow his child to live in a shelter while he sleeps in a mini mansion."

"He doesn't have a choice," Marlissa said, slowly standing, using the toilet for support.

"What do you mean, he doesn't have a choice?" Starla questioned. "Does Kevin know you're pregnant?"

Instead of answering, Marlissa leaned over the sink and rinsed her mouth.

"You are going tell him, aren't you?" Marlissa still didn't answer. "Girl, stop playin'!"

Marlissa gargled, then finally answered. "No, Kevin doesn't know I'm pregnant. I just found out two days ago."

"When are you going to tell him?"

Marlissa wanted to tell her friend she wasn't going to tell Kevin about the baby, but Starla wouldn't understand, not with her daddy issues. Marlissa wasn't sure that's what she really wanted anyway. She understood firsthand the effects of not having a father. In her heart she didn't want her child to experience that, but Kevin had hurt her. "I don't know. Right now, I can't stand the sight of him."

Starla placed her hand on Marlissa's shoulder. "Don't wait too long. That's not something you should keep from a man, especially one who wants to be a father."

"You're right. Tyson said he would contact me tomorrow, I'll decide after that." Starla left Marlissa to check on the boys. Marlissa was relieved when Starla didn't press her. The last thing she needed in her life right now was for her only female friend to take sides with her estranged husband.

Marlissa surprised Starla when she glided into the kitchen and announced she was going to church.

"Are you sure? Kevin might be there, he is a member now."

"Oh, yeah." Marlissa had forgotten that minor detail. "So what, I'm not going to allow that jerk to steal my praise." She prayed that her voice sounded stronger than she felt.

Chapter 28

The doorbell chimed four times before Kevin comprehended that the sound was live and not a figment of his imagination. The realization wasn't enough for Kevin to move from his location on the couch in the den. There was only one person he wanted to see and that person had a key. Whoever was on the other side of the oak door was irrelevant and insignificant to him.

"Kevin, I know you're in there. Open the door," a voice stated from the other side of the door.

"You can't hide forever," a second voice added.

It was Tyson and Leon.

Kevin moaned in resignation, then reluctantly rolled off the couch and moped to the front door. He didn't acknowledge his visitors; just slightly opened the door, dragged himself back to the couch, and reclaimed his position, staring at the ceiling with his hands folded behind his head.

Leon stood over him, demanding answers. "I asked you plain and simple what your plans for Marlissa were. Why did you lie to me?"

"Leon, he didn't lie to you," Tyson answered for Kevin. "He just didn't tell Marlissa the truth like I advised him to."

"Why is she on my couch crying about her life being over?" Leon wanted to know.

Kevin blinked. At least now he knew where Marlissa was. After calling her cell phone all night without an answer, he'd feared the worst.

Leon had the perfect solution. "You need to get over there and fix this, now!"

"Change your clothes first," Tyson said. Kevin was still dressed in his dress shirt and slacks from the night before. "Have you been out here all night?"

Kevin remained unresponsive. If not for inter-mittent blinking and sporadic chest inflations, Kevin seemed lifeless.

Leon retired the tough guy attitude and low-ered his tone. "Look, man, tell me the truth, do you love Marlissa or not?"

"Can't you tell?" Tyson had all the answers. "She hasn't been gone twenty-four hours and look at him. He can't brush his teeth, his eyes look like he poured in red dye." Tyson gestured toward Kevin's face. "I've seen dead people with more color than this."

Leon didn't understand. "If you love her so much, then why isn't she here?"

"Because he's a certified dummy, that's why," Tyson answered again. "You should have seen the good doctor in action last night."

"You're right, Tyson," Leon said after getting the disaster highlights. "That was dumb. But as dumb as he is, Marlissa still loves him."

"Not anymore. She hates me." Leon and Tyson looked at Kevin as if he had rudely interrupted a private conversation.

"I ain't too crazy about you right now either, but my girl really does love you," Leon tried to assure him, but it didn't work.

Kevin finally sat up. "You didn't hear the words. You didn't see the hurt." He leaned his head against the wall and exhaled. "I don't know what came over me last night. That sister thing was *real* stupid. I should have corrected him. I didn't even acknowledge her in my acceptance speech."

Tyson and Leon kept quiet now that Kevin was on a roll.

"And the things she said, she accused me of using her and said I lacked integrity." Kevin purposely paused, hoping the guys would jump in and defend his character, but they remained quiet. "She has this crazy idea that I don't love her anymore."

"Why does she think that?" Leon asked with a tone of sarcasm.

"Ah, man!" Tyson said in response to Kevin's silence. "Kev, please tell me that you have said the words to her at least once since she's been back. At least once since y'all been *cohabitating*." When Kevin dropped his head, Tyson threw his hands down. "Man, you must have graduated valedictorian from the Dummy Institute of Thoughtlessness with a PhD in Stupidity!"

Leon slapped his hands against his knees and sat down. "See, that's why I didn't want to attend traditional college, too much book knowledge saps your common sense."

Both Tyson and Kevin stared at Leon, but neither corrected his warped analogy.

Kevin had grown tired of the insults. He knew he'd messed up big time, but they made him sound like a moron. "She knows I love her. How can Marlissa not know how much I love her? Since she's been back I can't sleep in this house without her. Okay, maybe I haven't told her that, but she should know how much I've come to depend on her presence." Kevin tried to turn the tables to sound like the victim. "I take very good care of her. I make sure she has more than enough money, reliable transportation; she never has to worry about food or clothing or anything. I even gave her my time. I came home to her every night. Doesn't that prove how much I love her?"

"No, you would do the same things for a mistress," Tyson started.

"Or whore, but that wouldn't mean you love her. Just that you like what she's giving you and want her to look good while giving it," Leon finished.

With the wind gone from his sails again, Kevin fell backward as the possibility that he had in fact taken advantage of Marlissa became a reality.

"What you gave her were things. She wanted you. She needed to know that you loved her enough to forgive her," Leon explained. "One of the major concerns on the road to recovery for an alcoholic is whether or not our families and the ones we love will be able to forgive us and afford us another chance. Marlissa had given up on your marriage, thinking the damage was beyond repair. She didn't have any hope until you pursued her. People in recovery work extra hard trying to be the perfect this or that, to earn the love and trust again. If you weren't willing to give her that, you should have left her alone, especially after she shared her past with you."

Tyson didn't know what Leon was referring to, but his grave tone expressed the seriousness.

The tension in the room had escalated; the playfulness had evaporated.

Leon continued. "Look, Kevin, everybody makes mistakes, but Marlissa doesn't deserve to be taken advantage of. She loves you, but if you can't fully love her back then leave her alone."

The moment she took her usual seat, Marlissa second-guessed her decision to attend service. It was then that she realized how long it had been since she'd been to church without Kevin by her side. Praise and worship was barely underway when the tears and the emptiness returned with a vengeance. Marlissa didn't mind this emotional breakdown as much. That was one of the benefits of corporate worship. A person could cry all through service. People would assume they were feeling the Spirit and leave them alone. There were a few saints that would read right through the façade, though. Mother Scott was one.

In no time, Mother Scott had joined Marlissa in the row, and while holding her whispered in her ear. "Don't worry, baby, Mother will take care of it. When I get through with the good doctor, the only thing he gon' be good for is the altar."

The declaration made Marlissa chuckle. "Don't worry about it, Mother, I'll be all right."

"Me and Drake are gonna make sure. We gon' pray the devil out of him." Mother patted her shoulder, then went back to her seat, but not before giving First Lady Drake the warfare signal: forearms across her chest with fists balled.

"Thank you, Jesus. You always know what I need," Marlissa whispered as Pastor Drake preached a sermon about not allowing your circumstances to ruin your destiny. Marlissa listened intently as Pastor Drake broke down Philippians 1:6 to terms she could understand. His words encouraged and motivated her to move forward with her life and the life of her unborn child.

By the benediction Marlissa felt renewed. Her heart was still heavy, but she had the strength to face her future without Kevin and without alcohol. Being a single parent wasn't something she'd signed up for, but it wasn't the end of the world. Starla was right; Kevin would do right by his child. Their baby would probably enjoy a better life than she had. Despite her broken heart, Marlissa didn't regret carrying his seed. For her, their baby had been conceived out of love, and, to be honest, she enjoyed making a baby with Kevin.

"You're looking better," Starla commented after the customary dismissal hug.

"I am feeling better," Marlissa replied.

"Are you ready to talk to Kevin?"

"No, but I am ready to get off your couch." Starla looked disappointed. "Don't worry Starla, I will tell him soon."

"Promise?"

"In the house of the Lord on a stack of Bibles with blessed oil dripping down my face. Thank you, Starla," Marlissa said, once they stopped laughing.

"For what?"

"For allowing Leon to be my friend. A lot of women would have a hard time with their husband having female friends. Not to mention having one as a roommate. How many women do you know who would allow a female to beckon her man in the wee hours of the morning?"

"Not too many," Starla admitted. "But you are special to Leon, to both of us, actually."

"How so?"

"Leon told me about all the times you kept him from falling off the deep end and how you encouraged him to keep pursuing me and the boys after every rejection. At first I did have a problem with the living arrangements, but then I realized that although he shared a living space with you, his heart always belonged to me. I was just too scared to trust him again. Plus, the first day I met you, I knew you and Kevin were still in love. It was written all over your faces."

Marlissa held up the "timeout" sign. "You were doing good until you mentioned that name."

"Okay, I'll leave it alone," Starla conceded. "But, seriously, thank you for helping my baby get himself together."

"And thank you for befriending me. You know, it's your fault I'm pregnant anyway." Marlissa rolled her eyes at Starla. "It was your crazy advice that almost made me lose my mind. You really should write a book."

Starla chuckled. "You mean Mother Scott should write a book."

Marlissa giggled all the way back to her Lexus. "Laughter truly is good for the soul," she said as she exited the parking lot.

Chapter 29

Lewis stared at the paper in his hand with disbelief. Leon was quitting his job today and thus ending Lewis's connection to Starla. What was more shocking than Leon no longer needing his job was the reason for his departure.

"Leon, how did you come up with enough money to restart your own construction company so soon?" Lewis knew for certain he couldn't have done that on what he paid him. "What about your contractor's license?'

"That's already been taken care of." Leon smiled proudly, then handed Lewis a Star Construction business card complete with his logo and contractor's license number.

Lewis was almost speechless. What was he supposed to do now that Leon was on the right track? Lewis gave Starla her space and time, but only because he was waiting for Leon to mess up again. When he did, Lewis planned to be right there waiting to comfort Starla. Lewis pasted on a fake smile and extended his hand. "Congratulations and welcome to the world of entrepreneurship."

"Thank you, Mr. Mason," Leon said while shaking Lewis's hand vigorously.

Too much joy flowed from Leon. Lewis had to say something to burst his bubble. "Leon, you know, starting a small business requires a lot of hard work and money. You have a wife and two kids to support. Are you sure you don't want to keep your job here until you build up a steady flow of customers?" Leon stopped smiling; Lewis had struck a chord. "I'm sure you don't want to drop the financial burden of sustaining the household on your wife."

"Mr. Mason, you're forgetting, this is not my first time running a business. I know all about hard work and how much money it takes. I was successful before and I will be even more successful this time because I now have God in my life."

"Of course, eventually you're going to succeed," Lewis said, nodding. "But in the meantime, your wife and children need to eat. I understand completely how a man should go after his dreams, but it's not fair to do that at the expense of your wife and children."

Leon glared at him, and Lewis wondered if he'd made a mistake referencing Starla and the boys.

"Mr. Mason, I know what's best for my family; that's exactly why I'm leaving this place."

Lewis continued to dig. "What about money, Leon? Do you have enough to stay afloat? I could help you out."

"No, thank you, I have everything I need," Leon said with finality.

Leon turned on his heels, and, without looking back, exited the store and jumped into his truck. His days of working for someone else were over. Not that he was above it; it just wasn't what he was born to do. He wanted a legacy, something to pass on to his boys if that's what they wanted. Leon's desire to build Starla a house was stronger than ever. After making it through the fire of disappointment without her love for him getting consumed, Starla deserved the best of everything, and Leon was determined to die trying to grant her wishes. Their trip to Calistoga transported their love back to the early days of their courtship so much that Starla finally agreed to renew their wedding vows.

Naiveté was not one of Leon's characteristics. He was concerned about their future. To be honest, he was frightened. He prayed constantly for his courage to outweigh his fear. It did, and Starla's unwavering belief in him was the fuel that kept his engine running. "Father, I thank you for giving me more chances than I can count," Leon prayed before leaving the gas station parking lot as an employee for the last time.

"How are you this morning?" Mr. Atkins's smile showed nearly all thirty-two of his teeth. That's one of the things Marlissa loved most about her employer; Brother Atkins was drenched in happiness all the time. "The joy of the Lord," he called it.

Marlissa forced a bright smile at her boss, determined not to drag her personal business into the office. "Blessed and most highly favored. How is your Monday morning so far?"

Mr. Atkins nodded. "Just lovely. God woke me up and kissed me with His sunshine."

Marlissa quickly went over the day's schedule with him, pondering if she should tell her boss about her pregnancy. She decided to wait until she started to show.

Mr. Atkins's office door barely closed before Marlissa booted up her computer. She was on a mission. She needed to find an apartment she could afford on her insurance salary alone.

This morning's bout with morning sickness helped her realize that she wouldn't be able to work sixteen-hour days during her pregnancy. Prenatal care was another issue. Her job didn't provide health insurance. Marlissa was among the thousands of working poor in California. That left her with two options: apply for state assistance or ask Kevin for help. Right now she was leaning toward door number one.

Marlissa searched every Web site for housing within a ten-mile radius and grew more frustrated by the minute. Not one of the rental Web sites offered any hope. The nice apartments were way out of her price range. The ones in her range were in the worst neighborhoods. "I should take your daddy's house and make him find an apartment," she grumbled and rubbed her stomach. "You would love it there."

Her thoughts drifted to what her baby would look like. Would he be tall like Kevin or average like her? Would Kevin's chocolate skin dominate or would his chocolate blend well with her creamed coffee complexion? What would she name her son or daughter? "I'll just have to wait and see," she stated when the phone rang.

Her stationary smile fell once she heard the caller's voice. It was Kevin. She'd been avoiding his calls, but the insurance office phone didn't have caller ID.

"What do you want?" she said dryly.

"Can I see you today, please?"

"No."

"What about tonight?"

"No." She heard Kevin sigh after the second refusal.

"Marlissa, we really need to talk."

To her, Kevin sounded exhausted, like he hadn't slept in days. Marlissa stroked her abdomen. "I know, but not tonight. I'll let you know when I can pencil you in. Bye." She hung up before she gave into her desire to see him.

It hadn't been two whole days since the breakup, and as much as she hated to admit it, Marlissa missed him. This morning she cried through what would have been their prayer time. What about Bible Study? How was she supposed to sit in the same building with him? "He better take my advice and go back to his mother's church," she mumbled, and resumed her fruitless Internet search.

Two hours later Marlissa gave up the futile search and faced the hard facts. She couldn't have this baby without Kevin's help. She couldn't even find a one-bedroom apartment without his signature. "I should have kept that bank check card a little longer." She folded her arms and pouted. It was too late; on her way to work, she had picked up the rest of her belongings from the house and left the check card along with the house and car keys on the kitchen counter.

Marlissa brooded a while longer before she swallowed her pride. "Let's go see your daddy." She sighed and looked down at her still-flat stomach. She wasn't going to ask him for anything. Her intentions were to simply tell him about the baby and then wait and see what he offered.

Chapter 30

"Dr. Jennings, are you sure you don't want me to cancel the afternoon clinic? You don't look so well."

"I'll be fine," Kevin answered his nurse for the third time. "A brief nap during lunch time and I'll be good as new."

"If you say so." His nurse grunted and shook her head at him before leaving.

No sooner had his nurse closed the door than Kevin stretched out on his office couch and closed his eyes. Two sleepless nights were taking their toll on him. Every muscle in his body ached, and his prosthesis irritated him to the point where he wanted to snatch it off and throw it across the room. Kevin hadn't eaten much, either. His last complete meal was two days ago at the gala. Since then, he'd munched on rice cakes and fruit with occasional water. Thankfully, he only had one procedure scheduled this morning and it was a routine LASIK.

Kevin knew he couldn't continue with his diet and sleep regimen for long, but he couldn't help it if he couldn't sleep without Marlissa next to him. The first time she left it was easy; they were already in separate bedrooms and barely speaking. This time around she was the manifestation of every desire he needed and wanted in a wife. They had become one in every sense. Being separated from her was now unnatural to him.

Tonight, he'd hoped to put an end to the chaos, but Marlissa dismissed him like he was a stranger. "What does she mean, pencil me in?" Kevin grumbled. "I am her husband; I should go down to that insurance office and make her talk to me." Turning onto his side, Kevin realized that doing so would be a major mistake. The male-dominance approach never worked with Marlissa. He wouldn't get two words out before Marlissa would jump into her fight zone. No, he would just have to wait until she was ready to hear his pleas for forgiveness. A knock on his office door disturbed his mental ramblings.

"Who is it?" Kevin barked at the door.

"It's me," a female answered.

"I am not in the mood for this today," he grumbled, and started for the door. "Reyna, what do you want?"

Reyna was taken aback by Kevin's rude behavior. "Sorry, I'll come back later. Better yet, I'll write you a letter." She turned and left.

Watching her slowly walk, Kevin regretted his abrasiveness and started after her. "Reyna, hold on."

She stopped and turned around. "Kevin, I didn't come here to stalk you." Reyna lowered her head. "I came to thank you, but I should have called first."

Kevin leaned against the wall and folded his arms. "You came to do what?"

Reyna raised her head and took a deep breath. "I know this sounds strange, but I want to thank you for having me arrested."

Kevin raised his eyebrows. "Really?"

"Yes. You were right, one night in a cold jail cell opened up my understanding. Not just to the fact that I was chasing a married man, but the reason I was chasing after you became crystal clear."

Reyna piqued his interest, and he invited her into his office.

"As I was saying," she continued, seated next to him on the couch. "That night and every day since, I have been thinking about a lot of things. Important things, like who am I, why I do the things I do, and what I want."

"I'm impressed." Kevin smiled.

"I haven't figured it all out yet, but one thing's for sure, I don't want you, never have."

Kevin faked injury. "You hurt my feelings."

"No offense, Kevin, but I'm not attracted to you. I only chased you because that's what your mother wanted me to do." Kevin wasn't laughing anymore. "I idolized your mother and I was willing to do anything she wanted me to. I trusted her to have my best interest at heart."

"What about now?" Kevin asked.

Reyna stood and walked over to the window. "Kevin, Pastor Jennings is your mother and I wouldn't dare slander her, but she's not the person I thought she was."

"What do you mean?" He had a good idea, but asked anyway.

Reyna turned to face him. "Your mother hasn't spoken two words to me since she blamed me for you leaving the church. She claims that if I had tried harder, you and Marlissa wouldn't have reconciled and you'd still be with her."

Kevin closed his eyes and breathed heavily. In his head, Marlissa's statement about him being just like his mother haunted him. *Am I that cruel?* he wondered. "Reyna, I am so sorry for how my mother used you."

"Don't be sorry, I didn't offer much resistance. Tyson tried to point out the manipulation to me on Memorial Day, but I refused to receive it for what it was. I respected Pastor Jennings as a genuine woman of God. She was my pastor. The idea of her using and manipulating me was incomprehensible."

"Are you still attending church?" Kevin was concerned about her spiritual life.

Reyna shook her head. "No, but I pray and read my Bible on a regular basis. Tyson has been trying to get me to visit your church with him, but I don't know if I want to attend church anymore. Tyson seems to believe that if I'm around Christians who genuinely portray the love of God, my trust will be restored."

"I think Tyson is right. I recognized a big difference the first time I stepped foot inside Restoration Ministries. That place really does live up to its name. The people there care more about spiritual well-being than outward appearances. I can't say enough about Pastor Drake. Hearing him teach the Word has helped me to understand what God really requires and not what man desires of me."

"That's what Tyson keeps telling me. He's thinking about joining."

Kevin smirked. "That will really make Mother happy." He then lightened the mood by asking, "If I'm not your type, then what is your type?"

"Men and their egos." Reyna smacked. "Don't get me wrong, you're handsome, but I prefer bright-skinned brothers and I love bearded men."

"Aw, I see." Kevin had it figured out. "You prefer someone like Tyson?" He smiled.

"I'm not saying all that." Reyna shook her head and both of her hands to emphasize her point.

"What I heard you say was his name three times in less than a minute," Kevin teased.

"You better let that go," Reyna warned. "He's just helping me work through my issues. That's all!"

"All right, I'll leave it alone," Kevin conceded, but the beam on Reyna's face said that this wasn't the end of the story.

Reyna reached for her purse and Kevin walked her to the door. "Kevin, I am happy that you and Marlissa were able to work things out. It would have been a major mistake for the two of you to divorce, seeing how much you love her."

Kevin wondered why Marlissa couldn't see that. "Thank you, Reyna. I'll be praying for you, and please pray for me."

"Does this mean you accept my apology?"

"Of course, I accept your apology." Kevin reassured her by giving her a light hug.

"What are you so happy about?" Vangie asked, walking over to Starla's desk. "Let me guess: it starts with 'L' and rhymes with 'neon.'"

"Girl, flesh and blood didn't reveal that." Starla laughed. "That's my boo!"

Vangie shook her head. "You sound like a schoolgirl in love for the first time."

Starla smiled, thinking that that was exactly how she felt. Life with Leon was glorious; the only way they could be closer was if they were joined at the hip.

"Are you coming?" Starla inquired. To celebrate their reunion, she and Leon were renewing their vows in a small ceremony among friends.

"I'll try my hardest to be there since we're close family; you being my auntie's late husband's daughter. And you have the nerve not to let me be the maid of honor." Vangie walked away, laughing.

Starla directed her attention back to the wedding details. She'd just hung up with the florist when her desk phone rang.

"Lewis, what are you doing, calling me here at work? I told you not to call me anymore."

"I know what you told me, but I needed to talk to you." Lewis was indifferent, as if she hadn't thrown him out of her house. "I've waited long enough and it's time you made a decision about us."

"Lewis, how many times do I have to tell you there is no us? I am a married woman, now leave me alone!" Starla muffled her voice so no one in the office could hear her.

"Starla, please don't hang up, you'll regret it if you do."

Lewis's tone frightened her. "What do you mean by that?"

"Starla, I have waited patiently for you to come to your senses, but you're determined to ruin things by entangling yourself with bondage. I'm giving you one more chance to make a decision to divorce your pitiful husband and move on with your life."

"Who do you think you are?" Starla shrieked into the receiver.

"Starla, I'm the one who loves you, and if I can't have you, a worthless man like Leon Scott certainly won't."

"Lewis, don't ever call me again." Her fingers trembled long after she slammed the phone down. What on earth did Lewis mean? Could he, would he cause physical harm to her? Would he harm Leon? Would he harm the boys? Those questions troubled her for the rest of the day. Starla didn't know if she should tell Leon. One thing was sure: it was time to pray.

"I hate him!" Marlissa screamed, and threw her purse into her desk drawer, then slammed it shut. "Not even two full days and he's all hugged up with Reyna! Less than three hours ago he was calling me, talking about he wants to see me. Ugh! I can't stand that man!"

It was a good thing the insurance office was empty. Marlissa was livid after going to Kevin's office to tell him about the baby, only to find him hugged up in his doorway with Reyna.

"That lousy cheat!" she yelled, pounding her fist on the desk.

The office door opened, and Marlissa dumped her frustration and anger out on her visitor without mercy.

She stood up and demanded, "How much longer do I have to be married to that trifling, low-down, sorry-excuse-for-a-man friend of yours?"

"I guess you and Kevin haven't made up yet," Tyson said calmly.

"We're not going to make up, ever! Now about the divorce, I need to make an amendment to the agreement."

Tyson looked at her like she'd lost her mind. "Marlissa don't make any hasty decisions. You're angry right now."

"Oh, I'm way past angry. Trust me, you don't want to know what I am at this moment."

"What changes would you like to make?" Tyson asked, still a little too calm for Marlissa's liking.

She planted her hands on her hips. "Tyson, if you tell Kevin what I'm about to tell you, I'll beat you up worse than I did Reyna."

"I'm listening," he answered, totally ignoring her threat.

"I want health benefits and spousal support until . . ." She paused.

"Until what?"

Marlissa glared at him. "Tyson, if you tell him, I promise I'll hunt you down."

"What's going on, Marlissa?" His voice carried the sternness of a judge ready to impose a sentence.

She exhaled and plopped down in the chair. "I'm pregnant. I don't have any health insurance and I can't afford a nice apartment on my own."

Tyson shook his head from side to side and mumbled something she couldn't decipher. "When are you going to tell Kevin?"

Marlissa hunched her shoulders. "I don't know. I went to his office to tell him today, but he was too busy feeling up Reyna."

"I'm not sure what you mean by that, but I'm sure whatever you saw was completely innocent. Reyna told me she was going to make amends with him."

"Whatever." Marlissa rolled her eyes.

"Marlissa, believe me when I tell you that Kevin doesn't want Reyna. He loves you."

Marlissa didn't want to hear that. "What do I need to sign to keep from having my baby at the county hospital and bringing it home to a shelter?"

Tyson studied her for a long and intense moment before answering. "Marlissa, normally I wouldn't do this, but Kevin hasn't left me any choice. You're my friend also and I care about what happens to you." He pulled the legal-sized envelope from his briefcase. "This is a copy of Kevin's divorce petition. He has the original. I was hoping he would have discussed this with you by now."

Focusing on the envelope, Marlissa's anger seeped away. Did she really want to be free of Kevin? Her hands shook the entire time it took to open the envelope and read the contents. "Is this real?" she asked, after taking a deep gasp.

"Yes, it is."

Marlissa was totally confused. "What does this mean?"

"Exactly what it says," Tyson answered nonchalantly.

Marlissa, unable to contain herself any longer, buried her face in her hands and cried; first lightly then uncontrollably. "Why did he do this?" She wiped her face with the handkerchief Tyson handed her.

Tyson dropped the lawyer image. "Marlissa, if you honestly don't know the answer to that question, then you belong seated right next to him on a *big* yellow bus." Tyson picked up his briefcase and left just as quickly as he had come.

Chapter 31

Dreading what awaited him on the other side of the door, Kevin hesitated before entering exam room number five. It was one-thirty Tuesday afternoon: Mother Scott's new standing appointment time in order to ensure that she arrive by two o'clock. Kevin knew it wasn't the Lord that told her to arrive early today. No doubt his feistiest patient would have a smorgasbord of choice words for him. Kevin took a deep breath before opening the door, and prepared his ears for the tongue lashing of his life.

"Good afternoon, Mother Scott."

"Hi, baby, how are you doing?" Mother Scott's voice was so sweet and her smile so pleasant, Kevin squinted his eyes to make sure he wasn't seeing things. The name on the chart matched with the face before him, but the cool and calm demeanor didn't fit the profile.

"I'll be fine. How are your eyes treating you?" Kevin thought it best not to prolong the visit with idle conversation, since Mother Scott was in a good mood. He quickly pulled out his ophthalmoscope and began his examination.

"Baby, I told you, the Lord is going to fix my eyes." Mother Scott nodded, and then went on to talk about Leon and Starla's upcoming vow renewal and her children living out of state. She even went over her grocery list. Not once did she mention Marlissa.

God doesn't show her everything; she doesn't know about the fallout, he thought.

"I think you're right, Mother, your eyes are showing remarkable improvement," Kevin acknowledged at the end of the exam.

"Baby, you look tired. Maybe *you* should be examined by a doctor," Mother Scott stated, and, at the same time, placed the back of her hand against Kevin's forehead.

"I'll be fine, Mother." Kevin couldn't tell Mother Scott he'd been having trouble sleeping at night without Marlissa. Last night, he was able to sleep for six hours straight, but that's because he'd stayed at Tyson's house.

Kevin still didn't understand why Mother Scott was behaving so graciously. Mother Scott had addressed him as "baby" three times; she'd never done that before.

"Mother, you surprised me today by being on time."

"Baby, I know your time is valuable and I am not the only patient you have. I'm your favorite patient, but I'm not your only patient." Mother was really laying it on thick. "I don't want to throw your schedule off. I know you're a busy man."

Kevin still wasn't convinced. "Mother, are you sure there's nothing wrong?"

"Baby, I'm fine." Mother Scott shoulder-strapped her purse and casually started for the door. Holding the door open, Mother Scott narrowed her eyes and glared at him. "Kevin, if you're referring to how much I want to place you over my knees and whip your behind for hurting my baby, don't worry, I am going to let God take care of you. Drake and I know just how to deal with you." Mother's hand was now planted on her hip. "Why do you think you're so tired? We've been praying for the Lord not to let you sleep until you do right by Marlissa. Drake is in your office now, casting the devil out."

Kevin envisioned First Lady Drake slinging oil all over his chair, desk, and carpet. The vision caused him to chuckle.

"Don't laugh at us! We've tackled bigger devils than you, and God always causes us to triumph. You see Leon came back. David would have come too, but he didn't want to change. But you, on the other hand, you want to change. You are afraid to trust again, and, quite frankly, Kevin, you're a little slow when it comes to women."

Kevin wasn't laughing anymore. Mother Scott could see a lot deeper than he thought.

"We know you haven't been eating, so we brought you some food. It's in your office. Nothing much, just some roast beef, fried chicken, collard greens, candied yams, macaroni and cheese, cornbread, and 7-Up cake. Try not to eat it all in one sitting. Remember, you're a little slow, so you may be alone for a while."

First Lady Drake appeared in the doorway next to Mother Scott. "One Eye, my work is done in there. Are you ready?"

"Drake, is there anything you want to say to the good doctor?" Mother Scott asked.

First Lady Drake stepped inside, pointed her index finger at Kevin, and snarled, "You will do right!" then left. Mother Scott huffed and followed her.

Kevin was too hungry to care that he'd just been told off by two nosey women who obviously loved both him and Marlissa. He made it to his office in record speed.

"I was going to take tonight's lesson from the Gospel of John, but something else just dropped in my spirit," Pastor Jennings announced as she looked out into the congregation. "The Spirit is leading me to the book of Luke, chapter fifteen."

"That's a good one!" someone yelled.

Pastor Jennings scanned the small audience once more, then continued. "This familiar passage tells the story of an ungrateful son, who leaves the comfort and safety of home and gets caught up in the pleasures of the world. He leaves his father's house and is lured astray by the lust of the world."

"Say that, Pastor."

"After he loses everything, he finds that the hogs are in better shape than he is." Pastor Jennings wasn't sweating, but she wiped her forehead out of habit. "I don't know if this young man ever prayed, but he had enough sense to come to himself and remember his father's house."

"Come on now!"

"It was in his father's house that he learned the statutes of God. Um hah, he learned how to pray in his father's house. It was in his father's house that the Lord healed his body, not the hospital, 'cause y'all know the church is the saints' hospital."

"That's right, Pastor!"

"See, it was his father's prayers that helped him excel in every endeavor he undertook. It was his father's sacrifices that made him successful.

Saints, I believe he remembered that his success was tied to his father's house."

"I know that's right!"

Pastor Jennings paused for a sip of water. "After making a mess of his life, the young man realized his father was right, and went back home to beg the father's forgiveness. See, he knew his father was sincere in his care and our heavenly Father always knows what's best for us. We just have to be obedient as dear children and obey they who have the rule over us. Then we won't have to come crawling back after we've ruined our lives, begging for forgiveness."

"Say that in the mic!"

"Now, I am not God, but I love and care for every one of you as the sheep God placed in my care. I'll go with you to the end, but when you decide to live a life of disobedience and wickedness, that's where I draw the line. I'll still love you while you're running with the pigs, but don't expect me to get down in the pigsty with you. Don't expect me to dirty my white garments. I'm not going to do that, but like a good father, I'll be waiting for you once you get yourself together. Just like the father in this story, I'll restore you after you come home and repent, and then prove yourself."

Kevin didn't see his mother walking toward him; he only heard her words. Trying to hide his tears, he bowed his head and covered his face with his hands. He'd come to his mother's Bible Study to prove that Marlissa's assessment of him was wrong. He wasn't like his mother. He didn't only love when it was convenient for him. Kevin didn't use people to get what he wanted, and then refused to forgive them when they didn't measure up to his standards. He'd been feeding those thoughts to his psyche for three days, but now listening to his mother twisting the Word of God, he couldn't deny it anymore. Marlissa was right.

For reasons Kevin couldn't understand, he hadn't been able to forgive Marlissa, and, because of that, he had selfishly dragged her along all this time. Yes, he'd taken advantage of her. Subconsciously, he made Marlissa prove her remorsefulness by refusing to tell her how he really felt and by holding the divorce over her head. Deep down he wanted Marlissa to hurt as much as he had. The act of sleeping with her without forgiving her was wrong, plain and simple. Forgiveness was the only thing Marlissa had asked for. She was entitled to much more; he was prepared to give her the house, but all she asked for was forgiveness and he couldn't even grant her that.

Pastor Jennings hadn't spoken to him since he'd made it clear she wasn't going to have things her way. Now here she was preaching to him that the only reason he was successful was because of her, referring to Marlissa as a pig, and basically she told him she couldn't be part of his life unless he allowed her to control him.

A hand touched Kevin's head, and more hands went to each of his shoulders, breaking his concentration. Kevin raised his head to find his mother standing in front of him and church members surrounding him.

Pastor Jennings smiled into her son's wet face. "I forgive you for becoming entangled with the enemy. Aren't you ready to come back home, under the ark of safety?"

"Tell Him yes, son!" the church members encouraged.

"We've all made mistakes, but, Kevin, I love you. I am your mother; I'll never leave you, nor forsake you like that heathen did."

Kevin wiped his face with the backs of his hands, then stood up. The church members began clapping, thinking that Kevin was about to "give up."

"Mother, I didn't come here to be manipulated, nor did I come here to rejoin. I only came here to learn the truth about myself, and, thanks to you, I have."

Pastor Jennings's head jerked back and the church members stopped clapping.

"Mother, you should be more concerned with how you've destroyed Reyna's faith in the church and less concerned with my marriage." Pastor Jennings sucked in her breath. "You're my mother and I love you, but Marlissa is my wife and will remain my wife, and she will one day be the mother of your grandchildren. You are not to address her as a heathen, drunk, or any other derogatory title. If you can't handle saying her name, then you can address her as Mrs. Jennings."

Pastor Jennings was flabbergasted. "How dare you disrespect me in front of my members?"

Kevin wasn't going to play into the drama, but before he left there was one more thing he needed to clear up. "Mother, just so you know, you're not the force behind my success. True, you prayed for me, but most of your prayers were out of guilt because you caused the accident that impaired me. I don't hold the accident against you. I forgave you for that a long time ago. My success was earned with the help of God. He's the One in control of my destiny, not you."

As she watched Kevin leave, Pastor Jennings didn't know what role to play: the jilted mother or the humiliated pastor. She folded and unfolded her arms; her mouth dropped and drew up repeatedly.

Her church members were too busy talking among themselves, trying to figure out what she'd done to Reyna, to notice Pastor Jennings slowly walking back to her pulpit.

"Marlissa, please let me in, I need to talk to you," Kevin pleaded on his cell phone outside Marlissa's apartment complex after she refused to buzz the security gate open to allow him entrance. After the episode with his mother, he had to see her.

"No, I don't want to talk to you tonight."

Marlissa's voice sounded colder than it had on the security phone, but Kevin didn't care. He needed to see her to make amends.

"Baby, I am so sorry for what I did. You were right, I was wrong. Please give me the chance to explain."

"Kevin, you had months to explain and you said nothing. Don't think just because you sent me roses today that you can show up here uninvited."

"Baby, that's not why I sent the roses."

"Good!" Marlissa snapped before he could finish. "Because roses have thorns, Kevin, and I'm tired of getting pricked by your thorns, so don't send me any more! And stop calling me 'baby.'"

My name is Marlissa Scott-Jennings, for the next few days anyway."

Kevin took a deep breath. This wasn't how he wanted the night to end. He wanted to make up and bring his wife home and make love to her until he fell asleep, but Marlissa wasn't cooperating.

Marlissa waited for him to respond to her last statement, but he didn't, and that only served to infuriate her more. "Kevin, don't call me anymore!"

"Marlissa, I love . . ." Kevin didn't bother finishing the sentence. Marlissa had already slammed the phone down.

The following day, Kevin had Dr. Wheatley cover his afternoon clinic for him. Kevin needed help getting his life together. His pride had seeped from him when Marlissa refused to talk to him last night. It was then that the possibility of living his life without her became a reality. In the past she would talk to him if nothing else, but now he'd lost total control of the situation.

He needed divine intervention and soon. He'd been praying, and the more Kevin prayed the more he saw his shortcomings, and now comprehended that if he didn't work on himself first, he would never be a husband to Marlissa. His failure to forgive and trust had caused just as much harm to his marriage as Marlissa's drinking had.

He shifted in the chair that didn't adequately support his large frame, and waited patiently for his turn.

"Dr. Jennings," the secretary called to him, "Pastor Drake will see you now."

Chapter 32

"Starla, that's beautiful!" Marlissa exclaimed about the off-the-shoulder, sage-colored taffeta dress Starla had chosen to renew her vows in. Starla had convinced Marlissa to come shopping with her at the last minute in an effort to cheer her up.

"Do you really think so?"

"Yes, and it looks fabulous on you. Leon's going to love you in that dress."

"I hope so." Starla giggled. "Wait until you see the dress I've picked out for you."

Marlissa smacked her lips. "Girl, I can't believe I let you talk me into being your matron of honor. That's a little unorthodox considering my present circumstances, don't you think?"

"This is the twenty-first century, everything is unorthodox." Starla chuckled.

The sales associate handed Marlissa her dress, and she slouched into the dressing room stall. Starla waited patiently while Marlissa tried on the cream-colored version of the same dress.

"Oh, Marlissa, it's perfect for you." Starla beamed when she stepped from the dressing room. "You should wear your hair down, and I have the perfect 'genuine' pearl earrings and necklace set," Starla said while observing their reflections in the mirror.

Marlissa wanted to laugh in Starla's face, but the occasion was special to her friend, so she pasted on a smile instead. Starla saw right through her.

"Marlissa, cheer up. I know it's a little awkward for you and it is the last minute, but Leon wants the boys to stand with him. That means someone has to stand with me, and since you're like family, you're it."

"Ooh, don't I feel special." Marlissa's sarcasm dampened the mood.

"Marlissa, please cheer up. I have something I want to tell you, but I can't as long as you remain down in the dumps." Starla folded her arms and pouted.

Marlissa took a deep breath, and, once again, pushed the pain of her miserable life aside. Somebody deserved to be happy; it might as well be Starla. "Okay, what is it?"

"Promise to be happy for me?"

"I promise I will try to be happy." Despite Marlissa's best effort, the words dripped with bitterness.

Starla scrutinized Marlissa's face to see if she meant the words. Marlissa would find out soon enough, so Starla went ahead and told her the good news. "I'm pregnant! Can you believe it? We're going to have a baby around the same time?"

"Starla, that's wonderful." Marlissa was truly happy for her friend, but her present situation prevented her from showing much enthusiasm. She prayed the smile pasted on her face passed for genuine. "Have you told Leon yet?"

"Yes, and he's just as excited as I am, although he's concerned because he's trying to restart the business. He wants to move into a bigger house before the baby's born. Leon wants his daughter to have a room of her own."

"And just how do you know you're having a girl?"

"My father told me," Starla said, then stepped back into the dressing stall.

Marlissa shook her head, then stepped into the stall next to Starla's. "Girl, I am not going to ask how a man who died ten years ago told you the sex of the baby you're now carrying."

Starla laughed. "It's nothing creepy." She went on to tell Marlissa about the letter from her father. "Everything he prayed for, I have, except the daughters. That's how I know I am carrying a girl, maybe twin girls. Two for one, that would be a blessing and put an end to my baby-making career."

"How's the progress with your mother?" Marlissa changed the subject.

Starla sighed heavily and joy seeped from her voice. "I'm still hurt about the whole thing, but I still love her. We talk once a week, but it's not the same. She refuses to admit she was wrong."

"Is she coming to the wedding?"

"No, she said it didn't make sense to fly from Arizona to see me marry the same person. It's probably for the best since Odessa is coming."

They practically exited the stalls simultaneously. "Starla, you know I love you. You're the closest thing I have to a sister. I'm trying to be happy for you, but right now I'm jealous of you," Marlissa admitted. "You have a committed man who will not only love his baby, but he loves you."

Starla embraced her. "Kevin loves you, Marlissa. Just wait, once you tell him about the baby, everything will be different."

"But I don't want to tell him about the baby first. I want him to commit to me because he loves *me*, not because I'm pregnant."

"Hold on, Marlissa, he will," Starla encouraged her. They gathered the dresses and started for the register.

Marlissa looked down at the price tag. "Starla, I can't pay for this," she whispered.

"Don't worry about it. I have some money in addition to the money Leon gave me. Now, come on, we have to pick out my bouquet before the florist closes, and buy shoes."

At the flower shop, Marlissa admired the tulips while Starla selected a medium-sized bouquet made of white roses. "Since you like tulips so much, let's use them for your arrangement," Starla suggested, noticing the serene look on Marlissa's face.

"I like that idea, and the colors will go well with my dress."

No sooner had Starla paid the florist than her cell phone rang. "Girl, I know this isn't anyone but Leon, wondering where I am. He acts like he can't breathe without me." Starla giggled.

"I know what you mean," Marlissa responded, remembering what it felt like to be needed by Kevin. She stepped away to give Starla some privacy. Marlissa was looking at shoes through a store window when she heard Starla scream.

"Oh my God!"

Marlissa rushed to her. "What's wrong?"

"Baby, I'm coming . . . I . . . will . . . I know." Tears poured down Starla's cheeks before she disconnected the call.

"Starla, please tell me what happened."

Starla leaned against the store wall, and between tears managed to say, "It's Leon."

"What's wrong with Leon?" Starla wasn't talking fast enough for Marlissa.

"He's in jail!"

Chapter 33

The Lexus had barely stopped when Starla jumped out and ran inside the main police station on Broadway. Marlissa watched until Starla was on the other side of the glass doors before breaking down. The supportive, strong friend charade was over. "Oh God, how could this happen?" she cried. Marlissa didn't know the details of Leon's arrest, but whatever the charges were, she just knew Leon was innocent. "What about Starla and the boys? What about me?" she mumbled. "What am I going to do if he's in jail?" Leon was her friend, the rock she could always lean on.

Angry car horns interrupted her emotional breakdown. Marlissa forgot she had stopped in the middle of downtown Oakland after 5:00 p.m. on a Friday. Marlissa slowly removed her foot from the brake and searched for a parking space. She parallel parked after a Honda pulled out half a block down. Before stepping from the car and placing coins into the parking ticket machine, she prayed hard. She prayed harder to the point of speaking in tongues after she rested the parking receipt on the dashboard.

"This can't be real," Starla moaned as she stepped inside the busy precinct. She'd seen the scene before her a thousand times on television, but now the characters were real people and the guns were loaded with real bullets instead of blanks. The policemen seated behind the bulletproof glass were talking about real people and situations, not staging conversations for a camera. Starla wiped her face, and then swallowed hard and approached the window under the sign that read START HERE.

"Excuse me, officer, I am trying to find my husband."

"Is he missing?" A salt-and-pepper haired gentlemen, who looked like he should have retired years ago, manned the booth.

"No, he is not missing." Starla lowered her head before adding, "He's been arrested."

"Miss, speak up. I am busy, I don't have time to guess at what you're trying to tell me." The officer's lack of sensitivity surprised Starla. The officers on TV were much friendlier.

She raised her head and read the number on his badge before responding. The rude gentleman was licensed to disrespect her. "My husband was arrested earlier today."

"I see." The officer clicked the mouse on the computer, then asked, "Name?"

"Leon Scott," Starla answered as she leaned closer to the glass.

"Have a seat in the waiting room on the third floor. The officer handling his case will be out to speak with you."

"Officer, can you please tell me why my husband was arrested?" Starla held her breath and waited for the answer.

Officer #821 looked down at the computer screen, and then shook his head. "Mrs. Scott, your husband was arrested for stealing."

"What? Are you crazy?"

"So you can talk loud?" The officer smirked. "Mrs. Scott, lower your voice." Starla didn't realize she was yelling.

"Starla, what's going on?" Marlissa rushed to her side just in time to cool Starla down.

"They think Leon is a thief!" Starla answered.

It was Marlissa's turn to look at the tired officer and ask, "Are you crazy?"

"I'm sure he's innocent like all the other criminals." The officer chuckled. "But I don't want to hear it. Tell it to the investigating officer." The women gasped as the officer put his head down and pointed his index finger toward the elevator, in essence dismissing them.

"He better be glad I'm saved," Starla fumed, walking toward the elevator. "He don't know me; I'm from the hood. I will beat the slop out of him."

She punched the elevator call button and waited, then faced Marlissa. "Make sure you keep a cool head. It would only hurt Leon's case if both of us were arrested for assaulting an officer. Obviously, this whole thing is nothing more than a misunderstanding. Leon is a lot of things, but a thief he is not."

"Calm down, this mess will be over before you know it. Leon will be back home with you and the boys tonight, and tomorrow you'll renew your vows and life will be happy again."

Starla took a deep breath, deciding that Marlissa was right. But, just in case, Starla said a silent prayer.

The waiting room on the third floor resembled a hospital emergency room with the white walls and blue linoleum with white speckled flooring. The hard blue chairs connecting at the arm were overflowing with people, the majority of whom didn't appear worried at all. Some read magazines, a few even slept. Several men acknowledged Marlissa's and Starla's presence, but no one offered them a seat. Marlissa and Starla leaned against the wall near the door.

"I need to ask my neighbor to pick the boys up for me," Starla said after waiting over an hour. Both women were now sitting on the cold, hard floor.

"We should probably call Mother as well," Marlissa suggested. "I didn't want to worry her, but I'm starting to get a bad feeling about this; it's taking too long."

"I know," Starla admitted. "Maybe I should call a lawyer." Starla didn't know what to do, but passing the time on the cold floor in a room filled with strangers certainly wasn't the answer. She needed Leon out of jail. They were renewing their vows in twenty-six hours and she was having a baby and her daughter needed her father. Her sons needed their father. Starla tucked her face in her hands and cried softly.

Marlissa pulled her cell phone from her purse. "You call Mother and your neighbor. I'll call Tyson."

An hour later they were still on the floor, waiting, when the cavalry arrived. Mother Scott along with Pastor and First Lady Drake arrived first.

"Starla, what is going on?" Mother Scott didn't give her a chance to answer. "Have they let my son go yet?"

Starla shook her head slowly. "No." Pastor Drake handed her a handkerchief and assisted her to her feet. "Thank you," she acknowledged him, and, after blowing her nose and stretching her legs, she continued. "We've been waiting for over two hours, and the only thing they've told me is that Leon was arrested for stealing."

"What?" Mother Scott snapped.

Everyone remained focused on Starla and didn't see Tyson and Kevin enter the room.

"What's this I hear about Leon stealing?" Tyson echoed Mother Scott.

Kevin didn't hear the recap; he was too busy staring at Marlissa, who was still seated Indian style on the floor. Marlissa's attempt not to return his gaze was easily lost. She missed him too much, and right now she needed him, but she wasn't going to let him know it. After a prolonged moment, she folded her arms and redirected her attention back to the group.

Kevin wasn't deterred by her wall. He simply walked over to her and extended his hands to her. The gesture astounded Marlissa, and all of her defenses, without much resistance, tumbled down. She accepted his hands and allowed him to lift her to her feet. Kevin didn't stop there. He wrapped his arms around her and pressed her close to him. Marlissa shuddered, then released the emotions she'd been holding in for the past two hours, trying to be strong for Starla's sake. Kevin didn't say one word, just continuously stroked her hair and back until she quieted down.

"Starla, I'm not a criminal attorney, but I'll do whatever I can tonight to help," Tyson offered. "In the morning, I'll call a colleague who works in this area."

Before Starla could thank Tyson, Mother Scott went off on a tangent. "What do you mean in the morning? You better get my son out of here tonight! Do you hear me?" Mother Scott narrowed her eyes at Tyson. "If my son ain't going home tonight, then neither are you!"

"Scott, calm down!" First Lady Drake chimed in. "It's not his fault Leon's in jail."

Mother Scott apologized to Tyson, but not before rolling her eyes at First Lady Drake. She then walked to the front and set the room in order with First Lady Drake following close behind. "All y'all men in here, I know your mothers, fathers, grandparents, or somebody taught y'all some manners. If they didn't, I will." Mother Scott placed her hand on her petite waist and glared at the group. "It's improper for y'all to be sitting here all comfortable while we women stand around or sit on the floor. Now, y'all ain't got to leave, but in Jesus' name, y'all are going to get up out of these chairs so we women can sit down."

Pastor Drake started praying while First Lady Drake and Mother Scott started singing a duet version of "You've Got to Move." By the time they got to the chorus of "when the Lord gets ready," every man in the room was standing, along with some of the women.

Marlissa, who was still glued to Kevin's chest, laughed uncontrollably. She was so relaxed she allowed Kevin to kiss her forehead and tighten his hold on her.

Starla laughed. "You two are a mess!" She appreciated the change in the tension-filled atmosphere. The change was short-lived. Starla hadn't been seated one minute when a uniformed officer entered the room and called her name. Starla rushed to the officer, expecting to see Leon.

"Where's my husband?"

"Mrs. Scott, I'm Officer Grimes, follow me," the officer said without answering her question.

"Wait a minute. I want to know where my husband is."

"Why are you detaining my client?" Tyson asked, standing next to Starla.

Officer Grimes's demeanor changed from one of irritation to tolerance. "I'm sorry; I didn't know Mr. Scott had legal representation."

"Now you do." Tyson wasn't the least bit intimidated by the officer. "Tyson Stokes. Now I'll ask you again, what are the charges against my client?"

The tall, slender officer smirked as if it was an open-and-shut case. "Mrs. Scott, Stokes, please follow me."

Tyson nodded his consent to Starla and together they followed the officer to a small room that contained only a square table and four chairs. One side of the wall was mirrored. Starla figured it was a two-way mirror. Officer Grimes placed a file on the once-white table and began.

"Mrs. Scott, your husband was arrested for theft and embezzlement." Officer Grimes made the announcement like he was making a simple comment about the weather.

"What!" Starla jumped to her feet. "My husband didn't steal anything!"

Tyson stood and placed his arm around Starla's shoulder. "Hear him out." Starla reluctantly sat back down.

"His former employer, West Coast Alliance, alleges he stole over fifty thousand dollars over a four-month period."

"That's ridiculous! Leon's not a thief!" Starla countered.

Officer Grimes continued reading his notes as if Starla hadn't said a word.

"What proof do you have?" Tyson asked.

"Manipulated deposit receipts with your husband's signature, and purchases your husband's income can't afford."

Starla's head pounded as she reflected on the past three months. Leon had been spending more money than usual.

"Mrs. Scott, can you explain how your husband was able to purchase a brand new truck with cash?"

"I didn't know Leon paid cash for the truck," she mumbled, defeated.

"Can you explain the five thousand dollars worth of new tools found in the truck when we arrested him?"

Starla massaged her temples. "Leon's been doing side jobs."

"Can you explain how a man who works for minimum wage has a business account with a balance of over twenty-five thousand dollars?"

Starla didn't have any answers. Leon wouldn't tell her how he was able to restart the business so fast. Whenever she asked, he'd just say, "God made a way." Starla trusted him completely.

When sober, Leon was not careless with money. If Leon spent money, it was because he felt it was safe to do so.

They'd spent close to $1,000 in Calistoga and were spending more than that on their vow renewal. Leon said he didn't want her to use the money her father had given her, so he gave her enough cash to cover everything. He was talking about buying another house before the baby came, and he wanted Starla to have a new car. Leon wanted the boys to attend private school. Leon wanted too much to risk their future for $50,000. The Leon she knew loved his family too much for that. *He did throw us away for the bottle.* The thought pounded Starla's head with the force of a sledgehammer. She moaned and rubbed her temples.

"Look, Officer Grimes." Starla raised her head, looking him dead in the eyes. "I honestly don't know how Leon was able to buy all those things. But I know my husband, and he is not a thief. His family means too much to him. We're renewing our vows tomorrow and then we're having a baby. Tell West Coast Alliance to check the receipts again, my husband didn't take their money."

"She's right," Tyson said, pulling out his laptop. "Dr. Jennings and I can account for the money in Mr. Scott's business account as well as the purchases."

"What?" Starla's head jerked toward Tyson. Officer Grimes shifted in his chair.

"Dr. Kevin Jennings and I advanced seventy-five thousand dollars to Mr. Scott to help him restart his business, Star Construction, three months ago. We also set him up with work from several of our colleagues. Those are the side jobs he's been working on every day."

"I knew my husband wasn't a thief," Starla said repeatedly.

Officer Grimes cleared his throat. "Can you prove it?"

"I'm pulling up the banking transaction now. I can also open the file containing the repayment agreement."

"Thank you, Jesus." Tears streamed down Starla's face as Officer Grimes's countenance changed to a smirk.

"I'm in the wrong profession, I should have been a lawyer," Officer Grimes commented once he viewed Tyson's account online. Grimes leaned back in the chair. "That proves your half, what about this Dr. Jennings?"

"He's outside. I'm sure he has access to his accounts online as well."

Officer Grimes stood. "I'll be back."

"Can I please see my husband?" Starla pleaded.

"If Dr. Jennings can corroborate this story, then I'll let you see him."

As soon as Officer Grimes left, Starla ran to Tyson and hugged his neck. "Thank you so much. I am still going to fuss at Leon for not telling me about this little arrangement."

"Cut him some slack. He wanted to do this on his own, and from the reports I hear, Star Construction is well on its way back."

Starla smiled proudly. "He does do good work."

"Congratulations on your pregnancy," Tyson stated almost with excitement.

"Thank you." Starla studied the ultra-conservative Tyson, wondering if she'd ever seen him smile or heard him laugh. "Tyson, is there a special someone in your life?"

"If you mean other than Jesus and my law practice, no."

"Maybe you should find someone."

Tyson zipped up the laptop case. "Why? I get more than enough drama from Kevin and Marlissa and, now, you and Leon."

Starla shrugged and sat down. "Can't argue with you there."

Fifteen minutes later, Officer Grimes returned with another officer and Leon, who was still in restraints. The officers allowed space for Starla to embrace him.

"Star, I am so sorry about this," Leon repeatedly apologized. "I promise I didn't steal that money; you have to believe me."

"I do believe you," she answered after kissing him. "I've never stopped believing in you."

Officer Grimes cleared his throat. "Mr. and Mrs. Scott, please take a seat."

"Can't we leave now?" Starla didn't see the point in staying.

"You can, but he has to stay until his bail is posted," Officer Grimes explained.

"I don't understand, didn't Kevin's statement clear him?" Starla was confused.

"Dr. Jennings confirmed Stokes's story, but West Coast Alliance has filed criminal charges against your husband; they want their money back."

"But I didn't take it," Leon protested.

"That's what you'll have to prove in court," Officer Grimes stated flatly. Then he added, "Unless Lewis Mason drops the charges."

Starla gasped. "What does Lewis Mason have to do with anything?"

"He's the owner of West Coast Alliance," Officer Grimes answered. "He's the one who filed the charges."

"He was my boss at the gas station," Leon further clarified.

"I don't believe this," Starla said, shaking her head. "That no good . . ." Lewis's threats were clear now. She knew Lewis owned a trucking company, but had no idea he also owned the gas station at which Leon worked. Lewis had planned to set Leon up all along.

"Star, how do you know Lewis Mason?" Leon asked Starla. Everyone in the room anxiously awaited her answer.

"Lewis Mason is the man I told you about from my old church."

"Lewis is the one who wanted to marry you?" Now everything made sense to Leon. Lewis's intense interest in Starla and the boys and his constant prying into Leon's financial status, everything now fell into place.

"Yes, Lewis Mason is a low-down, dirty, sorry excuse of a man. I'll tell you all about that later." Starla kissed Leon's cheek, then started for the door.

"Would someone like to tell me what's going on?" Officer Grimes asked.

"Officer Grimes, you can start preparing the necessary paperwork. When I get back, Lewis Mason is dropping the charges, and my husband is coming home with me!"

When Tyson caught up with her, Starla was already in the waiting room demanding Marlissa's car keys. "Starla, wait, I'll go with you."

"Girl, what's going on?" Mother Scott demanded, breaking from the Bible Study session Pastor Drake had started with the waiting room visitors.

"I don't have time to explain." Starla shook her head and reached for Marlissa's purse.

Marlissa grabbed the purse before Starla could retrieve the keys. "You're too emotional, I'll drive."

Kevin didn't know where they were going, but he wasn't going to allow Marlissa to go alone. "Tyson and I are coming with you."

"I feel trouble in my spirit," Pastor Drake called after him. "I think we should have prayer before you all leave."

"You're right, Pastor," Starla said after opening the door. "I want you to pray that the Lord gives me the strength to lay hands on Lewis Mason and knock him out under the power if need be. Pray that I do just what Jesus did: whip his behind clean out the temple."

"Well Amen," Pastor Drake stammered as the four of them left.

Starla filled Marlissa, Kevin, and Tyson in with the details of Lewis's pursuit on the drive to her former church.

"Oh, no, he didn't!" Marlissa yelled. It was a good thing Kevin was seated in the front with Marlissa, because when Starla mentioned that Lewis had shoved the boys, Marlissa released the steering wheel and snatched out her earrings. Kevin had to reach over and grab the wheel of

the Lexus to keep the car from swerving into another lane. Starla was too fired up to notice and
Tyson didn't utter one word. He'd learned from
his numerous female relatives never to scold
an emotional pregnant black woman. Kevin
couldn't say anything; he was too busy praying.

"Good!" Starla said when Marlissa pulled into
the church's parking lot. "The monthly business
meeting is still in session."

The gearshift didn't make it into park good
before Starla jumped out of the car and stormed
through the doors of her former church. Tyson
hurried after. Kevin followed with a firm grip on
Marlissa's arm to keep her from running off.

"Lewis Mason, you low-down, triflin', dirty
devil!" Starla screamed in slow motion when she
barged into the conference room.

Lewis was seated at the head of the table. His
jaw fell. The remaining twelve people seated
around the oval oak table were taken aback by
the sudden intrusion. Most stopped what they
were doing and dropped their pens and paper.
The secretary continued writing.

Starla started for the stunned Lewis, and
Tyson followed close behind. "How dare you
accuse a decent man like my husband of stealing
your money, all because I refused to marry your
tired behind?"

Murmurs of, "Oh my goodness" and "What did she say?" floated around the table.

"Sister Scott, I . . . What brings you here tonight?" It was apparent the chairman of the deacon board didn't quite know how to respond to the outburst.

"Is that the best you can come up with?" Marlissa said from the doorway.

The chairman hunched his shoulders. "I had to say something. It's my job to keep order in these meetings."

Starla briefly glared at the chairman, then walked over and stood over Lewis. Kevin and Marlissa remained in the doorway. "You heard what I said," Starla snarled. "The man you have representing this fine church tried to talk me into divorcing my husband to marry him, and when I refused, he had my husband falsely arrested." She hit Lewis on the back of the head. "Tell them!"

The slap brought Lewis out of his trance. "Ms. Scott, you are out of order for bringing this ghetto behavior in here." Lewis's voice came across as cold and demeaning. He detested public displays. "You are no longer a member of this church; therefore, you have no right to be here. Now leave!" Lewis tried to intimidate her by standing and stepping to her.

The murmuring grew and the secretary kept writing.

Lewis soon learned how ineffective his tactic was when Starla stepped even closer to him, and, with one hand on her hip, pointed a finger in his face. Kevin wasted his breath instructing Marlissa to stay put. She arrived next to Starla the second after Kevin stood next to Tyson.

"First of all"—Starla's neck rolled rhythmically—"it's Mrs. Scott, and as long as my husband is in jail behind your lies, I will stay here. If you think my behavior is ghetto now, see what happens if you don't march down to the police station and drop those phony charges. You didn't know I am from the hood, did you? I'm saved, but I ain't forgot nothing!" Starla gestured around the room with her hand. "I will tear you and this place up and repent later!"

"Hold on a minute, Sister Scott, we don't want any trouble," the chairman stuttered, then turned to Lewis. "Mason, what is going on here?"

"Tell them, Lewis. Tell them how you sexually assaulted me and attacked my boys," Starla demanded.

Lewis's nostrils flared and his jaw flexed with the rapid pace of his breathing. "What did you say?"

The secretary spoke for the first time. "She said, 'Tell them, Lewis. Tell them how you sexually assaulted me and attacked my boys.'"

The murmurs instantly transformed into full voices and text messages were transcribed at a rapid speed.

Starla walked around Lewis and stood at the head of the table. "Go on, Lewis, tell the board how you pursued me and came to my townhouse and forced yourself on me after I refused you. Tell them how you physically attacked three- and six-year-old boys who were only trying to protect their mother." Starla folded her arms. "Tell them, Lewis, because when I get back to the police station, I and Officer Grimes are going to have a long talk." Starla cocked her head. "I wonder if Montel left any teeth marks."

Tyson and Kevin grabbed Lewis's arms before his clenched fist could strike Starla. Taking advantage of the opportunity, Starla kicked him in the groin.

"Mason, you've gone too far this time!" the chairman said, and pounded his fist on the table. "This is the third time you've run a good member away with your obsessive behavior. This time I am not going to look the other way. We don't need this type of mess." The chairman motioned to Tyson and Kevin. "Take him down to the police station. Mason, you're going to clear this up now!"

Lewis attempted to break free, but it was useless. He wasn't any match for Tyson and Kevin. "I'm not going anywhere!"

"Shut up, Haman!" Starla yelled back. "You're going to hang in the same gallows you set up for my husband." Her eyes narrowed. "I assume you read that big Bible you carry to know who Haman is," Starla said in reference to the man who'd plotted to kill God's chosen people.

Lewis grunted and jerked some more to no avail.

"Sister Scott, I am so sorry about this," the chairman apologized. "Mason promised he wouldn't do this again and I believed him."

Starla didn't have any words for the chairman or anyone else in the room. She turned to Tyson and Kevin. "Let's get back to the station. I want my husband home before midnight."

"Excuse me," the secretary called after Tyson and Kevin. "Can I have your names for the minutes?"

"Whew!" Marlissa sighed and leaned against the back passenger door of her car. "This has been some day."

After the confrontation at the church, Tyson and Kevin dragged Lewis down to the police station. After Lewis explained that he'd made an accounting error, Officer Grimes released Leon two hours later, but detained Lewis. Marlissa guessed it was for filing a false complaint.

"Tell me about it," Kevin replied while opening the door for her. "This has been the most chaotic day—week, actually—that I've ever experienced."

"At least Leon is free." An awkward silence followed. Momentarily, Marlissa surveyed her surroundings. The police station rested on the border of Oakland's Chinatown and Jack London Square. Surprisingly, the landmarks were over-shadowed by the homeless population living on the streets. *Thank you for your grace*, Marlissa prayed. *I was almost one of them.*

She turned back to the man who'd given her the greatest pleasure and had also caused her the most agonizing pain. "Thanks for helping Leon. I didn't realize the two of you were that close. He didn't mention the business loan to me, and I thought I was his friend."

Kevin smiled. "I know you didn't think all of our conversations and meetings were about you."

Marlissa shrugged. "What do you know, I was wrong again. I've been wrong about a lot of things lately." Marlissa paused before asking, "Kevin, why did you come here today?" This was Kevin's chance to finally level with her.

"Tyson told me what happened and I knew you would need me."

Marlissa rapidly blinked back tears. Once again, Kevin refused to give the one answer she needed to hear. "Kevin, we need to talk," she announced while discreetly rubbing her belly.

"I know." He nodded. "But not tonight. It's after midnight and we're both tired. We'll talk tomorrow." Kevin motioned for her to get inside the car. "Buckle up. I'll follow you home."

Too drained to argue, she obeyed. Before closing her door, Kevin attempted to kiss her and didn't appear disappointed at all when she offered him her cheek and not her lips.

Chapter 34

Marlissa studied the room and debated how she was going to tell Starla she was pulling out of the wedding. Marlissa just couldn't do it. Throughout the night and all morning, Marlissa tried to convince herself she could do this, but standing at any altar without Kevin wasn't something she looked forward to doing.

The small, intimate setting resembled the wedding she'd always wanted, but wasn't allowed to have. Starla had chosen the Yacht Club for its 360-degree exquisite views of the bay. The hardwood floors and vaulted ceilings gave the illusion of a much bigger space. The guest list was only fifty people long, but Starla decorated like she was expecting to have a spread featured in *Ebony* magazine.

Starla's color scheme was sage, cream, and silver. Cream-colored netting was draped through hooks on the ceiling, forming an impression of clouds. Across the center of each "cloud" was a silver ribbon. Starla selected this particular design to signify that there is a silver lining behind every cloud; good could come out of every situation. Marlissa thought the fragrance extracted from the cream-colored vanilla candles and the sage-colored cucumber melon candles, which centered the tables and lined the walls, was heavenly. The archway where Leon and Starla would stand was conservatively lined with cream netting and sprinkled with artificially dyed sage-colored roses and cream-colored tulips. Cream and sage tablecloths draped round tables of six with matching chair covers. The catered celebratory sit-down meal included prime rib and salmon, Starla's favorites. They were also Marlissa's favorites.

"I'm sorry, Starla," Marlissa whispered, heading toward the dressing room while squeezing the garment bag that contained her gown.

The hairstylist was putting the finishing touches on Starla's hair. Marlissa had never seen Starla without her braids. Marlissa had assumed the single braids were mostly added hair. It turned out that Starla's hair was just as long as the braids she wore. "Your hair is beautiful." Marlissa's voice communicated her surprise.

"Didn't know I had hair, did you?" Starla started to muse, but stopped abruptly when she noticed Marlissa wasn't dressed at all. She didn't even have on makeup. "Do you know what time it is?" Starla barked. "You better hurry up and get dressed. This is not a CP Time wedding."

Marlissa bit her lip before saying, "Starla, I'm sorry, but I can't do this."

"Why not?" Mother Scott appeared suddenly from behind a curtain.

"It's too hard," Marlissa whimpered.

"What's so hard about putting on a dress and walking down the aisle for your friends?"

Before Marlissa could answer, Mother Scott grabbed her by the arm, pulled her behind the curtain, and continued with her tangent. Starla never got a chance to say one word and she didn't mind at all, because when the curtain opened again, Marlissa was fully dressed.

Mother Scott was getting on her nerves so bad, Marlissa practically ran to the vanity and applied her makeup in record speed.

"Marlissa," Starla said, placing her freshly manicured hand on her shoulder. "I know this is hard for you. I saw how difficult it was for you to handle Kevin's presence yesterday at the police station. I just want you to know that I love you for pushing your pain aside and being here for me."

Marlissa had a list of sarcastic and bitter remarks she could say, but didn't. She simply smiled and said, "I love you guys too," then asked, "Where's my bouquet?" before leaving to prepare for her entrance down the aisle.

Starla frowned. "Marlissa, I should have told you earlier. When I went to pick up the bouquets, yours wasn't there," Starla explained regretfully.

"Great." Marlissa smirked. "What will I use now?"

"Here." Marlissa didn't complain. She took the single rose from her friend and quietly exited the room.

On cue, Marlissa inhaled and started down the aisle. With a pasted smile she strolled and almost tripped upon seeing Reyna seated next to Tyson. *What is that about?* she wondered. She quickly regained her composure by focusing on Leon and the boys. Montel and Jaylen were too adorable in those cream tuxedos and sage cummerbunds. What could she say about Leon, whose attire mirrored the boys'? She loved him. He was a God-given friend and her big brother. Marlissa took her place, then after Pastor Drake instructed everyone to stand, directed her attention to the door.

Starla was beautiful in her sage dress, and the love that radiated between her and Leon was so evident, even Tyson appeared moved. His bright skin had turned a shade of red. Before interlocking his arm with Starla's, Leon stole a quick kiss, causing the audience to chuckle. Marlissa was too busy laughing to notice that Leon and Starla had moved three steps to the left. Marlissa continued laughing until a song very familiar began playing through the sound system. It was the song she'd originally desired for her wedding march. She looked over at Starla and Leon for an explanation, but all Starla and Leon would do was smile. Montel and Jaylen were smiling too. Pastor Drake touched her shoulder and nodded toward the door. Marlissa still didn't understand what was going on.

"Turn around, baby," Mother Scott called from the audience.

Marlissa did as she was instructed and thought she was dreaming. The image of Kevin in a cream tuxedo and carrying her tulip bouquet, walking down the aisle to her, was better than any fantasy.

"Y'all set me up." Marlissa sniffled, accepting Leon's handkerchief. But to Kevin she didn't say anything; she couldn't, not yet. She bit her lip and her hands fidgeted with the single rose as she waited for him to approach her.

Kevin removed the rose from her shaky hands and placed it on an end seat. "I love you," he began after taking her hand and tenderly kissing it. "I never stopped loving you. I should have told you that a long time ago, but I didn't, and for that I am sorry."

Marlissa sucked in her breath.

"You asked me for forgiveness but I refused to grant it because I was afraid of being hurt again. You were right. I took advantage of you by making you prove your commitment to me repeatedly without once fully committing to you."

Marlissa inhaled deeply in an effort to control her breathing and to delay the tears, but it was too late. Tears pooled and streamed down her cheeks.

"'Lissa, I am so sorry for every hurt I selfishly inflicted on you, and I forgive you for everything that happened in the past." Kevin held out the bouquet to her. "Let's start over."

Marlissa released her hand and shook her head from side to side. "How can we do that? Too much time has lapsed; aren't we divorced?"

"We are not divorced," he answered plainly. "I rescinded the petition the day you walked into Tyson's office. I realized that day I loved you too much to live without you. I just didn't know how to tell you that. I was afraid."

Marlissa moved her mouth to say something, but then changed her mind. She calmly removed the bouquet from Kevin and placed it on a chair, then in one quick motion sucker punched him.

The entire audience gasped almost in unison.

"Hit him again," First Lady Drake called out.

"Yeah, you deserve that one, son," Mother Scott added.

"*Kevin Hezekiah Jennings, I could kill you!* Do you know how much heartache you've caused me? Do you have any idea how many tears I have cried over you?" Marlissa tried to soothe the throbbing in her hand by shaking it. Kevin's rock-solid stomach caused her more pain than the punch did him.

"Can you forgive me?" Kevin managed once he was upright again and the initial shock of being punched by his wife while wearing a tuxedo wore off.

Marlissa went off on a tangent, rolling her neck. "I have been going out of my mind for five days, waiting for you to come clean about the divorce. Not to mention the days and weeks I tried to regain your trust. I can't hardly hold any food down and can't sleep at night because I'm too busy praying for you to come to your senses." Marlissa snarled at him. "Kevin Hezekiah Jennings, you had better be glad I love you so much!"

Marlissa was scowling and Kevin was smiling.

"I love you. Will you marry me, again?" Kevin asked once more.

Marlissa wasn't ready to give in just yet. "Tell me again and say it loud enough to be heard in Mexico!" Marlissa softened, listening to Kevin repeat the statement and question again.

"Drake, did you hear that?" Mother Scott asked out loud.

"I think he needs to say it again, this time like he means it," First Lady Drake answered.

Marlissa giggled uncontrollably when Kevin lifted her into the air and yelled, "I love you, Marlissa Jennings. Please marry me again."

"Okay," Marlissa shrieked.

Kevin abruptly ended the celebratory kiss that followed her acceptance and set Marlissa on her feet. "What do you mean you've been waiting five days for me to tell you about the divorce? How did you find out five days ago?" Kevin followed Marlissa's eyes to where Tyson was seated. "Man, you told? You weren't supposed to do that."

Tyson nonchalantly shrugged. "I know, sue me."

"You should be happy Tyson told me, I was going to give up on you," Marlissa admitted.

"I'm glad you didn't."

Little Montel excitedly watched Kevin and Marlissa kiss again and everything made perfect sense to him now. He tapped her on the arm. "Auntie Marlissa, now you and your baby don't have to live in the car."

The room drew quiet.

"Montel!" Starla grabbed his arm and pulled him back. "You are just like your daddy." She grumbled. "Girl, I am sorry. This boy must have been listening on the other side of the bathroom door."

Kevin's eye fell to Marlissa's stomach, then traveled back up to her face, and then he smiled. "Is my baby growing in there?"

"Yes." Marlissa smiled back.

"Good, that's one down." Kevin handed Marlissa her bouquet then nodded for Pastor Drake to continue with the ceremony.

Both Starla and Marlissa shed many tears during the double ceremony and both screamed when it was time to exchange rings. Starla received a new, bigger ring and Marlissa got her old ring back.

Watching the couples kiss, Mother Scott and First Lady Drake exchanged high-fives. "Time for the next project," Mother Scott announced, and the first lady agreed.

***

The late Luther Vandross filled the air as the couples shared the traditional first dance. "Mrs. Scott, you're the greatest woman in the world," Leon said while nibbling on Starla's ear.

"That's because I'm married to the greatest man in the world," Starla answered between giggles.

"I'm trying to be serious here."

"So am I." Starla whispered something in his ear and Leon lost his train of thought. He gave up trying to talk and enjoyed the moment.

"I love you, Mrs. Jennings." Kevin couldn't stop saying the words and Marlissa didn't want to stop hearing them. "I can't believe you doubted that."

"I thought you did until the gala. That whole date/sister thing blew me away."

"What a difference a week makes." He sighed.

"Tell me about it." They shared a soft peck. "Kevin, promise me you won't hide your fears from me again. I know what it's like to be afraid. I still have fears, but they're easier to face when you have someone in your corner. Kevin, baby, I love you, and I'll always be in your corner, cheering the loudest, no matter what."

"Thank you." Following a kiss, Kevin adorned a mischievous smile. "Feel like cheering tonight?"

Marlissa pressed even closer to him. "I have to stop by the apartment for clothes first."

"We'll move you back home tomorrow, but you won't be needing clothes tonight. We're staying at the Ritz. You owe me a wedding night."

"I'm ready to pay up," Marlissa squealed.

A tap on Kevin's shoulder interrupted the moment. Kevin turned around. "Mother, you made it."

"Yeah, well, this is important to you." Pastor Jennings strained her neck to face her daughter-in-law. "Marlissa," she said dryly. "Welcome to the family—again."

"Thank you, Pastor Jennings," Marlissa answered cheerfully.

"Since you're determined to be family, I guess you can call me Rosalie."

The stress on his mother's face was undeniable; Rosalie was having a hard time. Kevin decided to put her out of her misery. "Mother, maybe we should start calling you Grandma." Kevin beamed, placing his hands on Marlissa's abdomen. "We're having a baby."

"This day just keeps getting better." Pastor Jennings smirked. "Excuse me."

"Your mother still doesn't like me," Marlissa said once Pastor Jennings left.

"I love you; everything else is irrelevant."

"I love you too." Another tap.

"May we please cut in?" It was Leon and Starla.

"Yes, you may, but I'm still going to get you guys for tricking me," Marlissa pouted.

"Whatever, brat," Leon said, extending his hand. "I tried to tell you it wasn't over, but you wouldn't listen to me."

With unspoken gratitude, Kevin relinquished his wife to her friend. While dancing with Starla, he took the opportunity to thank her for helping him pull off the double ceremony.

"Can you believe it? We did it, well, God did it. He gave us more than what we had." Marlissa beamed, falling into step with Leon.

"What did I tell you, brat? Love is always worth it."

"I'll never doubt you again, big brother."

"Congratulations, Dr. Jennings." Tyson slapped Kevin on the shoulder.

"Thank you, Attorney Stokes, for everything," Kevin said after the two shared a hug. "Especially for running your big mouth."

"After she told me about the baby, I had to tell her before she did something crazy. You know how your wife is."

"You knew about my baby before I did and you didn't tell me? I thought *we* were best friends."

"We are best friends and you can show me some appreciation for saving your marriage by naming your firstborn after me."

"Hey, guys." It was Reyna. "Congratulations, the ceremony was beautiful. I have never seen a wedding as romantic as this. Neither have I seen a man beg as hard as you, Kevin."

Across the room Marlissa chatted with Mother Scott and First Lady Drake.

"Come on, Drake," Mother Scott said, suddenly grabbing Marlissa's hand.

"Reyna, I hope you decide to visit Restorations Ministries soon, with Tyson, of course," Kevin teased.

Reyna rolled her eyes at Kevin and Tyson pretended not to hear the wisecrack.

"Young lady, let's get one thing straight. This is his wife," Mother Scott said, holding out Marlissa's hand to Reyna. "This ring means she belongs to him, not you. Do you understand?"

"Yes, ma'am, I do," Reyna answered. "Hello, Marlissa."

"Hello, Reyna." The former foes exchanged pleasantries.

"I don't want any problems out of you," Mother Scott warned Reyna again.

"Trust me, Mother, Reyna won't cause any problems," Tyson assured her.

Mother Scott glared at Reyna then at Tyson. "Now what's going on between the two of you?"

"Nothing," Reyna answered, while breaking eye contact.

"Not a thing," Tyson validated.

"Um huh," Mother Scott grunted.

"One Eye, leave them kids alone, and for once, mind your own business," First Lady Drake scolded Mother Scott.

"Drake, I'm about tired of you calling me One Eye. I have two very good eyes, you can ask my doctor," Mother Scott replied.

"You are just in time," Kevin said to Leon as he and Starla approached. "Will you get your mama?"

"The only person who can handle her is Jesus," Leon retorted.

"I don't have to ask your doctor nothing. I can look at your outfit and tell you can't see too well. Out here looking like the rainbow coalition." First Lady Drake rolled her eyes and Mother was ready to let her have it.

"Don't worry about my color coordination. I can see well enough to knock your old butt around this room and back."

"Oh goodness, they're going to fight?" Reyna exclaimed and pulled on Tyson's arm.

Mother Scott suddenly smiled. "Oh no, baby, that's my best friend in the whole world. I would never hit her."

"That's right," First Lady concurred. "We love each other to death."

"We're prayer partners," Mother Scott added. "We can pray the devil out of anyone." She then leaned in close to Reyna, "Do you have any devils you need us to help you get rid of?"

Discussion Questions

1. Kevin married Marlissa knowing she was an unbeliever, thinking he could change her. In your opinion, has this way of thinking added to the high divorce rate among Christians?

2. Leon complained of going to church too much as a child. Do you think this is a valid point among adults who no longer attend traditional church service? How can parents find a balance?

3. Marlissa was "sheltered" as a child and suffered sexual abuse as a teenager. At what age should parents begin educating their children about sex and dating?

4. Pastor Rosalie Jennings attempted to control everything and everyone around her. Why do you think this was? Was she a typical representation of female pastors? Do you support female pastors? Why or why not?

5. Leon and Marlissa were best friends and Christians. Do you think it's possible for

male/female platonic friends to live under the same roof without crossing the line?

6. Reyna compromised herself and lost her identify in order to pacify Pastor Jennings. Is her behavior common among church leader/church member relationships?

7. Due to her past, was Kevin justified in stringing Marlissa along?

8. Should Starla have let Leon back into her and the boys' lives?

9. Who was your favorite character(s)? Why?

10. What was your favorite scene?

11. Which characters would you like to know more about?

About the Author

A romantic at heart, Wanda uses relationships to demonstrate how the power of forgiveness and reconciliation can restore us back to God and one another. Wanda is a graduate of Western Career College. In addition to building a career in health-care, she is currently pursuing her bachelor's degree in Biblical Studies. She currently resides in the San Francisco Bay Area with her husband of twenty-two years and two sons.

She is an award-winning author of four Christian fiction novels. Visit the author's Web site: www.wandabcampbell.net or contact her at: wbcampbell@prodigy.net.

Wanda loves hearing from readers.

UC HIS GLORY BOOK CLUB!

www.uchisglorybookclub.net

UC His Glory Book Club is the spirit-inspired brainchild of Joylynn Jossel, Author and Acquisitions Editor of Urban Christian, and Kendra Norman-Bellamy, Author for Urban Christian. This is an online book club that hosts authors of Urban Christian. We welcome as members all men and women who have a passion for reading Christian-based fiction.

UC His GLory Book Club pledges our commitment to provide support, positive feedback, encouragement, and a forum whereby members can openly discuss and review the literary works of Urban Christian authors.

There is no membership fee associated with UC His Glory Book Club; however, we do ask that you support the authors through purchasing, encouraging, providing book reviews, and of course, your prayers. We also ask that you respect our beliefs and follow the guidelines of the book club. We hope to receive your valuable input, opinions, and reviews that build up, rather than tear down our authors.

What We Believe:

—We believe that Jesus is the Christ, Son of the Living God.

—We believe the Bible is the true, living Word of God.

—We believe all Urban Christian authors should use their God-given writing abilities to honor God and share the message of the written word God has given to each of them uniquely.

—We believe in supporting Urban Christian authors in their literary endeavors by reading, purchasing and sharing their titles with our on-line community.

—We believe that in everything we do in our literary arena should be done in a manner that will lead to God being glorified and honored.

We look forward to the online fellowship with you.

Please visit us often at:
www.uchisglorybookclub.net.

Many Blessing to You!
Shelia E. Lipsey,
President, UC His Glory Book Club

just go back and use the knowledge she now had in her old situations. No matter how hard she willed it, Paige couldn't go back and right her wrong. She conceded long ago the hole in her heart would remain there until the day she dies. During this time of the year, Paige wished that day would come sooner than later.

She reached for the terry bath towel she'd placed on the bed and wiped her face. She learned long ago that the strongest tissue was too weak to handle her heavy tears. After partially drying her face, Paige summons the strength to look at the one and only picture she had of her baby boy. It wasn't a good picture. The once white edges had yellowed with time and the fuzzy black-and-white image was only recognizable by a trained professional eye. Still, Paige was grateful to have the sonographic image, considering the sonographer went against the clinic's protocol by giving it to her. The older woman had hoped to change Paige's mind, but had failed. Thirteen years later, the image was all Paige had left of the baby fetus she once carried. Although, the baby's sex couldn't be determined at ten weeks gestation, instinct told Paige the baby was a boy with her espresso skin and the father's hazel eyes. She'd secretly named him Jonathan.

"Why didn't I keep you?" she groaned, cradling the worn picture. "I am so sorry. I really did want you. I was just so selfish." Like the twelve years prior, the apology turned into sobs that transformed into a prayer of repentance. "God, I am so sorry for destroying the gift you gave me. Father, please forgive me and give me another chance. I promise I won't place my will above Yours again. Just one more chance and I promise to be a better person. I'll help everyone I can. I'll feed the hungry and help the homeless. I'll be faithful to church. I'll pay my tithes . . ." Paige bargained with God until no words were left and only her sobs communicated the depth of her despair.